'Though historical, this book highlights the ongoing urgent need to think and talk about mental health.'
Margaret Brunskill, The Compassionate Friends

'Lots of the background details are fascinating (and fit with my understanding of what went on at the time). Some episodes/scenes in the mental hospital are very powerful.'
Dr Val Harrington, Mental health historian

'A powerful gripping story.'
Tony Higginson, Formby Books

'Brilliant. Couldn't put it down. Far-reaching, experience-based and extremely well written.'
John Nelson, Formby Times columnist

'It is quite an achievement to portray so vividly that slice of history. The use of dialogue is good, keeping the momentum going. Good portrayal of the characters reminded me a bit of those in *One flew over the Cuckoo's Nest*.'
Peter Sharkey, Community care author

Mad
Worlds

A Tale of Despair and Hope
in 1950s England

Bill Douglas

Matador
9 Priory Business Park
Kibworth Beauchamp
Leicestershire LE8 0RX, UK
Tel: (+44) 116 279 2299
Fax: (+44) 116 279 2277
Email: books@troubador.co.uk
Web: www.troubador.co.uk/matador

ISBN 978 1783065 875

British Library Cataloguing in Publication Data.
A catalogue record for this book is available from the British Library.

Typeset in Goudy Old Style by Troubador Publishing Ltd
Printed and bound in the UK by TJ International, Padstow, Cornwall

Matador is an imprint of Troubador Publishing Ltd

www.billdouglas.co.uk

For my dear wife Elisabeth
And all my family

An Introductory Note

This novel shows dramatic happenings – largely on the mental health scene – in 1950s England. The town of Aversham, Springwell Mental Hospital, and the characters, are all fictitious – but they reflect the realities of that time. I've also used the kind of language that was around then.

Generally, care and treatment will be more enlightened now than in the 1950s. Ignorance and fear should be less prevalent in public attitudes. Yet many who have 'breakdowns' will experience stigma and discrimination – and the public awareness campaigns must be ongoing.

I hope this tale will grip you and move you. And if you're interested in the historical mental health context, you'll find a brief commentary on this in a postscript to the novel.

Bill Douglas

A Timeline

The Prologue – in 1938   1

Part One: DESPAIR (Chapters 1 to 25) – in 1956   5

A Prologue to Part Two – in 1932   137

Part Two: HOPE (Chapters 26 to 50) – in 1956-7   143

The Epilogue – in 1962   276

Appendices

1.   The 1950s English Mental Health Context: A Brief Note   281

2.   Acknowledgements   283

PROLOGUE

Wednesday 8th June 1938 – in Dupton, North-East England.

In the night John hears Da shouting, Ma crying. He sees Dave – in the moonlight by the half-open door – poised, neck straining. He creeps from the bed to join his bruv in listening, but he can't make out what Da's shouting. He tiptoes back to bed.

"What's it about?" he whispers.

"Dunno. Go to sleep."

Next thing, Dave's shaking him by the shoulder. "Get up Johnny, we're late. I'm goin' now."

As he scrambles into his clothes, he hears Dave clattering downstairs and the front door slamming.

Must get to Danny's for his paper round. He takes the stairs two at a time. The room's dark, miserable – the curtain's not been pulled back. He spies a glint in the corner. The wheelchair – and in it his da, who has no legs since the pit accident.

Ma's in her nightgown and bending over Da. John stops. "'Bye Ma and Da," he shouts. No reply, so he takes a step nearer.

Ma twists round and points to the door. "Go, Johnny." A quiet command.

Gotta get to Danny's fast. He turns and runs through the open front door and slams it behind him.

He races down the hill to the shop. Big Danny standing outside, thunders, "Johnny Chisholm, I've been tellin' your brother – you pair o' blondies have to get your bums here by seven o'clock sharp. If you can't, there's other lads hungerin' after your jobs."

He feels like charging at the man, thumping the swollen belly. But he needs this job, this money. "Sorry," he manages, looking down. Maybe he's real late

1

– didn't look at the clock before he came out. Dave's his timekeeper. And he always trusts his bruv, who's two years older after all.

He gets his sack of papers and rights the heavy bike. He's eight now and just big enough to manage it. He wobbles, gets up speed, and he's on his round. Dave's already gone the other road.

Big bully – that Danny! And he hates the man calling him and Dave 'blondies', all because they've blond hair. "Makes us sound like girls," Dave says.

The Hawthorns, number ten. That dog yesterday – must be new – nipped his fingers as he pushed the paper through the letterbox. Still hurts. So he leaves the paper halfway, sticking out. He listens, and chuckles as the paper disappears to a snarling. The dog's ripping it up.

Something to tell Dave. Dave's always telling him stories. They've scrapped from when he was little, and sometimes Ma and Da had to pull them apart. The age gap never held him back. But Dave's his best mate, who always looks out for him.

Back home first – his round's shorter than Dave's (and he gets paid less). Ma's in the corner, sitting beside Da. She's whispering and Da's grunting. John can't see the porridge pan on the range.

"Get your own breakfast, son," Ma says.

Things must be bad. He gets the stale loaf from the bread bin and cuts himself a slice. Spreads the dripping on nice and thick. He pours a cup of water, gulps it down. He stands, chewing the bread slowly, making it last.

Dave bursts in. "Beat me again bruv." John feels a tap on the back of his head. It's solidarity, though Dave's also reminding him who's bigger.

"Davy, your sandwich and drink are in the cupboard for you." Ma points.

Of course, the class trip Dave told him about – to the sea, on a bus. Sounded great. He can go year after next.

There's a clatter in the corner. Da's crumpled on the floor. Ma shrieks. She's kneeling. Dave's there first, stands over them.

"He's been trying his new legs," says Ma.

Yesterday he saw the legs that came for Da. Even with no legs, his da would walk again. "Magic legs, my boys," Da said.

Da's scrabbling and cursing on the floor. Ma's still down there, crying. John stands with Dave, ready to help.

2

Ma stands up, and he and Dave move in. "Under the arms," says Dave. And they struggle, with Ma's help, to get Da, grunting and sweating, back in his wheelchair. Da's only little now, but weighs right heavy.

"Thanks, my boys. The magic in these legs isn't working yet." His da's smiling, but there's tears – or is it the sweat?

"You go to school, boys," says Ma, hugging Dave then him.

"We'll miss Assembly," says Dave. They're real late.

He grabs his schoolbag and trails Dave, charging down the hill and into the school. He hears Dave shout "See ya bruv," and watches him go to a classroom.

Afternoon, the last lesson's just started. John's yawning. There's knocking on the classroom door. Mrs Heggie the teacher goes to the door, and holds it open while she whispers with somebody.

Mrs Heggie turns round and calls out, "John Chisholm, the Headmaster wants to see you." He grips the desk. He'd been real late for school, and he'd maybe get the belt. Dave would still be on his trip.

Then a surprise. A woman greets him at the doorway with a smile, takes him by the hand. "Come with me John. I'm Miss Blake, the Headmaster's secretary."

"I'm sorry for being late," he mumbles as they walk along the corridor.

Miss Blake stops. "It's not about that, my dear," she says, looking down at him. He feels her squeeze his hand. She looks sad, like she's been crying.

They walk till they reach a door that reads 'Headmaster'. She knocks and they go in. The Headmaster sits in a black gown – with a funny hat on his head – behind a big desk. A red-haired woman's standing by the desk.

"Sit down, John." The Headmaster points to a chair at the desk.

He sits down. Miss Blake stands beside him, still holding his hand. Warm, sweaty, nice.

The Headmaster coughs, says "I'm sorry John, I have bad news." What? Da looked right ill this morning.

The Headmaster coughs again. "Your brother David has met with a very bad accident. We'll take you home to your parents."

No, not Dave! "But... he's... an accident?" Would Dave be like Da – in a wheelchair?

3

The red-haired woman looks his way and says, "John, I'm David's teacher. He fell into deep water and we couldn't save him. He's drowned."

He feels the hand tighten on his. He wrenches free, stands up, bangs the desk with his fist and shouts, "You liars!"

The teachers have gone, and John's at home with Ma and Da. Da's silent, staring from his wheelchair. Ma's wet face wrinkles up as she wails "that canna' be." John feels the warmth of her shaking body, smells her sweat, as she hugs him close.

He doesn't cry. He rages inside – at that teacher, at Dave for not coming home. 'See ya bruv' said Dave – huh! Ma releases him. He runs up to his bedroom and burrows into his pillow. After a while he lies on the bed and stares at the ceiling. He'll take Dave's paper round as well as his own. He'll give up footie after school, get straight home and help Ma with the housework, Da with his legs. He'll work hard at school, and when he grows up he'll be a teacher – like Dave would've been.

Sleep? He's too wide awake, and lies thinking of the times before Da's accident.

Da comes home in the evenings, always gives a roar – "Where's my boys?" – and gets down on his haunches. He and Dave race to be first. Da scoops them up, one under each arm, whirls them round, and stands them back on their feet. Da picks him up, throws him in the air and catches him, then nuzzles into him, makes him giggle. Then it's Dave's turn. Dave shouts and giggles too.

Da laughs, kneels on the floor, cuddles him and Dave, and says "My wee rascals – love you both." He likes it when Da's in his miner clothes, with a black face and smelling real sooty. "It's the coal dust magic, my boys," says Da.

He reaches across to punch Dave in the back – but he hits the mattress, and scrabbles with his hand to the other side of the bed. He buries his face in Dave's pillow.

Part One

DESPAIR

1

Thursday 19th April 1956 – in Aversham, middle England.

Noiselessly, John Chisholm opened the front door, closed it with care, crept into the hallway and slumped onto the chair. Home. What an afternoon! He craved solitude.

He looked up at the mirror. A wretched picture. Head and shoulders, like a police WANTED poster. He started filling in gaps: JOHN CHISHOLM... for child neglect... age twenty-five... height five-feet-eight and slim build... hair, fair... eyes, blue... occupation, teacher...

Enough! He forced a wry smile. He was no criminal. But a fool – yes. And a coward – yes.

The afternoon had started so promisingly. In warm sunshine, with a hint of a breeze, he'd spent an idyllic half-hour with a small party of his young pupils in Blyth Meadow – his favourite place of beauty and calm – helping his charges identify the wild flowers and showing them how to press specimens into jotters. He'd managed to engage all the kids, and a couple were obviously keen. Not bad for eight-year-olds.

Then they were en route back to the school. The path was longer than the shortcut they'd taken to the Meadow. Fine. He'd allowed time. He wanted the kids to get the most out of this all-too-short nature trip.

Walking a couple of steps ahead of the crocodile – the kids in pairs holding hands – he kept glancing round to check all was okay. One pair chattering, the others silent. No problems.

Pine needles glinted in the sunlight as they approached the tiny cluster of trees, and his nostrils caught the fresh invigorating scent he'd known from childhood. At the foot of the nearest tree, he spied a large pine cone.

He swung to face the column, motioned with his hand and shouted "Halt." After some jostling and muttering, all were still. "Stay there," he commanded. He walked over to select the cone. A perfect specimen; he caressed it, savouring the unique aroma.

He turned to his charges and held aloft the exhibit. "You know what this is, children?"

But the kids weren't looking his way. He followed their gaze.

Two of the girls were scampering towards the nearby riverbank! Yelling "Come back," he gave chase. One of the pair, at the water's edge, stretching to pat a swan, was toppling, and shrieking. She disappeared with a splash – and his outstretched hand clutched at a fountain of spray.

Screams and shrill voices bombarded him. The girl's head bobbed up further away. Natalie! He stood, frozen in horror, thinking – *that's what it was like for Dave.*

"Nat," "Sir." A crescendo. He had to jump in. He slung off his jacket and hesitated. He couldn't swim; he couldn't save Natalie. They'd both drown.

"H'rrah. C'mon Nat!" The kids were cheering?

Yes. The other girl was in the water, bearing Natalie back to the riverbank. Thank God the child was safe! But no thanks to him, their guardian, who'd been useless – rendered inactive by an overwhelming panic he'd never before experienced.

"John? What are you doing, sitting out here?" His wife, standing over him.

He sprang up, and kept his distance. "Heather – I've a splitting headache and need to go lie on the bed." Ignoring cries that smacked of puzzlement, he made for the stairs, started bounding up two at a time, and paused to yell over his shoulder, "I'm not hungry. Please – just leave me alone."

In the bedroom, he shut the door and flung himself onto the bed. No, he wouldn't sleep. But talking to Heather wouldn't ease this turmoil.

He could not have foreseen the life-wrecking events that would happen on the morrow.

Friday 20th April 1956 – in Aversham.

Natalie and Dave run hand in hand to the river and jump in. They're sinking. Natalie screams, "Sir." John, strapped into a wheelchair, watches – helpless. Natalie flies from the water, straight at him, cawing, pecking his shirtfront. Dave's blowing bubbles up from under the water and mouths, "Bruv, bruv."

John struggled towards a waking state. That noise – the alarm. He stretched across the empty space and crumpled nightdress to stop the racket.

He tugged off his drenched pyjama top and caught his own stink. He swung onto the edge of the bed, leaning forward on his elbows, digging fingers into his scalp.

A hellish night. Heather's snoring wasn't the problem – rather, a welcome distraction. In and out of consciousness, he'd kept re-living yesterday's horror.

Stupid kids. But the Head's tirade – "You, John Chisholm, are responsible... in disgrace" – blared like a record stuck in a groove.

He'd kept going to the lav and sat there, ruminating. Daybreak, he'd thought of getting up – and must have dozed off.

He dressed slowly. He did not want to go into work. Not that he was ill. That essay for his Diploma in Education on 'school refusal'; couldn't the term apply to teachers? Having to see the Head after Assembly would be bad enough – could even mark an end to his embryonic teaching career. But having to face the kids...

Still, he'd go into school, meet things head on. The way he approached tough situations. And he must keep this job. Teaching was what he wanted to do.

What happened to that zest for inspiring children? Halfway through last term, he began to struggle. 'Sort yourself out', he'd told himself, and spent evenings and weekends poring over lessons and marking. Like on a treadmill with the 'stop' button jammed. In class he'd sometimes lose track of what he was saying. The kids would gape at him like he was an alien; to keep control, he'd shout at them.

At night he'd lie awake, troubled about his teaching, and about

Heather. And memories of the day that Dave vanished were powerful. Not that he'd want them to go away; they were part of his heritage, his being. But they'd begun to gnaw at him more – maybe because Dave drowned on a school trip.

In the Easter vacation he'd re-energised, with workouts at the YM and going for runs. He'd kissed the wobbles goodbye – till yesterday.

He wrestled into his sports jacket as he plodded downstairs. He could hear the radio – the news on the Home Service. Something about Grace Kelly and Monaco.

"Do we have to listen to that?"

Heather, emerging from the kitchen, turned the knob and there was silence. "Thought you liked the news."

He sat down at the breakfast table. Becky, propped in the high chair, was staring at him almost accusingly.

"Hey Becky," he mumbled, and waved at her. He picked up the *Aversham Times* and opened it wide to block the infant's line of sight. The local rag was not a great read. It was, though, a great protective shield, helping him dwell undisturbed in his rich tormented inner world.

Becky's crying was even more disturbing than the stare. Heather knelt beside her. "There, Daddy doesn't mean it."

No, he didn't mean to hurt the infant – just keep her from gaping at him. Heather, putting the bottle into Becky's mouth, soon produced contented gurgles.

He laid down the paper and shook cornflakes into a bowl. They looked like bits of brown paper. He shoved the bowl away.

"Happy birthday, John." Heather was beside him, kissing his cheek. He coughed as the mesmerising scent hit his nostrils. Her best perfume!

"Thanks."

"You're twenty-six years old. You heard that – old?" She was smiling.

He grunted. Twenty-six going on sixty.

"Bacon and egg?"

"I'm not hungry." He caught the aroma of his favourite coffee beans from the steaming mug she set down in front of him. "Thanks,

Heather." Nice. But why was she suddenly like this – trying to butter him up, as Da would say about Ma? Well, it was his birthday.

"Okay, scarecrow." She laughed.

At him? He sipped more coffee and peered over the rim of his mug. Hair done up, her 'Sunday best' costume on, reeking of the special perfume he gave her every Christmas. She looked fabulous. When did she last dress up like this? Scarecrow, eh! Maybe he wasn't as amply endowed as the boyfriend.

Becky gurgled as she finished the bottle. Precious Becky. He pulled a funny face, and the babe squealed with laughter. He picked up the paper again, but held it low so that Becky could see him.

Things weren't brilliant at home either. The worst thing was a suspicion growing this few weeks that Heather was having an affair. No proof, but she'd been icily distant. Trying to tell her about the kids and his problems at school, had felt like delivering a monologue. Not the loving, good-humoured soulmate he had married.

"Why are you staring?" Heather's concern startled him.

He *had* been staring – feasting his eyes. Admiring her graceful gentle almost Hispanic beauty, with soft brown eyes that, when she smiled, could surely melt granite... "Sorry, nothing," he mumbled. He gulped more coffee, and held the paper up again. Heather was looking her sexiest. They hadn't had sex for ages. Easter after a run, he'd lusted for her. But she gave him the shove-off – pleading tiredness and her need to be alert for Becky. Yet Becky was a healthy babe, not over-demanding.

Okay, drained after the birth trauma, Heather seemed mostly in a wretched inner hell – uncommunicative, listless. Efforts to cheer her produced at best wan smiles a bit like grimaces. At worst she'd cry, say "I don't deserve you," resist cuddles. With Becky she was clinical – seemed to lack warmth. "Know I love her... can't feel or show it..." After three weeks, he figured all this wasn't just exhaustion.

"Baby blues, I'd say," the doctor stated. "Could be a postnatal depression."

Heather shook her head at mention of a psychiatrist. And when

11

John asked how long it might take her to recover, the reply was, "Weeks, possibly months."

For several months now she'd been active - doing housework, fielding the night-time baby care - and was clearly fit again. So what could explain her not wanting to hear about his troubles at school? Or giving a frosty 'no' to sex?

Becky shrieked. He laid down the paper and slurped the dregs of his coffee.

"John, how about a birthday kiss for our daughter?"

He walked round the table and planted a gentle kiss on the top of Becky's head. "Must go," he muttered, and made for the front door.

"Your briefcase." Heather was holding it up for him.

He turned to take it, but she held it back. Bending forward, he felt a kiss on the cheek. A tease? And that beguiling perfume! He snatched the briefcase.

"'Bye," he yelled over his shoulder as he set out for the bus stop. To school.

Half-dreaming, John boarded the bus and stumbled into the nearest seat.

"All right, mate?" His new companion was eyeing him quizzically.

He grunted, rose and moved to an empty seat.

"Wood Road," the conductress shouted. His stop. Kids were yelling as they clattered down from the upper deck. He stood up. He'd go into Assembly, see the Head after and explain.

He looked through the window at the playground. Swarms of kids and parents were arriving... He slumped back into the seat and his journey continued.

Horror images flooded his mind. Natalie's head bobbing in the water; kids screaming - at him, their teacher, immobilised, his mind seized by a real-life replay of the kind of accident that must have befallen his bruv.

"Terminus." An unreal-sounding voice. "Time to get off now, Sir."

The spare figure of the conductress loomed, her sharp features creased in a frown.

"Sorry." He rose.

"Your briefcase, Sir."

"Thanks." He rushed to jump off into the sunshine. For once, he'd scarcely noticed the stink of diesel and fags.

He doffed his jacket, thrust it over a shoulder and loosened his tie. He strode down the lane towards the river. Nowhere near yesterday's debacle. Between two trees short of the riverbank, he stopped and looked around. At last – solitude. Except for the midges, and they were innocuous company. He sprawled onto his back.

Unwelcome thoughts invaded his mind. Heather used to say she loved him, but she didn't now. He was a teacher, but with yesterday's calamity, would he still be? A fighter, resolved to champion the weak? Tosh! Yesterday and today he'd been a miserable coward.

His eyes were moist. He tugged out a corner of his shirt to wipe them. A loser, with fog swirling in his head! Thoughts came, and evaporated.

He sat up, trying to clear his head by shaking it. That scent, powerful in his sensual memory. From his earliest days with Heather, it could turn him on. And sure as hell he shared it, and Heather, nowadays with some guy she'd be seeing daytimes.

Nowhere to go. Home and school bad places. Ma, Da and bruv dead. Today, for the first time ever, he'd ducked shitty consequences.

His eye caught a ripple on the water surface. Suddenly he knew what to do. He stood up and thrust off all but his underwear. He straightened his shoulders and yelled, "Dave, here I come." He bounded to the grassy edge and leapt in.

The river's chill was okay. But the water stopped at his armpits! He crouched to submerge his head, open-mouthed and choking but determined.

He was floating. Of course – he had no shoes on, nothing to weigh him down. And an icy shaft was clearing the muddle in his brain. Well – not yet, bruv! He made for the bank, scrambled out and paused to stand, stretching his arms and legs.

It began as an inexplicable giggle and ended as a roar. What a fiasco – great slapstick! Crazy – him laughing. Miserable as hell and just messed up on suicide!

And as he donned the dry clothing over the wet, positive thoughts came. He must talk with Heather about his suspicions, and go face the Head (a guy who wasn't a monster – just got angry). He'd have been the envy of his old mates – with a luscious wife, baby daughter, council house, and a teaching job he wanted.

His mind went back to Heather's hellish birth ordeal. An age into her struggling agony of labour and non-birth, the doctor commanded, "A caesarean."

Heather shook her head.

Must back her up. "No. We want a natural birth."

"Without a caesarean now, both your wife and baby could die."

After minutes that felt like hours, he and Heather gave way. He was sent to the canteen, the baby was delivered safely, and Heather survived.

After the two were discharged, he'd happily embraced fathering – changing nappies, making up bottles and soothing Becky in the night. He swore a lot. Silently. Except one night he dropped the bottle in the sink, where it smashed and he lost the milk. Then he stood and bawled out curses – at the Almighty and the world – right through Becky howling. Eventually, with a mix of rocking and humming, he got the babe to sleep. When he'd climbed into bed, Heather's face was sunk into her pillow.

Tie adjusted, jacket on, he was dressed and ready. Next moves were clear. No watch, dammit, but it must be nearly midday. He'd go home, talk with Heather, and get a message to the Head that he'd been sick.

Uncomfortably soaking, but helped toward respectability by dry outer clothes, he was glad to find the bus stop empty. Dripping water and holding his briefcase, he must look weird. On the bus he elected to stand, shifting his feet to try and hide an embarrassing wet patch appearing. The conductress was preoccupied – chatting to the driver – and he successfully out-stared his two fellow passengers.

He alighted, a man with a mission. He walked slowly, rehearsing how to tackle Heather. Was this really a great idea? What if lover boy was there? Well, he'd teach the swine a lesson for messing with his beautiful wife.

He turned into his street. In the distance, a man in a suit dashed across the road from outside his – John's – house and into a blue car. The lover!

He sprinted after the mystery third party, who roared off down the street and disappeared round the corner in a cloud of mucky exhaust fumes.

He stopped, panting, by his house. He hadn't caught details of the car or the driver.

He raked his pockets. No key. He rapped on the door.

The door opened and Heather, cradling Becky with one arm, stared at him.

He brushed past them, catching the scent and noting her dishevelled hair. The dining room was the place to talk. He stood by the table. It hadn't been cleared since breakfast. What had she been doing?

Heather followed. "Why are you back, John? What's happened?"

Cool it. Inject some humour? "I fancied a swim."

"A swim – where?" She advanced towards him. Becky was moaning.

"The Yangtze River. Nice and warm."

"The what river? And why?"

This humour was sick! "Never mind, Heather – who was that?"

"What?"

"Lover boy – who is he?"

Her face crinkled up. "What do you mean?"

Lousy acting, Heather. "Just left – in a blue car."

"It'd be next door. Their front door slammed and I saw a man run to a car."

"A fib, Heather?" He banged the table and something fell onto the carpet.

He heard her shout "No" above Becky's screaming. She looked scared. He'd lost it, and he felt a mix of deep regret and not caring.

He glanced at the fallen item. The breadknife. He picked it up. "Who is it?" he asked quietly.

He glimpsed terror on Heather's face as she turned and ran out the front door.

2

Thursday 19th April 1956 – in and around Aversham and Springwell.

Sam Newman needed this fag. Leaning back from his office desk into the upholstered chair, he drew deeply, then exhaled in gentle short puffs, delighting in his blue smoke-ring creations as they drifted upward to join the cloud near the ceiling.

Last night had been hellish. Folk on his patch seemed to have conspired in a 'let's go crazy' jamboree. As the sole mental health officer authorised to get mad folk from the borough of Aversham into Springwell Mental Hospital, he'd had to sort out the lot. Maybe wouldn't have been so bad if Springwell had been nearer. It was a good eight miles out, built well away from the gentrified folk of Aversham, who didn't want to be too near their local loony bin. And much of the journey was along twisting country roads.

Seven damn phone calls from GPs. Three ending up call-outs! The first, triggered by an over-wrought husband hounding a panicky GP – to see a perfectly sane woman – took into the early hours. A bit of first-aid marriage guidance smoothed things. And he'd smiled as, home again, he rang a crusty, sleepy-sounding GP back at two a.m. to advise that the woman's hubby felt in need of a sedative.

While he'd lain unable to sleep, a second call-out came – then another as he was labouring to crank up his precious Morris Minor engine. He went to the latter call-out first, to find an agitated, depressed middle-aged woman being dissuaded by her daughter from taking an aspirin overdose. Sighing heavily and suicidal, the woman was certifiable. Her GP was there to sign the form and administer sedation, and the magistrate and duty psychiatrist complied in the certifying.

After pleas from the exhausted-looking yet compellingly attractive and persuasive daughter not to involve the police, he drove her and mother – huddled together in the back seat – the few miles to Springwell. The relieved-looking daughter hugged him – ah, the promise of that moment – but insisted on getting a taxi home.

"Damn!" A sharp familiar pain as the fag end singed the tips of forefinger and thumb. He re-opened the packet. Two fags. Better stock up soon as possible.

To get to the remaining call-out, he'd navigated the country roads speedily as he dared. He arrived outside a Georgian mansion to see an unconscious youth on a stretcher being lifted into an ambulance and an older man and woman climbing in.

He could still hear the ambulance-man yelling. "Casualty. Lad's lost gallons o' blood. Ran through glass. His folks are goin' too."

Following the blue-light-flashing ambulance on a five-minute drive to Casualty at the Infirmary, he had a thought. If he'd been there earlier, could he have prevented this? He rehearsed an explanation to the parents. At the Infirmary, he'd found them sitting in the waiting-room, looking stunned.

"Sam Newman, Mental Health." He flashed his card.

"We're Mark's parents," said the mum.

"Look, I'm sorry –"

"Spare us the drivel. What can you do to help our son?" The dad got up from the chair. A beer-bellied giant, eyes popping – in his face and ready for a punch-up.

"Cecil, tell the man what happened." From the mum, a command.

"Yes, it would help us find out what's wrong with your son."

The dad stepped back and puffed out his red cheeks. "In the night I heard thuds and shot downstairs. Our boy – he's seventeen – stood there in his pyjamas, with books all over the floor. I asked him what he was playing at, and he shouted 'the voice told me'. He was staring, like into outer space. Then he flung himself into an armchair and just lay there, in a funny position, with his eyes staring."

"Has he behaved like this before?" asked Newman.

The dad ignored the question. "I bawled at him, but couldn't get an answer. It was like I wasn't there. I got desperate, rang our GP – he's a personal friend – and he promised to send help right away." The dad paused, drawing breath. "I went back and Mark was still in that same damn position. Bloody weird. Mother came down and tried talking…"

"It was as if Mark had frozen into a statue," said the mum. "We didn't know what to do. We sat watching, and waiting for help." Her eyes were moist.

"In the end I grabbed his arm to get sense out of him. And…" The dad's voice was breaking.

"And?" Newman wanted the full picture.

The dad recovered his voice. "He sprang up, ran out the back door – I'd opened it to get fresh air – and dived straight into the greenhouse. I dialled 999."

Yes, a bit earlier and he might have prevented the bloodbath. So what! He didn't let the 'if onlys' get to him anymore.

Both parents were weeping. He'd seen it before – so often that he noted it without caring. Bewildered folk, struggling with the onset of madness in their midst.

At last, knackered and fighting sleep, he'd driven home. 5.30am! To avoid disturbing upstairs, he kipped on the settee – till he awoke to his startled daughter's scream at eight o'clock.

The internal phone was ringing. He picked up the receiver and grunted.

"Mary here, Sam. The boss wants to see you; his office, now."

"What's it about?"

"Dunno, but he's spitting nails."

He couldn't ignore the injunction. The Medical Officer of Health was boss of Aversham's Health Department – and liked to remind everyone of this now and again.

A glance in the wall mirror decided his next act. Bloodshot eyes glared from a swarthy face. Lathering up, he scraped quickly with his 'sword edge', smoothed his Brylcreemed hair – still jet-black – and limped at his top speed up the stairs, to knock on the MOH's door. At the command, he entered. "Sir?"

"Ah, Newman." The MOH stood behind the large oak desk. "Sit down."

He did as ordered, facing the desk. The MOH remained upright, frowning.

"You were out last night. I've had a complaint. Know what it's about?"

Images sped into his numbed consciousness. The daughter – anything sexual? He wished. That husband? Worked up – but he'd seemed friendly. The father of the lad that jumped through the glass? Yes – the delay! "I think so. I can explain."

"Good." The MOH's frown went. "An apology from you will suffice."

"I already apologised to the parents, but –"

"Parents? What are you havering about? It's Tickler you will apologise to."

The name rang a bell, but not regarding the youngster. Could the dad be the stepfather, with a different name? "To whom?"

"To Dr Tickler! Says you had the nerve to ring him in the middle of the night to advise giving a patient a sedative."

"What?"

"Is that correct?"

"Yes, but –"

"He says you were arrogant and questioned his judgment, and risked a shambles by refusing to organise certifying of a patient who was a danger to herself."

Steady, don't lose it. "No."

"Doubtless you had your reasons. I told him I would deal with it. I want you to ring and make a full apology. Herbert T. is one of our finest most conscientious family doctors – and an old friend."

"But the woman wasn't –"

The MOH held up his hand – a halt sign. "Make that call!"

Newman limped back to his room and his chair. He lit up and

propelled a cloud towards the ceiling. Pompous bighead; knew nothing about mental health. Nor did that fool of a GP.

He was calming. The boss couldn't be expected to understand mental health. Grasping the work of other sections in the Health Department would be easier for the MOH. Public health inspectors, health visitors, district nurses and home helps all did great jobs, but ones where intangibles weren't so critical.

But his thoughts were spiralling downward. Damn-all sleep, overworked and a target for aggro. Pay not rock-bottom, but being on call 24/7 without recompense equalled a measly rate per hour.

One good thing: Two lots with legal authority in certifying - the Justices and the G.P.s (bar Tickler) - bowed to his opinion on emergencies, and readily signed forms.

External phone. He grabbed the receiver. "Newman."

"Police, McNab. Keep your hair on, man. I've a nice one, specially for you."

Holding the receiver away from his ear, Newman groaned. He rubbed his eyes. "Sarge, I've been so bored. The good news?"

Even on the crackling line, McNab's broad Geordie accent was distinctive and - today - irritating. "Mattie's corner shop phoned. Woman with a baby ran in there - scared shitless. Husband tried to stab her. She's -"

"Did he?"

"Na, but he chased her out. She's in the back-shop. Uniform'll see you there."

"And the husband?"

"Young lad, teacher. Crackers."

Could be messy. "Where's he?"

"In the house - 90 Green Drive. Across from Mattie's, an' further along."

Not out in the sticks at least. "Name?"

"John Chisholm."

"Behave yourself, McNab." He slammed the phone down, inhaled, and puffed expansively. Yes, he was the department's mental health expert.

Adrenalin-fuelled, he limped to the car, revved away from the Department and slowed along back streets of terraced houses.

Crackers, eh? He'd see. He'd known guys who, tanked up with liquor, could chase the missus – maybe even with a knife. Didn't mean they were mad. Some women asked for it. Good chance the lad was crazy, though. Young teacher. Could be the stress. He'd seen it before. Or jealousy. Maybe paranoid as hell.

Turning into Green Drive, he espied at the far end, near where Mattie's would be, a small gathering. Vultures? Number 78. He slowed right down. Number 90, the green door shut, curtains drawn. Better see the wife first. He stopped a few yards further along, opposite the corner shop.

Walking over to the shop, he ignored a "what's up?" as he limped past the bystanders. Police would clear them.

He flashed his warrant card at the policeman. "Newman, Mental Health."

"Missus Chisholm's in the back-shop, Sir."

"And Mr Chisholm?"

"In number 90. I'm watching the front. Another constable's at the back."

Fine. He limped into the shop. "Newman, Mental Health," he said to the elderly couple behind the counter. "To see Mrs Chisholm."

The woman moved – fast for an oldie. "I'll tell her you're here, Sir."

He hung back and took the opportunity to buy fags.

The woman returned. "Go on through to the back-shop, Sir."

Approaching the open door, his nostrils twitched. Some perfume! In the small room sat a young woman, a dark-haired beauty, who gazed up at him with sorrowful brown eyes.

3

Heather didn't look back until she was in the shop and had her moaning infant seated on the counter in front of Mattie. No, John hadn't pursued her. She'd guessed not, hearing the front door shut, but hadn't dared pause to check.

"What's up, lass?" The white-haired man's gnarled face was impassive.

Breathless, she couldn't reply.

"I'll fetch the wife," said Mattie, and turning, shouted, "Elsie, it's Heather and the bairn!"

"Coming." Elsie appeared from the back-shop, advancing rapidly past the only customer – a woman studying the shelves. "Whatever's up, m'dear?"

"I'm in trouble."

"Come on through."

She picked up Becky and followed Elsie to a room at the back. She flopped onto a sofa, cuddling Becky and humming till the babe stopped moaning.

She declined 'a cuppa'. She must tell her story now, though the idea of doing so was scary.

The words weren't coming. She felt a reassuring pat on her hand as Elsie sat down beside her. "Take your time, m'dear." Elsie's careworn face radiated concern.

"It's John. He went funny, picked up a knife – and I ran." Her vision was clouding. "I'm afraid he's gone mad." She was shaking, teeth chattering.

"It'll be shock, m'dear," said Elsie. "Here, pass me the bairn."

Heather released Becky to Elsie, who started dandling the infant up and down.

The door opened. Mattie. He looked enquiringly at Elsie.

"Her husband went all funny and chased her with a knife. He's still in their house – number 90. She can't go back and she's worried sick about him."

Mattie scratched his head. "Maybe I should ring the police, see if they can help?" He looked at Heather.

Still shaking, though less violently, she nodded. She hated the idea, but couldn't think of any better course. John might harm himself.

"Can you mind the shop then, Elsie?"

"Yes. Nearly asleep, m'dear," Elsie whispered, handing back the child and closing the door quietly behind her.

Shaken up, but regaining control of herself, Heather cradled Becky in her arms. A sleeping little angel!

Mattie was using the phone on the wall in the far corner of the room. With his back to her, he was obviously trying to keep his voice down. But she heard snatches. "Mad... with a knife... 90 Green Drive... here with the bairn."

Mattie replaced the receiver and turned to Heather. "They'll be right round, and they're sending a mental man to see your husband. I'll join Elsie. She'll be back through soon." He returned to the shop, leaving the door ajar.

She continued to rock Becky. What was the 'mental man' – a psychiatrist?

Suddenly an image of John with the knife blocked out all else. Could he kill her – and Becky? Her eyes were blurring, her face moistening. Might he use the knife on himself? He'd looked wild and dishevelled. Said he'd gone for a swim in the river. He couldn't swim! So what was he doing there? Did he mean to drown?

"John," she whispered aloud. "My rock." Yes, through her depression he had been – tending to Becky each restless night. In the summer, he'd kept up the builder's labouring work to bring in cash.

What energy, in contrast to her apathetic negative state – but not too surprising from a guy whose approach to college was burning the candle at both ends. And when he started teaching, he'd spent hours telling her about every child in his class – their likes and dislikes, and problems he was picking up. She'd known what he was talking about, yet, uncaring, could barely pretend to listen.

Voices in the shop. Mental man? Holding Becky close, she crept to the door and listened. No. Mrs Allen at number 86? She returned to the sofa and her musings.

She must have been awful to live with after the birth. That whole experience, from the dreaded caesarean on, was seismic, and for a while she struggled through a cloud of gloom.

When some months back, the cloud began to lift, and she could experience joy in caring for Becky and tackling housework, she noticed John had changed. He was jumpy and distant and spent all his time preparing lessons. It stung to get the brush-off when she asked what was wrong.

She'd soon decided to stop questioning him. He was stressed, under pressure. And she wanted to concentrate her resurgent energies on bonding with her child.

Then Easter, and his going for work-outs and runs. "This exercise is shaking me up. Olympics next, eh?" he surprised her with one day. She'd thrilled to see a glimmer of a smile.

"Policeman's here, outside the shop, m'dear." Elsie was back. "Says there's others, watching your house front and back." She held up a jar of baby food and smiled. "I know what you get for Becky. All right?"

Heather nodded gratefully and handed Becky over. "Can I use your lav?"

"Of course, m'dear. Out the back door, on your left. It's not posh."

Relieved of discomfort, Heather stopped by the kitchen sink and looked through to the room. Becky, cradled by Elsie, was gulping down the spoonfuls. Nice. Elsie, her white curls dancing as she crooned to Becky, would have been a fine grandma.

"Your bairn's a grand wee eater." Elsie handed Becky over, then stood up, her cheeks glistening. Elsie - crying? "I'd better join Mattie. Make yourself at home, m'dear."

Yesterday's shock! Finding John slumped in the chair by the front door - hunched forward, head resting on his arms. Back from work early. Wild-eyed, he'd ignored her queries, insisted on going straight to bed and wanted to be on his own.

Later, when she tiptoed into the bedroom, he divulged something bad happened at school, and said he was wholly responsible. "My neglect," he added. Talking about it would not help, and he'd sort it out at school tomorrow.

A tapping jolted Heather from her reverie. Elsie was peering round the door. "Heather m'dear, you've a visitor. I'll leave you in private."

A dark-suited man entered, carrying a briefcase. "Mrs Chisholm?" The stranger continued in a low voice without waiting for a reply, "I'm Sam Newman, Mental Health." He sat down at the table.

"Yes. Heather Chisholm." This tanned, dark-haired little man looked nervous - smoothing his hair with one hand, briefcase (flat on the table) clenched in the other. "What do you mean, mental health?"

"I'm Aversham's Mental Health Officer, commonly known as the DAO - that is duly authorised officer, empowered under the law to take people of unsound mind to Springwell." He flashed a card with a photo on it. "Just to confirm."

Heather waved her hand. She didn't need to see his card. "The loony bin? John's no madman. Anyway, he wouldn't go there."

"Well, if your husband's having a nervous breakdown, that's where I have to take him."

"*Have* to take him? No! Surely you can treat him at home."

"Not if he's having a serious mental breakdown. Springwell's the only place to treat him. It's the mental *hospital*. Besides, there's your safety. The police said he tried to stab you."

"That's not true. He just picked up a knife. But..." She hadn't thought this through. Becky's and her own safety came first. Maybe John would have to go there.

The man produced a pack of cigarettes and motioned it towards her. "A fag?"

"No thanks."

"Mind if I do?" The mental man took out a cigarette and flicked at the lighter.

"No – I mean yes, I do mind." Her cheeks warmed. "The smoke would be bad for my baby."

The mental man looked disconcerted, but pocketed cigarettes and lighter. "I'm sorry, I didn't think." He sat down on a chair by the table, took paper and a pen from the briefcase, and faced her. "Tell me what happened," he said quietly.

Heather began her story.

4

John rushed to the front doorway and stopped, gripping the doorknob as he watched Heather speed with Becky towards the shop. He'd chase them – but no, she'd come back. God, he didn't mean to scare her like that! He slammed the door, retreated to the living room and slumped into an armchair. Thoughts rushed into his head, then faded – like some magnetic force was drawing them.

His lower back was aching. A dull ache. Yes, his underwear was sodden. He raised himself from the chair and began to strip off.

He suddenly imagined Dave, soaking and drowning. His body shook, and his eyes felt moist. Great bruv. Looked out for his 'wee Johnny'.

Yesterday! He'd panicked. Why did he go anywhere near the river?

He rubbed his aching forehead, massaging it. But this didn't relieve his cluttered mind. Was he going mad?

A strain of music. Hearing things? No, it was from next door. '*Heartbreak Hotel*'. A catchy tune, but he didn't want to hear it. Heather was always humming it. She was crazy about Elvis. Maybe 'the king' was her true love.

Tap-tap-tap. The front door? But nobody ever called. Heather! He ran to the door, and flung it open.

A stranger – a startled-looking little man in a suit – gaped at him.

"John Chisholm?" The man carried a briefcase.

He heard laughter. A couple of women across the road. What the hell. "So what?"

"Can I come in?" The man was dark-haired, swarthy, and stank of Brylcreem.

"No!" He made to shut the door.

The man stuck out a foot to stop it closing. "I'm Sam Newman, the duly authorised officer for mental health." With a smile (or a leer?), the stranger flashed a card with a photo. "I must come in and talk to you."

Arrogant sod. "No way. I'm not mental."

The man continued. "I've just seen your wife, and –"

"You've WHAT?" He glared at the man.

The man's face reddened. "I mean, I saw your wife at the shop over there, and from what she told me –"

"You *saw* her – at the shop?" The two women were laughing again.

"Yes. Oh I'd never seen her before. You'd threatened her with a knife."

"I didn't, and it's no business of yours."

"Ah, but it is. Look, can we talk inside?"

"NO! DAMN YOU TO HELL. SCRAM," he yelled. He didn't hear any laughter now. He saw a policeman outside the shop – near where the women were. "You do not want to mess with me," he added quietly.

The intruder had retracted his foot. "You need help. You can come as a voluntary patient into Springwell."

"The loony bin? Never! Get away from here and leave me – and my wife – alone!" The house shook as he slammed the door.

He stood, his thoughts churning. Perfumed little toad! The loony bin. He'd die first. Nobody was going to lock him up with madmen.

Trembling with rage had given way to shivering. Not that his thoughts were scary; he was starkers but for his socks. No wonder those women laughed.

Galvanised, he ran up to the bedroom and searched for dry underwear and a shirt. After rummaging through drawers fruitlessly, he struck oil in the laundry bin. All niffy – but so what?

The place reeked of Heather. He inhaled deeply. He struggled to order his thoughts. She used to say she loved him, but now she had a lover? Should he go over to the shop? He couldn't face that. Would she come home? Was he still a teacher?

He was pathetic. He'd messed up. He lay back on the bed under the quilt and pulled it up over his head. Maybe he could suffocate? Scarcely. Other options for self-kill? No rope, no gun. Cutting his wrists, or drowning – both possible.

Couldn't even decide if he wanted to live or die. He curled up on the bed, half-dazed, letting images come and go. If there was an afterlife, would suicide book him into Purgatory, or Hell? Not that he cared.

He's teaching the class about Heaven and Hell. Little Jimmy nods forward, head on desk, arms asplay. Natalie shouts "Jimmy's dead" and the class start wailing. He runs over, bangs the desk with a ruler and wakes Jimmy up. The Head appears, says this isn't Geography. He confronts the Head, argues these are places and the class should know about them. The Head sits on a desk. A giant hawk blasts through the window.

He was sweating. Must have dozed off. It was dark, and thunder was splitting the house? No. Someone'd been banging on the front door. The stink of Brylcreem! Catapulting off the bed, he took the stairs three at a time. The mental man stood in the hallway.

"I'm back," said the mental man, superfluously. "I knocked, then used the key your wife lent me."

"What!" He approached the mental man. Could be the sod Heather was necking. "Where is she?"

"Please, I want to help you." The mental man stepped back, and raised the briefcase belly-high. A protective weapon? "My name's Sam. Can I call you John?"

It would be easy to despatch this shit. But... get an answer first. "Where's my wife?"

"She and your baby are resting in the back-shop. I've come in to check if you're alright."

"I am, so you can go – Sam!"

"It's not as simple as that, John."

Another dark-suited man magically appeared beside the mental man. "Hello, Mr Chisholm." The mental man faded to the background as the speaker advanced and held out his hand. "John, you know me – Dr Smith."

His GP, a sad-looking old man he hadn't seen for months. A bit worrying, all this. He ignored the proffered hand. "Why are you here?"

"Can we go into your living room, John? It's rather cramped here," said Dr Smith. "Please, we need to talk."

Why? But what was the harm in shifting to the living room? He could throw this pair out anyway. "Okay." He stepped backward into the living room to allow the doctor entry. "But only you." He motioned with his fist. The mental man stayed in the hallway.

"Mr Newman told me you're not well. I think you should go to Springwell for treatment."

The loony bin. And this was his own doctor! He shook his head and banged it with both hands. "Never. Leave me alone. I've had enough – of you all, life, everything." He pointed to the door. "Get out!"

The mental man had slithered forward with his briefcase. Funny, the GP tapping the man on the elbow and nodding, before scurrying out.

"You need treatment. The doctor and I agree, and I know the magistrate will too," said the mental man, now further into the room. "If you won't come voluntarily, you'll be certified."

"Never!" Fists clenched, he advanced on the mental man.

A figure jumped in front of him. A barrel-chested giant in uniform.

Nothing to lose. A playground scrapper from earliest schooldays, John punched the policeman solidly in the stomach, drawing a groan, and followed with a head butt. He turned to grab a chair. A tornado hit his legs. Copper number two, with a crash-tackle that smashed John against the chair and onto the floor. Prostrate on his front, his legs were being crushed. He tried to move, but his arms were pinned.

The mental man said something about an order and taking him to Springwell. Dr Smith was kneeling with a syringe.

"NO!" he yelled, and heard "yes". Then his arm stung, and the scene faded.

5

Late afternoon, the mental man was shown by Mattie into the backshop. "Here are your keys, Mrs Chisholm. Thanks. Your husband's been sedated. We're taking him to Springwell. He's being certified, and he'll be kept in." With a "can't stop", the mental man turned and started back through the empty shop.

"For how long?" Heather yelled. Fear for her and Becky was now uppermost. The image of John with the knife, and that look on his face, were both scary. What if this mental man was wrong, and John came straight back?

The mental man paused, half turned and shouted. "A long time. Sorry, have to rush." And he disappeared.

Her questions would have to wait. In any case, Becky claimed her attention by waking and starting to whimper.

"You shouldn't go back to that house on your own tonight, m'dear," Elsie said, and Mattie added, "We want to see you and the bairn safe."

A welcome offer. "I'll need Becky's crib and a few other things."

"Aye, you go over the road and leave the bairn with me," suggested Elsie.

"I'll come and give you a hand with the crib," said Mattie.

Heather walked briskly across the road, followed by Mattie. She unlocked the door and remembered as she pressed the switch. Electric light had seemed a blessing – much brighter than the old gas mantle. But it broke down more often, and they'd had to learn about fuses and switchboxes.

32

She was glad of Mattie's presence - and the shaft of street lighting - as she walked through the hallway.

The living-room door was ajar and she entered, switching the light on. "Oh my!" she cried. One of the hard-backed chairs lay askew on the floor.

"He's no' gone without a fight." Mattie pointed to dark red blotches, highly visible on the pale blue carpet. He picked up the chair and righted it.

Those large bloodstains! Her new carpet ruined. And John must have been hurt. She'd never seen him fight. He was a peacemaker and tried to avoid conflict. But something was wrong with him. And he'd told her about tackling bullies at school. Yes, surely he could fight, and obviously had done here. "No!" she cried, as it struck her. Could this be someone else's blood? Had he used the knife?

"Do you need to sit down, lass?" Mattie drew out a chair from the table.

"No thanks." Back in action mode, she returned to why she was here. "Can you help get Becky's crib down, Mattie?"

They went up and carried the wooden crib downstairs.

"I'll manage fine on my own now," said Mattie.

"I've a few other bits and pieces to get. You go back to Elsie and Becky. I'll join you soon." She watched Mattie lift the crib with one hand, and with his other manage the front door. He was strong for a man that looked three-score plus.

She closed the door behind him and put the snib on to lock it. She stepped quickly through the living room, navigating obstacles while avoiding looking at the bloodstains, and ran upstairs.

She set about gathering things she and Becky would need. Quite a list, even for one night. Looking for her nightdress, she spied John's pyjamas. The same pair from their honeymoon, a million years ago. She picked them up and clutched them to her face, savouring the taste and his unique smell. The sex that was magic had been 'no go' for her, for so long. And when suddenly she fancied it, he spurned her. That hurt. And at Easter she'd turned him away. If only!

She was welling up. She'd tried to make his birthday special, but failed to lift him from his misery. And he came home deranged and aggressive.

All their life together he'd had spells of brooding. She recalled the time they first met. After a packed Students' Union debate on 'Can War Be Just?' - when he'd argued passionately against the motion she was defending - he'd sought her out.

"Fancy a drink downstairs, Heather?"

Steely blue eyes, hair the colour of corn, and smiling rugged features. Instant magnetism. "Yes."

Sitting in the S.U. bar, ready to continue debating, she was surprised by his opening: "Any brothers or sisters?"

"No, I'm an only child. Spoiled. You?"

His expression darkened. "I had a big brother." Then, waving his hands around, he poured out the story.

She'd felt moved by the tragic tale. Subsequently, she could recognise that melancholy look; and always his brooding was about Dave. He'd kept going on about it - so repetitively that she'd stopped listening.

But this was different from past tragedy, or stress at work. More sinister. Accusing her, banging on their table...? Maybe he had gone mad.

She threw herself on the bed and sobbed into the pillow. John, her beloved husband and sweetheart, her champion, was in the loony bin. Maybe forever.

She sat up and dried her face. The suitcase. Heavens, Mattie and Elsie would be wondering what had happened to her. And Becky?

She scrambled off the bed, stuffed her suitcase, flew downstairs and over to the shop. The shutters were down, and she knocked on the door next it.

"The bairn's near asleep," Mattie whispered, and closed the door softly behind her. He led her upstairs and stood aside to motion her into a room.

Elsie sat in an armchair, cradling Becky, rocking her gently and humming.

Heather whispered "Hello." She'd stay out of the picture and let Becky fall asleep. But the infant jerked up to look towards her and started crying.

"You have the bairn, m'dear."

The infant cuddled in close. This was stirring something in Heather – joy, fulfilment as a mother. Affirmation, at a time she needed a boost – and a sensation that would help sustain her through the nigh-sleepless hours ahead.

The rich aroma needed action. Holding Becky with one arm, she got a nappy from the case, while Elsie went to fill the nappy bucket with water and steriliser.

"Put the bairn there, m'dear." Elsie pointed at the settee, laying out a sheet.

"Thanks." She laid Becky on the settee and removed the sodden and hugely soiled cloth – inhaling the odour. This aroma in nappy changing was special, a perfume only Becky could produce.

"I'll put the mess down the lav," said Elsie, disappearing with the soiled nappy and returning to drop it in the nappy bucket.

Heather put the fresh nappy on and reached for the safety pin. Her eyes blurred. That evening she'd come home from hospital, exhausted. John nuzzled Becky, then held the babe in the air. "She pongs. I'll sort it – been practising for this." He put the clean nappy on correctly, then yelled "Ouch," drew back and sucked his bloodied thumb. He laughed. "Practice didn't include a safety pin." He completed the task, then hugged her close. She couldn't manage a smile. But she wouldn't be alone in caring for their baby. He'd be a brilliant dad. And so he had been.

"What's up, m'dear?"

She brushed her sleeve over her cheeks. She didn't want to talk about this. "Nothing." Forcing a smile, she picked up Becky and dandled her in front of Elsie.

"Mattie'll get fish and chips for tea," said Elsie. "What would you like, m'dear?"

Such kindness. She nuzzled her face into Becky's midriff to wipe her own eyes. "Thanks, but I couldn't eat anything." True – the bile was in her stomach. "I'm tired. I'll feed Becky, then go to bed, if that's okay."

Elsie nodded. "M'dear, that makes sense to me."

Heather cajoled Becky into swallowing a few spoonfuls, then followed Elsie to the dimly lit 'spare room'. Warmer than expected, thanks to a one-bar electric fire.

Elsie whispered, "If you need anything in the night, give us a shout. We're in the room over the landing. Night-night and God bless."

In the crib sat a teddy with large brown eyes and outstretched arms. How thoughtful of Elsie. She lowered Becky gently into the crib. "Teddy," she whispered, holding up the bear. "Becky – nice cuddle." Her child clasped the teddy and lay hugging it.

She sat on the bed alongside the crib, crooning softly until, surprisingly (as teething had been a problem lately), Becky dozed off.

Heather slipped into bed. The soft mattress, well sprung, unlike their aging second-hand one, felt warm. Yes, a hot-water-bottle.

She was being treated like a favourite daughter, the prodigal returning. She'd known the pair only through her shopping, and now they were her best friends.

She lay awake. Was John mad? Would he get better? Would he be tormented by lunatics? Would he be cooped up forever? She didn't hear of people coming out of there. Was this the end for their relationship – how could she and her beloved ever be the same? What of Becky's future – with a lunatic father? And if he did come home, how could he keep his job after being branded a loony? How would she meet the bills? John's pay wasn't great, but it paid the mortgage. Would his pay stop now?

Her world was collapsing. Her parents! At least they had money – with Father an ex-bank manager. Only fifty miles away, but they hadn't visited for ages.

If only she could rewind to before that fateful evening – two years ago – when she took John to meet her parents. It was okay at first, though uneasy, stilted.

Mother saying, with obvious admiration, "First class honours indeed," and John blushing, staying silent.

Father's opening salvo: "What does your old man do?"

John's: "Old man? You mean my da – he's dead. He worked as a miner."

Silence, Mother glancing at Father, then saying, "Oh dear, what did he die of?"

John's: "Lost both legs when a tunnel collapsed down the mine. He was stuck in the house, in a wheelchair, and died of a thrombosis a couple of years on."

Mother's: "Oh dear – and your mother?"

John's: "My ma took on three jobs slaving for filthy rich families. She died of overwork."

Silence, then Father's: "I'll uncork the wine."

John never drank wine. But after his second refill, Mother's: "What about your religious belief, John?"

John's: "I'm with Karl Marx. Religion is the opium of the people." Her lapsed Catholic fiancé – saying something that went down fine in the Students' Union.

A cooling in the atmosphere, as her churchgoing parents exchanged glances.

John's continuing with pronouncements in similar vein, raising his voice. She trying vainly to help him modify his comments, lighten the tone.

Her parents wouldn't want him for a son-in-law! An atheist and a socialist?

And Mother's penned 'we decline' to their registry wedding invitation – 'Sorry darling, we'll be abroad' – radiated with unspoken vibes. Vibes whispered in her ear by Mother later that evening. "Uncouth, not good enough for you, darling."

They'd come once since Becky's birth. When she was sunk in misery, not up to talking much. When silent unease between husband and parents screamed at her.

But this was a desperate time. Surely they'd rally to help their daughter and grandchild? She'd ask Mattie in the morning if she could ring from the shop.

6

Friday 20th – Saturday 21st April 1956 – in Springwell.

John came to in semi-darkness, his head exploding. And that stink – of sick? He tried to raise his hand to wipe his brow, but couldn't. His arm was trapped in some coarse material. Damn! He was wrapped in a sort of tent – yes, maybe a canvas sheet. And his legs rubbed against each other. Had he been stripped? He struggled weakly and unsuccessfully to free his limbs, then lay, blinking his eyes and trying to figure where he was.

A dim nightlight on the ceiling gave some help. He lay on a mattress – rubbery and lumpy – that was on the floor and in a corner against two walls. The other walls looked close, and he couldn't see any furniture. Surreal. A prison cell? He rolled along, off the mattress and onto the floor. Hey, this floor felt a bit like the mattress.

Growing fury helped him struggle from the canvas sheet. Yes, he was starkers but for underpants. Well – some kind of elasticated rubbery pants, covering a wet towel. He lifted himself to sit on the edge of the mattress and bowed his head into his hands. A familiar stink. Hadn't peed his pants since he was a kid.

It was coming back in an eerie dreamlike way. The mental man, the GP, scrapping with the cops, helplessness. This had to be – not prison, but, worse, the loony bin.

Click. A small shaft of light appeared and he roused himself to stagger towards it. *Click.* The light went out, and he felt his way along padded walls, cursing, shouting for help. This was weird too – no echo. And he couldn't find a door! As he made for the mattress again, he tripped over something. He fumbled the object. A piss pot, made of rubber. Empty at least.

Click. The shaft of light. A distant voice said, "You are awake, Mr Chisholm." The voice was unfamiliar, but reminded him of Panjit, his pal from uni.

He could make out where in the wall the light was coming through. Tensing, he sprang up towards it, but it vanished with a click. Where the light had been, he slammed both hands against a padded wall. "I'm awake all right. Let me out!" he yelled.

But the conversation had ended, and he was left in semi-darkness. He tried digging his fingers into where the light had shone through. The surface was impenetrable. Maybe a hatch operated from the outside? There had to be a door. He crawled along by each wall, his fingers probing unsuccessfully. Maybe this was Hell, and he'd never escape.

He again raised himself to where he thought the light had come from, and, yelling, beat against the wall with his fists. Noiseless and utterly futile. He slumped back across the mattress. His body ached, right through his bones and muscles. He lay drowsing.

Becky sprouts wings and flutters away. A butterfly? He tries to follow, but can't get his legs to move from under a heap of coal. Heather swoops past on a broomstick, shrieking, laughing at him.

He awoke, sweating. A horror dream. He recalled where he was – in a cell, in the loony bin – and the helplessness returned.

The shaft of light was there again. He lay still, listening, then shouted, "Hello?"

The voice replied. "Hello Mr Chisholm. How are you?"

How did this character think he was? Better try a different approach. "Where am I?"

"You are in Springwell Mental Hospital." A man, same as before, with a foreign accent, was speaking through the hole where the light shone from.

"What am I doing in here? I'm not mad."

"Well the people who brought you in say you are." A pause, then the voice continued. "They also say you were violent and dangerous, so we gave you knockout medicine and put you in this padded room."

"This what?"

"It is a padded cell. You are there for your own protection."

"For my protection! I don't need protecting. My imprisonment, you mean?"

"Well, that is also true. You were, as I said, violent, and you are also in here for the protection of other people."

Rubbing his sore eyes, he rose to sitting on the edge of the mattress. This guy could hold the key to his release. "Who are you?"

"I am Dr Singh, psychiatric registrar." Not Panjit – Indian sub-continent, though.

"Can you let me out of here, please?"

"No, not yet. We must be sure it will be safe to do so."

"For heaven's sake!" he yelled, "I can't even see you." He sprang up towards the light, which immediately vanished with a click. He hammered at the walls and then slumped onto the floor. He was helpless, beaten.

Click. The shaft of light. "The nurses will bring medicine to help you sleep," said the doctor.

Click. Semi-darkness again, and silence. He fumbled for the mattress and lay on it.

Click. The shaft of light. Yes, a hatch. A voice barked, "Chisholm, wakey! Time for your medicine." A very different voice – rough, gravelly. Sounded familiar, but where from? "Be a good boy," the voice continued. "Any trouble and we'll do for you."

That was it. The pig of a sergeant major at Aldershot for his induction to National Service and that delightful square-bashing! He'd dreamed of a reunion with that jumped-up little sadist – in a dark alley.

He heard, "Go." A door magically swung open and a large man stood in the doorway. From behind this heavy, the sergeant major voice growled, "Chisholm, you bloody stay where you are."

He did this and braced himself as the heavy, and then another equally big, squeezed into the cell. He sat up on the edge of the mattress, watching the white-coated incomers.

Sarge the Voice now blocked the doorway. "There are three of us

40

nurses, Chisholm, and we're coming in to give you knockout medicine."

Nurses! Not like any he'd known.

He raised himself to standing, facing his guests as Sarge the Voice also entered the cell. Getting crowded. They expected trouble. Why shouldn't he oblige? Dammit, he'd nothing to lose.

"Sit down, Chisholm," Sarge the Voice commanded. This man was twice the size of the Aldershot beast, though the rasping voice and offensive manner were uncannily similar. Sarge stood in the centre of the trio, blocking the open doorway.

John could feel the adrenalin. *Take deep breaths, and wait for them to move.*

The two heavies moved in concert to grab his arms. He slipped through between them, charging at Sarge the Voice, who stepped to one side. Freedom. But no. He hit a concrete abdomen and, caught in a headlock, was forced to the floor. Another heavy!

Cursing bodies crashed onto him. A steamroller might hurt less, and he couldn't move his weighed-down trunk or limbs. His head was being raised, his nose pinched and his mouth forced open. Foul-tasting liquid trickled down his throat. He was gulping. Maybe they were poisoning him. Everything faded.

He was back in the cell, on the mattress. His mouth was dry and on fire, with a taste like sewage. He made to sit up. Just moving hurt. His head was packed with splintered wood. But images of the invaders were clear. He'd charged them, and been done over.

Slowly, painfully, he raised himself to sitting and blew out his lips. Breathing in, he caught a sewer pong. He blew and sniffed a few times. Whatever it was stank, though it hadn't killed him. Maybe better if it had. He was a mouse in a trap.

Nauseous, he managed to crawl to the rubber potty and retched. His guts were being ripped. Only liquid came up, and that stank like a drain.

He lay on the floor, sweaty and shivery, with a thudding like roadworks inside his head. He'd had enough, feeling like dying but not like doing anything about that. Struggling to think, everything was jumbled. Images of Heather and Becky at breakfast, of Natalie floating, of the Head shouting, blurred as he drowsed into the land of nightmares.

7

Sam Newman motored at fair speed along puddly country lanes. This morning's escorting to the loony bin hadn't been a problem, as the patient came voluntarily. Not like that mad teacher yesterday. Sam used to like action – but maybe he was past it. As well the police were there. Smashing wife the man had. Must call on her some time; check she knew the score about visiting, try to comfort her. Not that he'd be expected to call. His obligatory visits were nearly all pre-admission.

He looked forward to Saturday afternoons. The boss had decreed that Mr Newman show up at the office five-and-a-half days weekly; but from Saturday noon, the building mercifully closed for the weekend. And though on standby 24/7, Sam was rarely troubled on Saturday afternoons. Thus free to indulge his passion for watching football, he had this season got to all Rovers' home matches. Today was special. Last game in the league, and Rovers, one point behind United, would entertain the enemy. 'Champions at last', the *Evening News* crowed.

He pulled into the driveway just on noon. Something he blessed his employer for – this nice two-bedroom semi. Opening the front door, he met a torrent. "With that hussy again? You've no time for me." His once-lovely wife Ella was going through a bad spell. She'd always been prone to jealous outbursts, and the disseminated sclerosis didn't help. It was ten years since a neurologist gave the diagnosis, and said the illness must have been there for well over a decade. "We have no cure, and sadly it's progressive – though you can expect periods of remission," wasn't great news.

"What's her name?" she whispered.

"I've been working. And there is no other woman." True. Right now.

"You'll be leaving me alone again." Yes, with a 3pm kick-off, he wouldn't be back before six; and their beloved child Helen worked at Woollies till then.

He applied himself to his Saturday task – making the scrambled egg on toast. Ella struggled into her wheelchair and manoeuvred to her place at the table.

They ate in silence. When the phone rang, he was glad to escape to the hall. But he didn't feel so good when he heard the voice.

The secretary to Springwell's Medical Superintendent was a spry ex-schoolteacher who clearly knew she spoke for the boss.

"Mr Newman, we need your help urgently."

She'd rung him only twice before, but each time the command (definitely not a request) started like this. He'd been obliged to drop other things and comply pronto. First week on the job, he'd gone with the MOH to meet the loony bin's Medical Superintendent (a wizened, fiery-looking man who grilled him about his job and why he'd come to work in mental health). The boss, keen on decent relations with Springwell, had made it clear he should jump if the Med Super asked him to.

"Yes, Miss Bewlay," he growled.

"One of our patients, whom you admitted, is on our Infirmary Ward, critically ill with pneumonia. John Chisholm, 90 Green Drive. We need you to contact his wife, Mrs Heather Chisholm, and bring her to Springwell." She paused. "Now."

"Isn't she on the phone? And doesn't she have a car?" Must see the match.

"No and no. You should know that, as you took her details when you admitted Mr Chisholm yesterday."

That stung. But there was still something odd about this. "Don't you take the ill folk into town?"

An impatient sigh? "Yes, but Mr Chisholm is too ill to be moved. Our physician advises that we summon the nearest relative immediately."

Better get on with it. "Yes, Miss Bewlay. Shall I take her to the ward?"

"No. Report at the main entrance and seat Mrs Chisholm in our Main Hall. They will ring for the charge nurse, who will send someone down to escort her. I suggest you wait in the Main Hall until she needs escorting home."

Blast. He'd miss the match. "Yes Miss." He slammed down the receiver and, turning, almost stumbled into Ella. She'd moved in her wheelchair to sit behind him. He cursed aloud, and immediately regretted it. Ella suffered enough without that.

"That was *her*, wasn't it?" Ella said, her brow knitted.

He took a deep breath. "No, that was Springwell. I've to take a patient's relative –"

But Ella had rotated her wheelchair and was making for the settee. She struggled onto it and buried her head in a cushion.

"The man's dying," he said quietly. He cleared the dirty dishes and washed up. Another Saturday job.

Better go. He checked his pocket for fags. One thing – at least he could light up outside. Ella wouldn't let him smoke anywhere inside. "Disgusting and filthy," she'd said on their first day together. After a volcanic row that nearly blew them apart, he'd decided he loved Ella more than the fags. So he, a chronic smoker accustomed to lighting up wherever and whenever, agreed to comply – and managed to stick to this. Nights, he'd often creep out for a drag by the back door.

He saw Ella watching him. Her eyes closed as he approached. He leaned over and kissed her on the forehead, then picked up coat and briefcase and left.

As he journeyed through nigh-deserted streets, Miss Bewlay's imperious tones rang in his ears. Talking to him like her slave! He could see her in a classroom, terrifying the poor kids into submission. Give some women power!

Funny thing to ask. Chisholm must be on the way out. Bet you – at Springwell they felt responsible. He'd maybe have been within his rights to refuse this escort job, but he didn't want the hassle of being snapped at by that witch, then dragged through hot cinders by the boss. And if the patient died... No choice, Sam.

Stopped by traffic lights, he looked in the car mirror and smoothed his hair. Mrs C was a stunner, and being with a beautiful woman always gave him a buzz.

He had married *the* beauty. But even from their earliest days together, his urges to play the field were irresistible. He felt an urge now – powerfully.

He swung into Green Drive and screeched to a halt outside number 90.

8

Saturday 21st April 1956 – in Aversham, then to Springwell.

Heather awoke to a knocking. Her head throbbed. Where was she?

The door opened. She sat up. Of course – at Elsie's.

"How are you, m'dear?" Elsie stood cradling Becky.

She yawned. "Alright." Though she didn't feel it, after a night spent mainly on tending to her restless child. Even more troublesome were the periods of quiet, when fears and imaginings plagued her over-active mind.

"You had a fair old night of it with the bairn, m'dear."

"Yes. Sorry for the noise – must have kept you both awake."

"Och, I'm never much of a sleeper. And Mattie can snore through thunder."

"Did I sleep through Becky crying?"

"No, m'dear. After we got up at seven, Becky was making wee noises. I peeked round the door and you were asleep, so I took her downstairs. She had one of her jars and baby milk. I sang her to sleep and stayed with her. She's a grand bairn."

"Thanks, Elsie."

As if on cue, Becky started crying. "Might be that she's hungry, m'dear."

"I don't normally feed her again till midday."

Elsie smiled. "It's gone half-past twelve, m'dear."

Goodness! She'd last looked at her watch at six a.m... "Gosh, Elsie."

"I'm happy to feed the bairn now, m'dear, while you get dressed."

"But what about the shop?"

"Mattie'll manage. Now, shall I go and feed the bairn?"

47

"Please, Elsie." Heather downed a couple of aspirins. Dressing, she switched into action mode. After something to eat, she'd ask about phoning her parents.

She'd just sat down at the table, when Mattie shouted through the doorway. "You've a visitor, lass."

A face peered round the door. The mental man!

"Sam Newman. I thought you'd be here, Mrs Chisholm. Can I come in for a minute?"

"Yes, Sir," said Elsie, rising from her seat.

Newman remained standing and told Heather his reason for calling.

"But – John – how ill?" was all she could manage.

Newman repeated what he'd been told. "When you come, you'll find out more." He looked away and added, "Must be serious for them to summon you."

"I'll have Becky, m'dear. You go and see your man," urged Elsie.

That settled it. She donned her coat as she followed Newman outside. She wanted to run to the car, but he was exasperatingly slow – seemed to have a limp.

She perched on the front seat beside Newman. The tyres screeched as he rounded the corner. At least he drove fast. She sat back in her seat – and on the journey, through the outskirts of town and along winding roads with high hedgerows and glimpses of fields, could think only about John. She heard Newman speak occasionally, but the words were intrusive. She was replaying memories of happier times with John and feeling the pain of impending loss.

"Up there," Newman was pointing towards the horizon, "the chimney." She looked up to glimpse the top of a chimney belching smoke. "All the old asylums have them – I mean of course the mental hospitals."

She glanced across, and imagined his face had reddened. "Sorry – they used to be called asylums," he said.

Yes, or loony bins. She peered through the car's front window, but saw only hedgerows and trees.

"This is it, coming up." Newman swung the car left and chugged slowly down a tree-lined road.

She now had her first real view of Springwell, still a distance away. The place looked grey and austere. She hadn't known what to expect, but this made her shiver.

"Grim-looking, eh?" Newman said.

"It looks like a prison. That high wall – and the building, what I can see of it." On her Social Studies course, she'd visited a prison – a depressing experience, in a scary, drab place.

They stopped, facing iron gates within a high stone archway. Through the gates on the right was a tiny stone cottage. From this a burly uniformed man emerged, and lumbered towards them through a narrow side gate.

"The Lodge," Newman said. "Their motto is 'they shall not pass'." He got something from his pocket. "My warrant card; he damn well always wants to see it." He thrust the card out of his window towards the unsmiling man.

The gates were opened and Newman drove down a winding road towards the front of what looked like the main building, at the obligatory ten miles per hour. She noted the lawns with beautiful flowerbeds on both sides nearly all the way down. Nice, in contrast to that prison. Maybe the inside wouldn't be as bad as she feared. They stopped alongside other cars in an area marked 'staff'.

"Follow me," said Newman, and started labouring up a flight of stone steps towards a large imposing door. "This is like Fort Knox and we have to be let in."

At the door he rang a bell, and kept his finger pressed on it. There was a clanking of keys and creaking as the door was unlocked and slowly opened.

9

A big man in a white coat stood smiling. "Aye, it's you disturbing the peace, Sam." He beckoned them inside and slammed then locked the door.

Newman introduced him as "Jock Mackenzie, one of the good guys," and explained the purpose of their visit.

Heather smiled at the man. Must be older than Father, and looked avuncular. What would the bad guys be like, though?

"Och, I'm sorry your husband's ill," said the man in a broad Scottish accent. He turned to Newman. "So the boss said she's to come. The lad must be special."

Newman grunted. "Has to be for me to miss the big match."

She didn't see the significance of this remark – which seemed to go unheeded by Mackenzie – but didn't feel that mattered. Of course John was special. Couldn't they get a move on? John could be dying. She followed the men along a well-lit and high-ceilinged hallway – grand, posh-looking – for a few steps to another large solid-looking door. Mackenzie unlocked it, and locked it again after they'd passed through.

They were in a vast space – austere and bare. "Our Main Hall, Mrs Chisholm. Come with me to the office," said Mackenzie, pointing to a small room in one corner. She followed as he lumbered across and found the key to unlock the door. He gestured toward a desk with an open ledger-type book on it. "I have to make a note in the Visitors' Book, about the patient you're visiting and your details."

This was so slow! She gulped out "John Chisholm" and went to stand beside the desk, waiting while the man sat down and took a fountain pen from his pocket. She watched him write the date in one column, then pause at the next.

"What's his name again, lass? I have to get it right."

She repeated John's name and spelt it for the man as he wrote laboriously in copperplate handwriting. Then, confirming her marital status, she gave her name and address, with spellings, and saw him write 'Infirmary' in another column.

Mackenzie pressed the sheet with blotting paper, pocketed the pen and stood up. Thank goodness that was over. Where was the urgency?

"You wait over there with Sam, lassie." Mackenzie pointed to a row of chairs against a wall. "I'll ring the ward, and they'll send a nurse to take you there."

Heather went and perched on the edge of a seat next to Newman. "Do they always have this palaver? John could have died by now."

"It's always the same procedure, even on an emergency visit. The only difference will be them bringing your husband down here to see you. I've never before known them let a visitor – even me when I admit a patient – onto their wards."

He sounded angry. Nothing to how she felt. What were they playing at? She must see John – now! An age passed. Newman limped across to Mackenzie.

A clanking of keys? Yes – a door was opening in the far corner. A white-coated man appeared.

She leapt to her feet.

Mackenzie shouted, "Mr Niven's here from Infirmary, Mrs Chisholm, and –"

She'd reached the open door.

The sullen-looking giant Mr Niven grunted and stood aside to let her pass. She watched impatiently as he fiddled with keys and locked the door behind them.

The next few minutes were a blur of walking in silence behind Niven along gloomy empty corridors. This was eerie, Dickensian, but at least she was being led to John. If only this giant would get a move on. He shambled, with no hint of urgency. Now and again she got a whiff of something nasty and unfamiliar – but this didn't bother her. She'd brave Hell itself to see John.

"We're here, Ma'am." The man wrestled with his bunch of keys and unlocked the door marked 'Male Infirmary'. "Wait there behind me," he said, and opened the door a fraction, shouting, "Sir, she's here."

More delay! The door opened to reveal another white-coated man. Niven stood aside and motioned her to go in.

The other man extended a hand. "Mrs Chisholm, I'm Mr Macnamara, the Charge Nurse here. Come with me. Your husband's near the other end."

Walking between the rows of beds reminded her of visiting her uncle on a general infirmary ward, but here really stank. She risked glancing from side to side, glimpsing beds – some empty, others with huddled figures on them – until she saw a leering pyjama-jacket-clad man sitting legs apart on his bed. Cheeks warm, she kept her eyes on the Charge Nurse as he walked ahead of her.

That smell. Same as the corridors, but stronger. Sick-making. And was that howling – and a wolf whistle – somewhere behind her?

Macnamara slowed and halted by a bed where another white-coated man stood. "Your husband," he said, "and the nurse is Mr Maclean."

No! Propped up in bed was a strange figure. Something covered his face and a tube ran down to a machine.

"The mask is to give him oxygen," said Macnamara. "And," he pointed at the machine, "that's the oxygen cylinder. He's got pneumonia."

She hadn't been prepared for seeing John in this state. She resisted her impulse to rush over and hug him. That might kill him. She walked over and knelt beside the bed. She took his limp hand and held it, burying her wet face in the blanket covering his loins. "John," she said. "It's Heather."

John's breathing sounded laboured; his eyes were open but stared vacantly. She heard Macnamara say "A seat," and, still clinging to John's hand, rose to sit on a small hard-backed chair.

She wiped her face with her sleeve. Raising herself, she bent over to kiss his brow. It was hot, soaking. She sat back again, holding his hand and squeezing it gently. An unnatural pink spot blemished each of his paler-than-usual cheeks.

Did he know it was her? The unblinking eyes gave nothing away and his wet hand was limp. Did he mumble something? She held her ear close to the mask but couldn't pick up anything coherent. "John, darling. It's me, Heather. Can you hear me?"

No visible reaction. Macnamara's voice intruded. "Your man's delirious, with a high fever. He rambles, but it doesn't mean he's conscious."

Surely John was dying. She relinquished his hand and stood up to face Macnamara. "He looks very poorly."

"He's on the critical list, but sure your man's a fighter."

John was a fighter all right, but was this his last battle? Her eyes blurred.

"Mrs Chisholm, we'll leave you alone with your husband a few minutes." Macnamara motioned to the nurse and they moved away.

Alone at the bedside, she sat down again, took John's hand and kept pressing it, but she couldn't feel any reaction. She kept talking to him, but got no apparent response. He mumbled again, but her best effort to make sense of this left her feeling more desperate. There was nothing she could do. John was dying.

She heard movement behind her. Macnamara. She bent over to kiss John's brow, then followed the Charge Nurse in silence back along the ward.

He stopped outside the door of a room partitioned from the ward. "Come into my office a minute, Mrs Chisholm. There's something I must ask you."

She followed him into the office. They remained standing.

"Sure, your husband has a fair chance of survival. This last hour, the fever abated a little." He coughed and looked away. "But just in case - what's his religion?"

What? "Why?" she demanded.

"Well, if he's Catholic and if it looks like he won't make it, we'll –"

No. "You'd better not let him die," she yelled, advancing on the man. "You've made him ill. You cure him, or –!" Macnamara was staring down at her.

"All right boss?" Behind her. She swung round and collided into a huge solid white-coated figure. "Steady, Miss," the man growled. She was a helpless rag doll under the powerful hands, one on each shoulder, that restrained her.

She collapsed onto the chair Macnamara pushed toward her. Her eyes swam. She'd lose her beloved John. And even her temper – which she never lost – wasn't under her control.

She calmed and dried her face with a tissue. "Sorry." She addressed Macnamara's question. "He's Roman Catholic – though I think he's lapsed. We've not been to a church for ages." Now she was regretting that.

"Thanks, and I'm sorry for upsetting you." Macnamara looked haggard. "I'll let our RC chaplain know right away. Our Church of England man called earlier and – because your husband was unconscious – gave some kind of blessing."

"The last rites," Heather murmured. Confirmation of her fears.

"I don't think so. Sure it's only Catholic priests give the last rites."

She had a question. "How did John get pneumonia? He didn't have it when he went into Springwell."

"I don't know, as he went to our Admissions Ward first." He hesitated. "Your husband might have had hypothermia before he came in."

Hypothermia – people could die of it. "No! He certainly did not have that when he was taken to Springwell," she replied.

She was ready to go, and stood up. "Don't let John die – please."

"Maybe that's a plea for the Almighty too, Mrs Chisholm? Be sure we'll do our damnedest to see John right again."

Niven was summoned to escort her. She trailed him through dimly-lit corridors, passing trolleys with urns being trundled along by men in brown coats. The trolleys probably bore food and drink. Smelt like cabbage. A pleasant change from whatever foul chemical stank in the corridors earlier.

Her taciturn companion unlocked and locked doors, and finally she was back in the Main Hall. Newman was with Mackenzie and another white-coated man.

"You're shaking, lassie, like you've seen a ghost," said Mackenzie.

"I don't want to talk about it, thanks." Ironic. Maybe she had seen a ghost.

She went with Newman, and doors were unlocked and then locked behind them. They proceeded in silence towards the car. She walked slowly, eyeing the ground. Newman, limping along beside her, kept looking at her. Irritating, but this gave some distraction from her dark thoughts. What a boring little man.

When they reached the car, Newman asked, "How was your husband?"

"He's alive – for now."

She wanted to be alone with her thoughts. She had questions that maybe Newman could answer. But her weary befogged mind just wanted rest. On the journey back to Elsie's, she feigned the sleep she was craving.

10

Saturday 21ˢᵗ – Sunday 22ⁿᵈ April 1956 – in Aversham.

Drawing to a halt outside Elsie's, Newman passed Heather a card. "That's where you can contact me. First number's my direct line."

She put it in her handbag. "Thanks."

He switched off the engine and turned to face her. Was he going to make a pass? "If anything happens to your husband, Springwell will contact you. And if you've any queries, or need to go again, ring me. I'll help if I can."

"Thanks." She opened the car door.

"Before you go – are you okay?" he asked as he revved up.

"Yes." She was too played out to feel anything but a dull headache. She forced a smile and waved as he drove off.

Mattie greeted her in a shop packed with customers. He pointed to the back-shop. "Through there, lass."

She tapped on the door and, as she pushed it open slowly, caught the welcome pungent, unique aroma.

Elsie was removing the full nappy. "She's been a clever girl for Mummy."

Heather picked up her child and cuddled her. "Becky, my Becky," she murmured, letting her tears flow.

"I'll deal with this nappy, then make us a cuppa." Elsie rose.

Nappy change completed, Heather laid Becky in her crib and soon the child was asleep.

Elsie returned with the tea tray, poured two cups and sat down beside her. "You look right weary, m'dear. Do you want to tell me about it?"

The uplift from cuddling Becky went as she started her tale. "It was horrible." She brushed her eyes.

"There, m'dear, take your time."

She continued in a low voice with her main worry. "John's dying of pneumonia." Encouraged by Elsie, she found strength to tell of her fears, and the agonies and frustrations of the visit. When at one point Becky started crying, Heather realised she'd been shouting. Standing up, she lifted the child and cuddled her. "Elsie," she said quietly. "It's worse than a prison, and I fear for John in there."

"M'dear, it must be terrible for you." Elsie's homely face looked strained and her blue eyes shone with compassion.

"I feel helpless. I don't know what I'd have done without you two."

"M'dear, we'll help you and Becky all we can." Elsie paused and looked at Becky. "We had a bairn once, but she lived just two hours. And we couldn't have any more."

"Oh." She wanted to say something comforting to Elsie about this, an overwhelming tragedy, but didn't know how.

Elsie, her eyes glistening, continued, "Ailsa would've been a grand wee bairn like Becky, then a fine young lass like yourself, but the Lord took her."

How sad and unfair. She took Elsie's hand and gave it a gentle squeeze. She still couldn't find anything to say. A dead baby. The grief must have been unfathomable. Elsie and Mattie would have been great parents. They'd already gone further in helping than any parents – never mind her own – could.

Elsie stood up. "M'dear, I've never talked about that. It was long ago – back in Newcastle, where we both grew up. We came down here just after, kept quiet about it and got on with our work."

"Thanks for telling me." And she meant it. Of course she'd told Elsie her deepest fears. But this was different – the older woman, a rock in a crisis and a support-giver, choosing to trust her with a tragic secret from long ago.

The door swung open. "The shop's closed," Mattie announced. He turned to Heather. "You're fair worked up, lass. Will you and the bairn stay with us the night?"

"You must, m'dear," said Elsie.

"Yes please." She didn't want to face the empty house yet.

That evening, though not hungry, she ate egg and chips. Must keep her strength up, for Becky. She yawned. "Sorry, Elsie, I'm exhausted –"

"Your room's ready, m'dear," said Elsie. "I'll make up a bottle for the bairn."

The support she needed. She hugged Elsie. "You're brilliant friends," she told the pair before retiring with Becky to the bedroom.

She downed two aspirins and, after Becky fell asleep, lay on the bed in the darkened room. She dreaded bad news about John. If only she could have stayed with him. That charge nurse said he'd 'a fair chance'. And they'd let her know if he died? Not good enough. She must find out how he was. Springwell would have a phone. Tomorrow she'd ask about using the shop phone.

What about her and Becky? Particularly if John had got the sack? Surely he hadn't. Yet awful injustices happened. John had known this first-hand – he'd told her how officialdom treated his father after the accident, and she knew from Social Studies.

She didn't want to ask her parents for help, but she must. Tomorrow?

The crying was insistent. She switched on the bedside lamp. Nearly 3am. Must have drifted off. She picked Becky up, nuzzled her and changed the nappy.

Tiptoeing out to the bathroom, she heard snoring from Mattie and Elsie's room. En route to her bed, she stopped outside their door and listened. Yes, they both snored.

Back in the room, she wondered if she snored. John never mentioned it, but then he wouldn't. He was too nice – or had been. When he lay on his back, he snored like a crackling loudspeaker. On honeymoon, she'd told him he sounded like a tiger. He growled, "I am a tiger," and sprang to crouch over her. This led to heavenly sex. Everything was great then.

Some weeks ago – she was clear of depression, and John's brow had started to furrow – he awoke and sat up in bed after snoring. She said, "Tiger, go for it," and tried to hug him. He grunted "Let go," and got out of bed. No magic sex. She hadn't called him 'tiger' since. Would she ever hear her tiger snore again?

She swallowed two more aspirins, then lay meditating on what Elsie told her. Tragic. At least she had Becky. Her child's welfare was all-important.

Bells. Church bells. It was light, almost ten a.m. She'd dozed off. And the crib was empty. Panic. But no, Elsie would have Becky safe.

Heather dressed hastily and followed the smell of frying bacon. There indeed was Becky, cradled on Elsie's arm.

After breakfast, Mattie opened up the back-shop for Heather and got Springwell's number from Directory Enquiries.

"I'll be in the shop looking at the shelves, lassie. When you finish on the phone, just give me a shout."

"Thanks, Mattie." She dialled the number.

"We do not give out information about inmates, Madam," said Springwell's switchboard operator.

"But I have a right to know. I am his wife."

"Madam, we do *not* give out information about inmates."

She inhaled deeply, and yelled, "Did you hear me?"

"Perfectly, Madam. There's no need to shout." He wasn't going to shift.

Stay cool, Heather. "Listen then, please. My husband is at death's door in your infirmary. The nurse in charge, Mr Macnamara, said to ring." Untrue, but...

A sigh? "I'll see then, madam. What is your husband's name?"

She told him again and the line seemed to go dead. She hung on for ages. And then she heard the Irish brogue. "Macnamara, Mrs Chisholm. I have good news. Our physician Doc Burn just popped in. Your husband's on the mend."

Thank God. "Is he conscious?"

"Still a tad delirious, but he's responding to the penicillin. Sure and he'll live."

"When can I see him?"

"That's not up to me. Visiting's once a month, except for emergencies. Could you ring back in a few days?" Then, "Excuse me, I must go." The phone went dead.

A relief, though still worrying. Sufficiently reassuring to risk being away at her parents' a few days. But she'd stay on here a couple of days–in case Springwell rang.

11

Ringing her parents was something of a long shot as they were often abroad on holiday. Heather never felt that close to them or experienced the warm affection she got from Granny. Mother's "You can do better, Heather," contrasted with Granny's "Well done, Heather." Why did Granny have to die?

Her parents had supported her in schoolwork and hobbies. And despite the coolness over John, she'd still got Christmas cards and postcards – all addressed to 'Heather and Becky' – from her parents' exotic holiday destinations. And they unfailingly remembered her birthday with a welcome cheque.

She waited till noon to ring as they might have gone to church earlier.

"This is Bolsall 516." Mother's voice, a cultured Edinburgh accent.

"Mother – it's Heather."

"Heather. What a surprise. Darling, how nice to hear from you." A pause. "So you have a phone now?"

"No. Our friends at the shop across the road let me use theirs."

"Not Becky – is she all right?" Mother sounded anxious.

"Becky's fine, Mother."

Sounded like a sigh. Mother used to sigh a lot. "What's wrong then? Do you need money?"

She swallowed. Mother was always direct in her comment, and this hurt. No real concern – but an assumption she'd get in touch only about money. Mother was spot on, though – the last time she'd phoned her parents was for a top-up to help eke out her student grant. "Well, yes Mother. But it's not as simple as that."

Another sigh. "Just a moment." She heard, "Who is it?" in the background, and Mother whispering "Heather." "Does she want money? Has she left that rascal?" Definitely Father. Mother again: "Carry on, Heather. What's not so simple?"

"Well, it's John. He's very ill in hospital and might be there for ages. He's got pneumonia and nearly died."

Another sigh. Then Father whispering, "What does she want us to do?" "I'm sorry," said Mother. If only she meant it. "What do you want from us?"

"Can Becky and I come to see you and stay a few days?"

"I'm sure... Here, speak with your father a minute."

"Heather." Father's voice, but quieter than she remembered – almost strained. He'd always sounded like he was addressing a meeting. "I'm sorry to hear John's ill." Hypocrite. "We'd be glad to have you and Becky over here."

"Thanks."

"Which hospital's John in? We'll send a card."

"Actually," she hesitated. She hated reinforcing their negative view of John. But she had to tell them. "He's in the infirmary at Springwell."

"Whew." A whispered aside (Father to Mother): "He's gone off his rocker." Then, "Right, we'll get details when we see you. When do you want to come?"

"I'd like to come on Tuesday, if that's okay?"

"Yes. We'd be happy to come and collect you on Tuesday evening."

Collect – like a parcel? However, she hadn't fancied a journey that would mean catching one bus then changing to another. "Yes. Thanks."

"Good. See you both on Tuesday."

"Oh, hang on a minute, Father." With a hand firmly over the mouthpiece, she shouted to Elsie. She did not want her parents going into her house in its present state.

After a quick consultation with Elsie, she added, "We'll be here across the road, at number 81. It's the flat above the shop."

"Right-ho. 'Bye."

Not entirely a comfortable experience, but not bad, and a good result. Her parents sounded disposed to help her and Becky.

Tuesday 24th April 1956 – in Aversham, then Bolsall.

As Springwell hadn't rung, Heather felt okay about going to her parents. Three or four days should be long enough – to get help, also check on how they were doing.

Just after six p.m., they arrived in their Riley, a grand red car, ageing but shining like new. They tooted, and Heather went out with Becky asleep in the crib, followed by Mattie with her bag and Elsie the pushchair. Her parents got out of the car to embrace her and shook hands with the older couple, but declined a cup of tea.

As Father revved up, she wound down the car window, shouted "'Bye," and waved to the pair. Elsie's eyes glistened.

She brushed her wet face with her hand and closed the window.

Mother twisted round from the front and whispered, "Mustn't waken Becky."

The journey passed in silence. Mother's brow was more lined. Father's black hair was snowy-white. Just getting older? Or were they under pressure? There was of course a big age gap – they were both forty-two when she was born. Funny, she'd never thought of her parents as vulnerable. Both always presented a strong front. Father's words to her some time in her childhood – "Stiff upper lip, young Heather; some things are sent to try us" – epitomised their approach to any kind of setback.

Not that much seemed to get in the way of their affluent lifestyle. Even in the war, Father continued as a bank manager and Mother as a medical secretary at the hospital – leaving her in the care of Granny (who lived in the 'granny flat').

Yes, cared for by her wonderful granny until that fateful day. Her tenth birthday party over, friends gone, she'd kissed Granny goodnight. Next morning, Father stood in her bedroom doorway. "Granny's ill, Heather."

She'd never known Granny to be ill. Tiptoeing through to Granny's, she slipped past Mother and crawled onto the bed. Mother yelled, "Come back, darling."

And there Granny lay – mouth open, eyes staring from her lifeless face.

Aching with grief for ages after, she'd got no comfort from Mother's repeated "I gave up a good job for you, Heather." Sacrifice and an eternal grudge. Mother's switch to part-time work in the typing pool had meant a slump in status and pay.

The car was slowing. They were near her parents' home. Throughout the journey, she'd hardly given John a thought. From deep in her core, she began to experience again the anguish threatening to overwhelm her.

She didn't want to face talking to her parents this evening. She fed Becky, then, pleading fatigue, went up to bed, to seek the rest she craved.

12

John was burning. He heard a funny noise, a rasping – his own breathing. Something was on his face. He couldn't move. Everything was swirling, then fading.

In and out of dreams, he fancied he could hear Heather's voice, feel her holding his hand. She floated among the white-coats.

Now he was awake. Everything was blurred. Funny smell. He wriggled, uncomfortable and sweating. He was in a bed, lying on something smooth yet lumpy, like a horsehair mattress.

A white-coated man was peering at him. "You're awake."

He tried to speak, but couldn't. He felt up around his mouth – he was wearing a mask of some kind. He moved it to one side and managed a hoarse whisper. "Where am I?"

"You're on Infirmary Ward, in Springwell Mental Hospital. That's an oxygen mask." The white-coated man put it back on his face.

What was he doing here? Felt like he'd survived a good kicking. His chest ached and his throat was on fire. He wanted to raise himself, but his left hand felt shackled.

"Don't move!" A crisp command. "You're on a drip." The white-coated man put a hand on his shoulder to keep him still.

What? This was *his* face. He lifted the mask with his right hand. "Why?"

"You've been critical with pneumonia." The man leaned over – and John felt the mask back on his face. "Keep that on. You still need it to breathe properly."

That was better. Anyway, talking hurt.

"Doc Burn gave you penicillin right away and it's worked wonders. You're out of danger."

'Out of danger'. Nearly died. Helpless, sleepy, he slid into unconsciousness.

John awoke. Something stank – like fumes, powerful and nasty. His head felt it had been stamped on. But he could see more clearly. And that mask was off his face. He could breathe okay. He shifted his body and realised the drip had gone.

Using his hands and elbows, he raised himself and looked around. Giddifying, but he could see. His bed was near the end of a long row.

He heard demented crying. White-coats were clustering round a bed, opposite and along the row. The crying ceased.

A dressing-gowned man was coming his direction from down the ward. Head bowed, the man shuffled to the bottom of John's bed, then stopped, mumbling. Gibberish? The man looked up, gripped the bedstead's iron rail and stared, wild-eyed, straight at him.

Disconcerting. Was this madness? Closer now, the man looked younger – middle-aged, maybe.

"Hello, what's wrong?" John croaked.

"You," shouted the man, pointing at him.

"Me?" He braced himself.

The man whirled round and, muttering, with head bowed, shuffled away.

He watched the man go slowly down the ward – head still bowed and not turning to right or left.

The white-coats now stood talking. Were they doctors – or these wretched 'nurses', like Sarge and his henchmen? He closed his eyes and slumped back onto the pillow. He didn't want to see Sarge and co again – except some day in that dark alley.

His bed was shaking. An earthquake? No. The dressing-gowned one had reappeared at the end of the bed, tugging at the bed-rail with both hands and yelling.

This man was strong – and crazy.

He dragged himself up onto an elbow. Through a wave of stars, he saw a white-coat appear and take the man by the arm. "C'mon professor. Back to your own bed." The man said something that sounded unintelligible but abusive, released his grip on the bed-rail, and raised a clenched fist towards John. A white-coated reinforcement came, and the man was led off muttering.

The dizziness gone, he raised himself to sitting and watched the party go down the ward to near the other end. He heard shouting as the man was bundled into bed. Loud groaning was followed by silence.

He lay back, grateful for the white-coats' intervention. He could normally handle all this, without hurting anyone. But right now...

He remembered from long ago the words of his grandpa – a Great War soldier, standing looking very sad – to his da. "Some men went doolally, right off their heads. Fought like wildcats. Didn't know their own strength."

A white-coat was at his bedside, holding a thermometer. "I'll take your temperature and feel your pulse." The same Irish voice as before.

"Wait," he croaked. "Who are you?"

"I'm Mr Macnamara, the Charge Nurse – that means I'm in charge of this Infirmary Ward. Now, can you please open your mouth, Mr Chisholm."

He did so, staring back at Macnamara, and accommodated the thermometer under his tongue.

"Take his pulse, Tommy." Another white-coated man, that he hadn't noticed on the other side of his bed, leaned across and grabbed his wrist. "Mr Niven here's a nursing assistant," the Charge Nurse said, "and," nodding towards the end of the bed, towards another white-coat, "that's Mr Maclean, who's a staff nurse and my deputy."

Intensive caring – or a show of strength?

"Like me," Macnamara continued, "Mr Maclean is doubly qualified – the only other man in Springwell that knows his physical as well as his mental."

The man's tone and demeanour were calming, though he was a show-off. The 'doubly qualified' – did that mean like ordinary nurses as well? Or did 'physical' mean they could take care of themselves in a fight?

Macnamara added, "As well as knowing my physical and psychological medicine, I'm trained in martial arts." The man had read his thoughts. "Mr Maclean is too. So if you're thirsting after a fight, don't try anything here."

He wouldn't. He couldn't take a handshake, never mind a beating.

Macnamara smiled and laid a hand on his shoulder. "It's okay – I know you'll be done in." Reading his mind again? "It'll be a few days, maybe weeks, before you're real fit. Sure I'm glad you pulled through. I'd have bet against it. You must have one helluva constitution."

He felt the thermometer being removed. Macnamara examined it. "Still up a bit. Pulse, Tommy?"

"Eighty-six, Sir."

"Right, you're on the road to recovery, Mr Chisholm. But I guess it'll be a while before we can let you go from here."

"Home?" His spirits lifted.

"No," said Macnamara, stepping back as though shocked. "Another ward."

Trapped in this bin. "Why?"

"You'll need treatment for your breakdown. I guess you'll have to stay in Springwell a long while yet." Macnamara held up a hand as if to signal the end of debate. "Now, John Chisholm, we need to give you medicine."

"I don't want it." He was hopelessly weak and achy. His voice was stronger again, though his throat was scorched.

Macnamara frowned. "You must have it. First, the penicillin that's saved your life. We've given you injections every few hours since you came here." He smiled. "And now it's time for that. We'll give your arms a rest. Go on your side, facing Mr Niven over there, and bare your bum for the needle."

He didn't like this. But he complied with the order, and faced Niven, whose bulging black eyes stared through him. He closed his eyes.

He heard Macnamara's "Over to you, Eddie," and glimpsed

Maclean moving round from the end of the bed. Ouch. The jab in the bum.

"Now a couple of spoonfuls of paraldehyde to knock you out. Go on your back again and sit up."

He could smell the horrible stuff. "I'm not having that."

"You are, and if you won't swallow it, we'll jab it into you. You'll need it to help you sleep." Macnamara smiled. "Right?"

"I'll take the dope." Turning to sit up again, his vision blurred and then cleared.

Macnamara, now at the end of the bed, was passing a bottle and spoon to Maclean. Spoonfuls of the now familiar foul-smelling liquid went down John's throat.

At least, he thought, I know what it's called. Paraldehyde. Everything faded.

13

As both parents were out almost all day, Heather had welcomed having a quiet pressure-free time with Becky.

Now – the evening meal over and Becky asleep upstairs – Heather settled into an armchair opposite her parents on the settee. It was time to talk.

"Tell us what happened." Father sucked a biro pen. (He used to smoke those dreadful cigars. Could he have given up?). "How did John end up in the loony bin?"

"It's not a loony bin." Heather's cheeks were warming. It wasn't just the words – there was something about his tone.

"Father means the asylum," said Mother, glancing at Father, who grunted.

She'd known it wouldn't be easy. And hadn't she herself always called it the loony bin? She took a deep breath, straightened her back and leant forward. "No. Springwell is no longer an asylum. John is in a hospital," she said, firmly and slowly, looking squarely at each of her parents in turn, "a mental hospital."

Her parents huddled together more closely. "Well, whatever," said Father. "It's where they always send the nutters."

"Ssh," said Mother, glancing at him again and nudging him with her elbow. "You mean the lunatics." Both now seemed to be frowning.

Something volcanic within was about to erupt. They classed John as a madman, a creature somehow inferior. She stood up and glared at them. She could see the shock on Mother's face, the unchanging bland expression on Father's.

How dare they talk about her beloved John like this? Ignoring her father's curt "Sit down, Heather," and her mother's "Yes dear, do," she paced over towards the drawn curtains - taking deep breaths. She calmed, walked slowly back and sat down.

"We've got off on the wrong track," said Father, and Mother added, "Sorry."

"Well, I know you don't much like John " - she ignored the protestations - "but I love him. And he's not really mad. He's been critically ill with pneumonia and he nearly died." She paused.

Both were looking contrite, Mother possibly sympathetic.

Heather added, her eyes moistening, "He shouldn't be in that dreadful place. He could be there months, or years."

Now they both looked uncomfortable. Father scratched among his white mop of hair. Mother was looking down - studying the pattern on the carpet?

"And he might never get out." She drew her sleeve across her face.

It was clear they were struggling for words. "Surely he will," said Mother. "Look, I need another cup. I'll go fill the teapot."

Mother never was strong in emotional situations. Avoidance and distraction. "Good idea, Mother. I'll check on Becky."

Father stretched and yawned. Or more probably he feigned a yawn - "A tried and tested way to give yourself space to think," he once told her. He was never one to display his feelings either. "I'll help," he said, following Mother to the kitchen.

She crept upstairs. Becky lay on her back, eyes closed, breathing softly.

Heather stood entranced. She'd always be there for her child, like Granny was for her. These terrible months after the birth would have been tough for Becky - something she'd never considered while she was depressed. She was doing her best to make it up and would never again let Becky down.

John was a great dad; but he couldn't be there for Becky now. This insane jealousy that surfaced recently – and led to the loony bin! She'd never had an affair, but he didn't believe her.

What went wrong between her and Mother? On the Social Studies degree, she'd been moved by Bowlby's research on maternal deprivation. Bonding in the early years was considered important to later wellbeing. She'd bonded with Granny, and could still draw support from imaginary talks with her.

"How's Becky?"

Heather jerked round, half expecting to see Granny. Mother was tiptoeing from the doorway, to stand looking into the crib and whisper, "My lovely granddaughter. She reminds me of you as a baby; you slept on your back too."

Mother turned away and began moving quietly out of the room. "Tea's made. Come when you're ready," she whispered, and disappeared.

Heather continued standing. She'd glimpsed a different side to Mother – something maternal. All these years ago, Mother had watched her sleeping.

"A reminder – tea's brewed." Father was in the doorway.

She enjoyed one last look at Becky – a picture of contentment and peace. This, she reminded herself, was what really mattered here. She'd come to ensure help for her and Becky, not John.

She went downstairs. Mother finished pouring tea into the china cups and sat down on the settee beside Father.

She took her cup and sipped the warm liquid. "Thanks. Having a break was a good idea, Mother." She paused. Both parents looked anxious. "I'm really worried, not just about John, but about Becky and me."

"Yes dear," said Mother. "So are we."

Sounded encouraging. "I mean, I'm not sure we'll have enough to live on. John started teaching only last September and I don't know what sick pay he'll get – if any. Or if he'll keep his job." She paused. She hated playing the sympathy card. "It's Becky and her future, that's what I care about. And," she added, aware she was blushing, "as well as being my parents, you're the only folk I know with money."

Her parents were looking at each other. "Well," said Father, "it grieves us to see you in this situation."

"And we do care about you and Becky," Mother added.

"You could come and live with us," said Father. "It's only a council house you're in."

She hadn't expected this. She didn't want it. And the insinuation about her home being 'only a council house' was derogatory. "No. What I'm saying is, can you please, if need be, see I get enough money so that Becky doesn't suffer?"

Her parents were again looking at each other. They were hesitating. Their only child and grandchild needed *their* support – and they were hesitating! "Of course," said Father, "we'll do what we can to help." He coughed. "You know, Heather, you probably have grounds for divorce if he's pronounced insane."

They wanted her and Becky away from John. She rose. "Time for bed – I'm tired." On the way out of the room, she looked back. Her parents sat staring at her. They looked wretched. "Goodnight and thanks," she added. "See you tomorrow."

She tiptoed upstairs and pulled the door to. Becky was asleep.

She stretched out on the bed. Shocking, how they talked about John! And their hesitation about helping – and the way they'd looked at each other – was odd. 'We'll try, do what we can' was scarcely reassuring. Had the well run dry? Was there a worrying secret?

Lurking deep within her was a vision of the workhouse Granny had feared. A grim safety net for the poor, but this was the Britain of the welfare state.

Through the night, haunting spectres of her Springwell visit wouldn't let her rest. Something was gnawing at her. When she'd asked how John got so ill, the nurse mentioned hypothermia. And she'd been outraged at the idea John might have had it before he went in. But of course, John had been soaking – said he jumped in the river.

Did he mean to kill himself? And if so, what brought him to that? Had she been too engrossed with Becky over the weeks before Easter to listen to him when he was troubled? And he was monosyllabic when she asked about work that last evening together. Had he been sacked?

Did she overreact when he picked up the knife? He scowled and shouted – but would he have done anything? She'd panicked. His removal to the loony bin was her fault. If he hadn't gone there, he'd have been treated for pneumonia at the local infirmary. She must ring Springwell.

Next day, with Mother at work, and Becky asleep, Heather got the okay to ring Springwell. She went into the front hall and dialled. Mr Macnamara was off duty, she was told, and nobody was available to speak to her. The brush-off!

She stomped back to the living room and told Father about the call. He shrugged and sighed.

She paced round the room. "The trouble is, they don't let you just drop in. Visiting's only allowed once a month. I'm worried about John. They thought he was dying. That's why they summoned me. I must see him, or at least find out how he is."

"How can you see him, if they won't let you in?" her father queried.

Not Father of old. He might have offered to blast fortress walls for her. She walked over to gaze out the window. An unmown lawn, weeds galore. Something was wrong. Tonight, she'd press them about this – Mother's headaches, and a 'terrible thing' Granny referred to mysteriously long ago.

She should get home. John was now her main worry. She could use Elsie's phone and, if need be, enlist the mental man's help. Tomorrow, maybe. Tonight – her parents!

"Father, can you drive me back tomorrow, please? I meant to stay longer, but I really should get home, in case Springwell ring for me. And someone I know could probably get news of him."

Father scratched his head. "Mother will be disappointed. But yes. I've got something on here that'll swallow up most of the day. I'll take you after I've brought Mother home."

In the evening, Heather was the disappointed one. Mother arrived ashen-faced, pecked her on the cheek, said "Raging headache, need my bed, darling," and went upstairs.

Later, with Becky settled upstairs, Heather returned to the living room. "Look Father, I know there's something not okay with you. Before I went to university –"

Father cut in. "Right, Heather. My health is fine." He cleared his throat. "But I had to leave the bank earlier than planned..." He was gazing at the carpet. "Mergers, a managerial cull, and I lost out." This would be painful, for a proud man that she couldn't remember ever moaning to her. "Mother went back part-time to boost finances, but finds it hard." He rose, yawning. "Must go up." He looked her in the eye. "Heather, we'll see that you and Becky have the support you need."

"Thanks." It was enough for now. Some light on Granny's worrying comment from long ago (though vivid as yesterday) – and on Mother's headaches – would have to wait.

That night, she lay awake thinking. For as long as she could remember, Mother had often gone to bed early with a headache. She could still see Granny, brow furrowing, standing over her and saying, "Heather, there are bad days when dark clouds come over your mother – and me."

Even more powerful was the day (she was nine) she saw Granny staring at the ceiling and shaking a clenched fist. As though kind caring Granny, always there for her granddaughter, had gone into another world.

It'd been scary. "What is it, Granny?"

Granny, looking down at her, said, "Once a terrible thing came to try us, Heather dear – you'll understand when you grow up," then smiled and changed the subject.

But she never did learn what that 'terrible thing' was, and she hadn't asked her parents about it. She knew what she'd heard. It was time they told her.

After tea next day – still pondering a surprisingly tearful goodbye to Mother – Heather was homeward bound. Seated in the front beside

Father – with Becky asleep in the crib at the back. They were on a clear stretch of dual carriageway. Her opportunity.

"Father, I'm worried about Mother's headaches and what's causing them."

"They started long ago, but they're worse now she's working again."

"When I was a girl, Granny said something terrible happened, and I was too young to be told."

He was frowning, "Ancient history. Can't talk without Mother, anyway."

So the 'terrible thing' remained a mystery.

At the other end, Heather got her father to drop her outside the shop. She'd welcome having tea with the older couple, but she would not stay overnight. It was time to face the demons lurking at home.

14

John lay half-awake, musing on the grim times after Da's accident.

"Da's in hospital," Ma says, "hurt bad." Da's away ages. He's afraid Da's gone forever. Ma goes to visit twice a week, but the miners' hospital is two bus rides away, so on those days he and Dave do for themselves after school. Dave looks after him – takes him to football, includes him with the big boys. Ma says Da's getting better. Nights he hears her crying. He asks Dave about this, and is told "Go to sleep."

Da comes home with no legs. The big wheelchair makes the living room look small. Prosthetic legs come. Da says, "Magic legs, my boys. I'll be a great big giant."

Then Dave vanishes. For ages, he half thinks Dave'll burst through the door. He takes on Dave's paper round as well. Through all weathers on a big bike, he rages, feels the tears.

And there's no magic in the new legs. They're too short and Da keeps tumbling over. Ma wants to try and get another pair, but Da says not to fuss and learns to use the legs to get around the house.

After school he stays in for the household chores and doing homework, and often falls asleep downstairs before Ma's home. They're real hard up, even with help from Miners' Relief and neighbours. Ma takes three jobs charring for families in the snobby part of town. He's proud of his Ma; wearing herself out to keep them going.

He blinked himself fully awake. A hand was gripping his shoulder. He glanced up. Black bulging eyes glared at him. Niven.

"Make sure Chisholm's awake, Tommy." Macnamara's Irish brogue. "Doctor'll be coming soon."

He didn't want to see anybody. He shut his eyes and lay still.

"Get the hell up!" A low voice, menacing. Niven threw the bedclothes off, jerked him up to a sitting position.

"The patient stinks, boss," Niven shouted.

"Change the drawer sheet and the mac. Eddie, you take the man walkies."

Maclean appeared beside Niven. "I'll take you to the bog. No funny tricks!"

Some chance. He closed his eyes and saw stars as a tug under each arm hauled him out of bed to standing.

"I'll manage, Tommy," said Maclean.

He began to totter down the ward, glad of Maclean's support. He saw from the corner of his eye an old man with a shock of white hair, sitting up in bed and pointing at him – and it dawned. He looked down, to see that he was naked apart from the coarse pyjama jacket.

"My trousers," he said. He felt the white-coat's grip tighten.

"You haven't got any yet. You've been too incontinent."

Nausea hit him after a few steps. This exercise was tough, but worse was the pungent smell of urine, even stronger than the paraldehyde. Maclean halted him by the end of one of the beds. A pail stood half-full of stinking dark yellow liquid.

"Glaekit," Maclean yelled. "Get this shit-pot emptied – and any others!" A young brown-coated man appeared, lifted the offending pail and walked off rapidly. "Damned orderly – it's his job," Maclean muttered.

John was thankful to continue the walk. They went slowly until Maclean said "Here," and guided him towards an opening between the beds. "The bog. I'll stay with you."

Great cocktail. Piss and shit, plus disinfectant? A chain was pulled in one of the cubicles. He saw the brown-coated youth emerge with an empty pail and speed out onto the ward.

"I'm right here, laddie." Maclean was talking to him. The shame of being watched like this!

Ablutions finished, he felt Maclean's grip tighten again as they walked back into almost welcome paraldehyde territory. He inhaled. Mustn't pass out!

At last, his bed. He flopped onto it, welcoming the bedclothes being pulled over him. He started to doze.

"Sit the patient up, Mr Macnamara!" A man's voice, like Panjit's. Ah, from the padded cell?

He was gripped under each arm and lofted to sit up. He sat, blinking at the white-coated man. A beard and a turban – like Panjit.

"This is Dr Singh, the psychiatrist," said Macnamara, stepping back to let the doctor come nearer. Yes, the guy from the padded cell.

"Mr Chisholm, you have been very ill with pneumonia, and on a drip to give you nourishment," said the doctor. "How are you?"

"Okay." Slipped out automatically. He was anything but.

"We have also been worried about your mental state."

So what? "Can I go home?"

"No, Mr Chisholm. You are a certified patient."

A loony! He shut his eyes.

"Mr Chisholm, are you listening to me?" Like he was a naughty child.

"No."

"You will be detained a long time while we treat your mental condition. After you have fully recovered from the pneumonia, you will be moved back to our Admissions Ward. Good day."

Trapped. And they held all the cards. He saw the doctor and Macnamara move off down the ward, leaving Niven by the end of the bed. His minder?

He slid down the bed and curled into a ball. Befuddled. A word he'd seen in books, but never felt applied to him. His mind felt vacant – like his thoughts had been pulled out, into the ether somewhere. Maybe he was crazy, living out a nightmare.

The bedclothes were jerked back. "Wakey wakey." Niven leaned over to whisper into his ear. "Sit up, you bastard, or I'll tear off all your clothes."

John sat up, leaning his head against the bed railings.

"Boss says you've to drink this. I hold the mug and you drink."

Well, what if it was poison? He gulped the liquid down. It tasted like water.

Over his remaining days in the infirmary, John endured being shaved each morning – by Niven, who said "Bloody hayfield" the first day. Pointing out he could do this himself now led to being grabbed by his pyjama jacket and told that "Patients never get razors." The shave that followed was painful and bloody, but at least he felt cleaner.

He also experienced the Niven bed bath. "You mad bastard," Niven kept muttering as he sponged, too vigorously.

"I can wash myself," he protested, then endured agony as his crotch was squeezed. Like Sarge, Niven was for that dark alley someday.

On trips to the bog, he had to be accompanied, they said. Utter humiliation. After that first trip, he could walk unsupported.

The meals came – breakfast, lunch, tea – with monotonous regularity. There was nothing appetising about them – and the soup had to be dishwater – but he forced everything down. He must get his strength back.

He began to welcome the nightly paraldehyde. Could it be addictive? And the penicillin injections were important to his getting well. Macnamara had explained about this life-saving medicine.

That wasn't all Macnamara explained. One afternoon the Charge Nurse came across and sat beside the bed.

"How're you doing?"

Sounded like the man cared. "I'm getting stronger. Why was I in that cell?"

"You were out cold when you came to Springwell. They took you to Reception to complete the certifying, then, as you'd cut up so rough, put you into seclusion on the Admissions Ward."

"Seclusion?"

"That's officially what being put in a cell is. It's padded so that you can't hurt yourself if you're violent, and you're put in there to help you cool off. We call it the cooler." Macnamara smiled. "Sure, you can see why?"

John nodded. "'Cooler' is a euphemism. You should try it."

"Sure I have done – and I'd heartily agree. Then after a few hours they came to take you to a bed on Admissions, and you cut up rough again."

"Hell, you should've seen them square up. And one of them had a syringe."

"That would be in case you resisted, for sure. They knocked you out and put you back in the cell. But this time the doc said you'd to be watched, and visited once an hour. He didn't like you being there on your own too long."

It was coming back. Doc would be Dr Singh.

"When they went in later, they saw you were breathing funny, gasping, and thought you were off with the angels. Lucky old Doc Burn was around – he's a GP, lives out here as his wife's a nurse on the female side. Doubles up on psychiatry, doing outpatient clinics. He diagnosed pneumonia, said it would be dangerous to move you into town as you could be dying."

"Why didn't you let me die?"

"Sure, we don't want that. You were brought into Infirmary. We got you onto penicillin right away. After a bit longer for recovery, you'll be for the Admissions Ward, where they'll assess and begin treating you for the mental trouble."

"When can I get out from Springwell?"

"I don't know. You're certified, and surely you'll be in a long while."

"But I'm sane. What do they say's wrong with me?"

"You haven't been diagnosed yet. They said your behaviour was disturbed."

Disturbed? "Well, I put up a fight."

Macnamara glanced at his watch and started to rise.

A reminder. "Where's my watch?"

"In safe keeping. Could go missing if you kept it on your person. I've to go. One more thing – Doc Burn said to summon next of kin, and your wife was brought out to see you." Macnamara stood up and started to walk away.

So he hadn't dreamed it.

Macnamara paused and turned. "She was very upset."

Well... Maybe Heather did still love him. But it could have been an act. "I've been suspecting she doesn't love me anymore."

But Macnamara had gone.

"Trouble with the missus, son?"

Two beds away, the old man with the shock of white hair was sitting up, gesticulating towards him. Must have heard something. Great privacy in here. "Who wants to know?" he shouted back.

"Fred. I've been on this ward longer than any. Had trouble with my missus. That's what brought me into these places."

"Well, Fred. And –?" He twisted round to face the old man.

"I was in the Great War, joined up 1915. That damn Kitchener's poster! I came home on leave after Mons and found the missus in bed with a lout. I beat him up and left him for dead. Trouble was, the weasel did peg it some time after and the police said it was from the hammering I gave him. I'd given the wife a thrashing too. She was whining, said she wouldn't tell who'd beaten the lout up."

"Did she?"

"Yes, she testified against me, said I'd gone right mad – and other things that wasn't true. But I'd gone back to France, went over the top at the Somme – so by the time the trial came I'd lost a leg and a lot more down below. The court said I was insane. Meant I didn't swing, but they put me in Broadmoor's infirmary. Then they reckoned I couldn't escape nor do no damage, and moved me in here."

"Oh." He wanted to say more, but his head was pounding and he sank down under the bedclothes.

Another patient appeared at the end of his bed. Looked familiar. It was the man who'd startled him the other day.

He sat up, and felt the bed being shaken, then the shaking stopped. The man stepped back and pointed at him, shouting "You," before turning and going back down the ward – head bowed and muttering. The same routine as before.

"What's all that about?" he shouted to Fred.

"Poor bugger, Larry. Came onto this ward in 1952. He'd been in the infantry and got decorated at Monte Casino. But he'd gone around shagging Italian women and got the clap. They brought him here in a straitjacket. Made a right shindig till they silenced him with their dope. He's GPI."

"What do you mean – GPI?"

"General Paralysis of the Insane – a nurse told me. There's a couple of other lads in here with it. They say if Larry'd had the medicine earlier he could've got better. But he's got worse. When he had your bed, I used to get right deafened with his swearing."

So, it was nothing personal. He was just in the wrong place at the wrong time. The sooner he got away from here, the better. "What happened to your wife, Fred?"

"Don't know. She divorced me long ago. And I don't want to know."

John slipped down under the bedclothes again. His head was bursting. He drowsed until tea arrived. A generous though marginally edible offering. He gobbled the lot and finished by licking the rubber plate. Survive!

When Maclean came with the medicines, it was a relief to gulp down his passport to oblivion.

15

Cajoling Becky into accepting the spoonfuls, Heather could feel her resolve weaken. She and Becky didn't *have* to face the cold unwelcoming darkness at home tonight.

"You look fair played out, m'dear."

"It's been a long day, Elsie." Heather managed a smile. "Tea's helped revive me."

Elsie's arms reached out. "Let me have the bairn. I'll change her nappy."

"Thanks." She passed the inert bundle across.

"Was everything all right with your folks, m'dear?"

This intruded. "Yes, Elsie - except that Mother had a bad headache." She didn't want to start discussing her parents, even with her friend. Her resolve strengthened.

"Must be terrible that, m'dear. Sure you won't stay?" That concerned look.

"No, thanks. I must get on with things in the house."

"Could I go ahead of you, lass?" said Mattie. "To take the crib and sort your lighting - while the bairn's being seen to?"

"Please, Mattie." Managing the crib would have been okay, but that dark hallway was spooky.

Mattie went off with the key while Elsie helped Heather get her things ready and prepare Becky. "All's sorted, lass." Gosh, Mattie'd been quick.

After the goodnights, she took the key and went with Becky to the empty house. The hallway radiated brightness. It was almost welcoming.

She carried Becky upstairs to the crib and stayed on in the bedroom. She didn't want to linger downstairs with the bloodstains on the carpet. Her eyes would surely keep being drawn to them. She'd tackle removing this gruesome reminder of what must have been an uneven gory struggle for John. But not tonight.

Fatigued yet restless, she lay watching Becky. When Mother similarly watched her all these years ago, was it pleasurable or a chore? No doubt Granny had done this (surely not as a chore) with Mother when a child, and with her. These motherhood thoughts were sustaining.

Lying under the bedclothes without John was strange and lonely. Not that there had been, for ages, even tenderness. But while his snoring kept her awake, it was a sign of being alive. Oh for that snoring now!

Through the night, Becky kept waking and needing nappy changes. Welcome relief from half-waking nightmarish thoughts and fears.

Gnawing at her was anxiety about John. She must get a visit.

Wednesday 2nd May 1956 – in Aversham.

Feet on the desk, Sam Newman was enjoying his cigar. Woodbines were his stock-in-trade, but this morning he'd splashed out.

He'd spent a boring half-hour yawning over a backlog of paperwork, then at nine o'clock the internal rang. The MOH. "Newman, come to my office now please." Shit! At least the boss said 'please'. Okay – he hadn't phoned Tickler. En route to the MOH's office, he rehearsed his excuse and braced himself.

But the Medical Officer of Health, beaming, greeted him with excellent news. "The Health Committee have agreed to the appointment of a second mental health officer. And from the first of July, you will be titled 'senior', with one extra increment on your salary."

"Thank you, Sir!" He couldn't have guessed this was coming. He accepted the handshake, got back to his room and slapped the desk. No, he hadn't misheard.

Five minutes had changed his world. Senior! He went straight to the tobacconist's.

Now he was savouring his recognition. It was well earned. And the killer workload would ease. He'd questions to ask. How would the incomer be recruited – and would he, Sam, have a say in this? Where would they put the man's desk (as his own room was too small to accommodate that)? But whatever, the world felt good.

He looked at his watch. Half-past nine. Better get on with the paperwork before the planet went mad. He stubbed the cigar and hunched over the desk again.

He was up to last Saturday. Missing the match had been a right downer. But Rovers lost seven-nil and his presence at the ground couldn't have worked the needed miracle. "One-way traffic," the team coach said, "worst day of my life."

So the trip to Springwell with the beautiful Mrs Chisholm had been a damn good alternative. Mrs C had been in a mess after, and would hardly speak, but then having your mate at death's door in the loony bin probably wasn't much fun. He'd felt for her. Like a father would – though boy, he'd love to get her into bed.

Saturday night, one call, but he hadn't needed to go out. Sunday, two calls. Only one a callout, ending in a woman agreeing to a voluntary admission. He'd been glad of the excuse to leave home for a while as Ella had been in a grumpy mood.

Ella. He laid his pen down and, leaning back in his chair, resuscitated his cigar. He puffed, enjoying the heady aroma. Ella was the other reason the world felt a better place. Monday, Tuesday and this morning, she'd been in good humour. Smiling at him. No mention of an affair. Even trying a few steps out of the wheelchair yesterday evening and laughing as she collapsed onto the settee. They'd kissed. Glimpses of happier times together. Of course it wouldn't last; the specialist said there would be 'up' periods, though the long-term prognosis was grim.

The external phone rang. He snatched up the receiver. "Newman."

"Mr Newman, it's Mrs Heather Chisholm. Please can you help?" Sounded desperate. "I want to visit John, but I keep getting blocked when I try to phone Springwell."

He could picture her – naïve and seductive. "I'll do what I can when I'm next out there." He'd love to be able to comfort her. He took down the phone number of Mattie's shop.

That afternoon, Newman had cause to visit Springwell. McNab rang. "High wire act, Sam. Trinity church caretaker, Bert Knowles, is on their tower with a loudhailer – says he'll jump."

Why didn't they let him? "Okay – Tarzan coming." He took details, carefully stubbed out his cigar and went straight to the car.

He arrived at the church to find a crowd being kept back by two policemen. The voice from the loudhailer was distorted and unintelligible. With a policeman's help, he pushed through, into the church, and gained access to the tower steps.

Dodgy this. Softly softly, or the guy might jump. Attract attention, invite an explanation. He could see through to the top now. Things had gone quiet. Maybe the guy had jumped. Then he saw the loudhailer and, holding it, the man.

"Hello," Newman shouted. "I won't come any closer. I just want to hear what you're saying. The loudhailer isn't clear." He had the man's attention – maybe.

"I am the Messiah, returning to my people."

Delusional? Don't argue, or challenge in any way. "Yes, so you are the Messiah. Look, my name's Sam. What is your earthly name?"

"Bert. I have been told I am the Messiah." The man was looking down at him.

"Bert, you've gone up high to tell everyone you're the Messiah? Not to jump or anything like that?"

"A space has been cleared for me below, so that I can throw myself down. The scripture says God will give orders to the angels, and they will hold me up, so that not even my feet will be hurt on the stones."

Tough one, this. "Look Bert. You are the Messiah. You've proclaimed it, and people are listening. Do you think jumping down could seem like showing off? Though of course I'm sure you would not intend to show off."

"I do not want to show off – just show people I am immortal."

"But people will know you are immortal, as you are the Messiah."

Bert had lowered the loudhailer and was still looking towards him. "Bert, another thing's struck me. If you jump, it could scare people, and make them run away, instead of welcoming you – which is what you'll want them to do."

The man disappeared from view, surely to jump. He heard the loudhailer blare unintelligibly. He waited. Silence. Bert had jumped.

Then came a hoarse shout. "Sam, my disciple, you go ahead and clear the way. I am going through the door to meet my flock."

"Will do, Bert." He went down the steps, through the door, and waited with the police. His leg ached.

Poor guy, Bert – wrinkled, getting on. Looked bewildered as the police escorted him into their van. "Unhand me. I am the Messiah. Where is Sam, my disciple?"

Sam was in his car – and followed to ensure the emergency admission into Springwell. While he was there, he'd try getting Mrs C a visit.

In Springwell, then Aversham.

The business finished – forms completed, Bert sedated – Newman's thoughts turned to Heather. Jock Mackenzie agreed to his using the internal phone and gave him the number he wanted. He dialled, his hand trembling.

"The Medical Superintendent's office. Miss Bewlay speaking." Who else? A voice to rally the troops.

He explained his whereabouts and reason for ringing – reminding Miss Bewlay of last Saturday's visit and emphasising how distraught Mrs C. had been.

"Mr Newman, stay there and I will ring you."

Well, she hadn't exploded. He told Jock what had happened and waited by the phone. After an age, it rang.

"The Medical Superintendent has consented to Mrs Chisholm paying another special visit. Her husband is recuperating in our Infirmary and will shortly be transferred to our Male Admissions Ward. It is permitted for Mrs Chisholm to visit the patient there on Friday 11th May at two o'clock."

Over a week? Still... "Thanks for your help. I'll pass that on today."

As if he hadn't spoken, she continued, "Mr Newman, I assume you will escort Mrs Chisholm. You will please ensure she is in our Main Hall while the patient is brought down from the ward."

That was a cheek, but he relished the idea of spending time with the luscious Mrs C. "Yes," he replied, "though –" The phone had gone dead.

He had a laugh with Jock, then drove back to the office. He rang the shop to leave a message, and found he could give the news directly to Mrs C.

"Springwell have suggested I give you a lift – there and back," he volunteered.

Silence. Was she turning him down? "Yes please. But you must be busy?"

"No problem. I'll call around one o'clock. If something does blow up, I could be late, even very late – but I'll still come. Okay?"

"Okay, thanks. I'll be ready whenever you come."

He went back to his cigar. And his paperwork – though he abandoned this soon after, to luxuriate in dreaming about the lovely Heather Chisholm.

16

Monday 7th May 1956 – in Springwell.

Early in the morning, John lay in the darkness, replaying that sunny day long ago – when Dave vanished. Over the years, he'd often replay the happenings on first waking– though some days the haunting would catch him at odd moments. And he'd found that anger can fuel a determination to survive.

They could strip him of his clothing, belongings, and dignity, but they could not strip him of his treasury of memories – good or bad.

"Watch out for yourself on Admissions," was Maclean's parting shot from Infirmary. "You get all sorts before some are moved on – and there's the odd violent psycho."

John could take care of himself once he was fit. And if somebody killed him – so what! Would anyone care?

But now, having been escorted pyjama-clad to sit on the edge of a bed in Admissions, he looked around warily. The ward seemed nigh empty.

A white-coat appeared and tossed a bundle onto the bed. "Chisholm. I'm Mr Mullen, the Staff Nurse – that means second-in-command here. Change into these."

Not his. "Where are my clothes?"

"Patients' personal property is removed and kept for them. Change pronto. The consultant psychiatrist – he's the god – is coming to see you."

The god? Chilling. Better get on with it.

He struggled into a grey shirt. The grey trousers would grace an elephant's wardrobe. Ludicrous. "These trousers are too big."

Mullen laughed. "So's you won't try and escape. No belts either."

So be it. He finished dressing by squeezing into a grey woollen jacket and sat on the bed, awaiting the god's arrival.

He rubbed his eyes and massaged the top of his head. If he could demonstrate his sanity, maybe the god would let him out of this crazy place.

"Chisholm." Mullen's voice. "Move it. God wants you in the office."

John rose, and paused till his vision cleared. Another big white-coat was at his side, nudging him towards what looked like a side-room on the ward – the office.

After a step, he had to grab his trousers. Clinging to the waistband, he followed Mullen, who entered through the open doorway. He shuffled in, the white-coat beside him, and heard the door close. Seated behind a large desk was a bespectacled, bird-like man – gazing down at an open folder. The god?

"Chisholm, sir." Mullen stood to attention. Reminiscent of that hellish parade-ground. Must be in the presence of hallowed authority.

There was no chair. He stood slouched, a white-coat at each elbow. A prisoner awaiting sentence?

The bird-like man looked up at John and pronounced with emphasis. "I am the consultant psychiatrist." Yes, this funny little bald-headed man was the god.

John couldn't suppress a giggle. He listened for further introductions, but none followed.

"Emotionally labile," he heard, as the god shifted round to nod in the direction of another white-coat standing to attention in the far corner.

"Sir," came a barked acknowledgement.

Ominously familiar. Sarge the Voice!

"Tell me your name." The god was staring at him.

"John Chisholm. Look, I want to –"

"This is not about what you want, Chisholm." The god was shouting, his pale cheeks colouring. "You are a patient, you have been certified insane and detained here as you tried to kill yourself and your wife. I will diagnose you and you will have the treatment that I prescribe." The god jerked his head downward to look at the folder.

John remained silent. There was no future in confronting this guy, who held all the cards. He must cooperate.

The god looked up from the folder and, leaning forward, peered at him. "What age are you?" The tone was gentler.

"Twenty-five – no, twenty-six."

"And what is your date of birth?"

Stupid – the god obviously had this information. "Twentieth April 1930."

"And when did you come into Springwell?"

"Twentieth April 1956, on my twenty-sixth birthday."

The god appeared satisfied, grunted, and returned to looking at the folder.

John glanced at Sarge. The man stood erect, his eyes fixed straight ahead. The god's specs glinted as he looked up. "Why did you try to kill your wife?"

"I didn't. We had a row." He paused. The god was peering at him, nodding as if to say 'continue'. More encouraging. He added, "She has a lover."

He stopped. The god was staring at him like he was some curiosity.

"Have you seen your wife at intercourse with this other man?"

"I haven't, but I know –" He halted, searching for words that wouldn't come.

The god looked away, towards Sarge, and said loudly, "Deluded, skits."

"Sir," replied Sarge.

"I'm not skitting – I'm serious," he yelled at the god, who was looking down and writing something. Now both his elbows were gripped tightly.

The god laughed and nodded at Sarge, who barked out a laugh.

What a pantomime. Mad. They must all be mad in here.

"Hm." The god studied the folder again, then looked towards Sarge. "ECT, course of twelve. Start three weeks from today. But get the patient back to full strength first. We mustn't be seen to kill him. Call Singh to do a physical on the day. Meanwhile, paraldehyde twice daily and the airing court. The patient can go now." The god looked down at the desk and picked up his pen.

"Sir," boomed Sarge.

"But I'm not –"

"Shut up." A loud whisper in his ear as he was forcibly led off, protesting his sanity while hanging onto his waistband. This encounter had been a shambles.

As soon as they'd exited the room, Mullen said, "Shouldn't have tried skitting him, man," then burst out laughing. His fellow white-coat, one of Sarge's heavies from the padded cell, also guffawed. Was everyone mad here?

Freed from the grasp of his minders, he shuffled to his bed, flung himself onto it and lay seething. He'd been ridiculed. Some damned excuse for a psychiatrist! But his mind was too cluttered for him to focus clearly.

He swung his legs off the bed, and when he stood up had to grab his trousers. He stumbled to the reeking bog – aware of being watched and shadowed by a white-coat. Ablutions completed, he sought out Mullen. His anger had a focus.

"I need braces if I'm not allowed a belt."

"Patients don't get braces either. And the boss said you've to wear these trousers." Mullen started to walk away.

"But –" he struggled to think. "Who is this boss?" he yelled at the retreating figure.

"You heard Mr Mullen." The white-coat now stood facing him.

"Yes. And –"

"Chisholm, I am the boss." The emphatic gravelly rasping from his rear told him it was Sarge the Voice. "Look at me when I address you."

Half expecting a punch, he turned to face Sarge. The swarthy face glowered down at him.

"See these," growled Sarge, holding up both arms to show a broad blue ring round each sleeve of his uniform. "I am the Charge Nurse here, which means I am the boss of this whole ward." The face was only inches away – tempting for an uppercut – the voice menacing. "Have you got that?"

"Yes." The man's breath was straight from a sewer.

Sarge drew himself up, puffing out his chest. "I am Charge Nurse Parker. And if you dare to address me at any time, you will call me 'sir'."

John stood motionless and silent. Sarge's hostile green eyes were boring into him.

"Is that understood?" Sarge was bawling now.

No point getting another hammering in a no-win situation. "Yes – Sir."

Sarge turned away.

John shuffled back to lie on his bed. He imagined giving Sarge a hiding. And let him have one minute alone with the shit they called the god!

He must have dozed off. Next thing, he was being shaken and a voice thundered in his ear. "Wakey – tea." The heavy pointed to a room beyond the beds, where a number of men (presumably fellow patients) were gathering, with white-coats in attendance. "Go to the dayroom and sit at the table."

He went as directed and sat down at the wooden table. Certain he was being stared at, he kept his eyes averted. He didn't want confrontation with madmen. Amid a confusing babble he heard shouts – some of them abusive. Though far from hungry, he ate the fish paste and margarine sandwiches put in front of him on a black rubbery plate. Some feast! Then he gulped eagerly at the lukewarm brew (funny flavour – could it be laced with parahaldehyde?) from a rubbery mug. Must take anything on offer, to build up his strength.

He sat with head bowed and elbows on the table. After an age, Mullen yelled, "Stay in your seats. Mackay and Snoddie, do your stuff."

He was aware of the table being cleared. He heard muttering among white-coats at the end of the table, then, "All okay, Sir."

He looked up and glanced to each side. The table – or rather, the row of tables – was clear.

"All leave the table," Mullen shouted.

The room was bigger than it had looked – with a couple of broken-down armchairs. Some patients made for those, some stood around, others went toward the beds. He made for his bed and stretched out on it.

"Medicines. Come up when you're called." Mullen's voice.

When his turn came a white-coat escorted him to a hatch at the office, where he gulped down the now familiar liquid. Then he was hustled towards bed.

Lying in bed, before the blessed paraldehyde kicked in, he had a fleeting image of that bird-like god horror. What was this ECT?

17

Tuesday 8ᵗʰ – Friday 11ᵗʰ May 1956 – in Springwell.

John awoke to a hullabaloo. "You're pigs, filthy pigs!" A ginger-haired pyjama-clad man was sitting up in the bed opposite and being restrained by white-coats. "You pigs," the man bellowed. A great voice. The whole ward must know the guy's opinion of the white-coats. The newcomer had some presence!

Suddenly all was quiet and, raising himself to sitting, he could see an unmoving blob of ginger on the man's pillow. Another protest snuffed out.

He lay, starting to doze. A figure loomed over him. "Chisholm – shaving. Keep yourself still or you'll get your throat cut." A white-coat heavy. Another Niven? Well, maybe it wouldn't be so bad if his throat was cut.

"I'll keep still." He stuck out his chin and shut his eyes. But the big man, with quick confident strokes, was gentler than Niven – and this process couldn't have lasted more than a minute or two. At least something was better on this ward.

"Get yourself dressed," said the white-coat, and went away.

John put on the ill-fitting clothes and, after the mandatory visit to the bog, went to the table for breakfast. He sat, his head aching, eyes fixed on the table, trying to ignore the hubbub.

A dark rubber bowl appeared in front of him, containing a kind of thin watery gruel. He excavated most of the contents with the rubber spoon, then raised the bowl to slurp the remainder. 'Seconds' were two slices of bread and marge. The tea was weak and lukewarm.

"Snoddie, Mackay – get cracking." Mullen's voice.

He sat with head bowed while the table was cleared and awaited the order to get up. This breakfast was reminiscent of hard times. After Da's accident, Ma had carried on making porridge (watery and saltless), every morning. Usually there wasn't margarine on the (often mouldy) bread; after Da died, sometimes there was no bread.

At last, after talking among the white-coats, Mullen yelled: "Medicines."

When summoned, John downed a tiny spoonful of paraldehyde, then asked one question he'd awakened with – and learned that 'he skits' was 'he's schiz'. "Short for 'schizophrenic'," Mullen said, and called the next man for medicine.

He stood for a moment, stunned. A white-coat ushered him away without explanation, but he knew what was meant. The god had pronounced him mad.

Maybe he was mad. En route to his bed, he heard a loud groan and saw the ginger mop opposite moving on the pillow. Big Voice lived.

He threw himself onto his bed. He recalled overhearing the deputy head last year in the staffroom tell a colleague about an ex-teacher. "Gone crazy. Schizophrenic, her mother says. Poor Bess – very sad."

Fascinated, he'd stared at them. The deputy glanced across and remarked loudly on the weather.

It was none of his business. But in the library, he found a medical textbook.

Now they said he was schizophrenic. Was he really? And whether he was or not, the term 'schiz' was derogatory, de-humanising!

"Chisholm!" Mullen stood over him. "Raise yourself. The boss said last night you've to go on the airing court."

"What's the airing court?"

"Outside, an exercise yard. Move it – sharp."

John went as directed to join a gang of men assembled by a door. 'Airing court' sounded interesting. Outside. A chance to escape this hellhole?

His hopes faded when he shuffled out. The courtyard was forbidding, with high walls that were surely not scalable. He was lined up with two other patients and required to walk round and round. Though glad of the fresher air and a reviving cold wind, he'd scarcely call this exercise. Still, it was better than nothing. At each corner, greatcoated men wearing peaked caps stood guard.

First time round, keeping his head down, he heard a familiar voice. "Chisholm, your card's marked." Niven? He glanced up. Yes, those bulging eyes were glaring across at him. Well at least that bully wasn't on his ward.

He tried talking to the patient walking next him, but the man eyed him suspiciously, grunted, and looked down at the concrete. He tried again, but the man remained silent. The other man in John's threesome seemed to be staring into the far distance as he walked. There wasn't much chatter anywhere else either – but an occasional "shut up", presumably from a guard.

The only relief from the boredom came when a patient ahead of him yelled "Kill", broke ranks to charge at a guard and was repelled, then frogmarched off.

An idea came. If all the patients charged at once, they could overpower the guards.

His head wasn't right, but maybe the cool air was helping. Plodding round, his mind churned with misery. Heather, his beloved beautiful soulmate, surely had a lover. Yet she'd come to hold his hand? Becky – he loved their baby, and missed her cries and chuckles.

A whistle blew. Half-time? He wished! Mullen had re-appeared and shouted, "Admissions, line up in your threes over here." From the other end of the court, someone else bawled out a command, and men started to line up by a different doorway. So that was it. There were patients from another ward. He could see Niven with them, shouting orders. Looked like the sadist had moved wards (as the patients were too fit for the Infirmary), but thankfully not to Admissions.

John moved slowly with the queue into Admissions and made for his bed. "Lunch, Chisholm," he heard a white-coat shout. Yes, something smelt good. He sat down at the table. For the first time since imprisonment, he was hungry! The large rubber plate before him held mince and mashed potatoes, cauliflower, turnips and carrots. The rubber knife and fork were hardly up to the task, and he finished by licking the whole plate surface to get all the goodness – something he'd done as a kid.

He gobbled the stodgy pudding amid watery custard, drained the rubber mug of its lukewarm tea, then sat with head bowed.

"Mackay and Snoddie, get moving," commanded Mullen.

This time he looked up and watched. Mullen and two other white-coats hovered while the two named patients – one huge, the other small – went along the rows, collecting up items, clanging and clattering. Hey, most of these things couldn't be rubbery. Why didn't they give him proper cutlery?

Impressive, the deftness and lightning speed with which the two patients were sorting the items – knives, forks, spoons, plates, mugs – into separate piles. Skills that were wasted in this dump. Job done, they returned to their seats. Then the two white-coats went through each pile and shouted numbers to Mullen.

Weird. They really did count everything back in. Were they that short of cash? But of course, this was the loony bin.

Shuffling back towards his bed, he figured it out. They were scared he might get something to use as a weapon, or an escape tool. Yes, a real knife could be useful – even a fork, or a bit of crockery. That was why they counted everything back in, and why they gave him rubberies.

"Get back in the day room, Chisholm!" A booming command from Sarge, standing by his office. "This isn't a holiday camp. Move it, you lazy bastard."

He hesitated. The day room? Of course – where they had the meals. He turned and walked back. Must behave, lie low for now.

Tables clattered as they were dismantled and stacked and Mullen kept shouting to direct the operation. Patients stood around, with one or two sitting.

John found an empty broken-down armchair and leaned on the back of it.

He swung round as someone prodded his elbow. A ginger-haired man – must be middle-aged, though with a boyish face – surely the guy from the bed opposite.

"What's the take, old boy?" said the man, sinking into the armchair.

"What do you mean?"

"I'm a new boy. These pigs messed me about today and I haven't got over it." Ginger-hair rubbed his eyes. "Damn them all. What happens now?" The man had a posh accent – posher than anyone he'd met, even the lecturers at uni.

"Dunno. I'm a newcomer too."

"These guttersnipes have no respect. I'm a baron, you know. A nobleman."

He'd heard of barons, and recalled seeing one on *Pathe News*. But he never anticipated meeting in person a guy from those so-called ruling classes – anywhere, never mind in a loony bin! He could still see Da stomping round the room, shouting "Damned nobility and gentry, they're the problem," – and Ma, who'd been in service with a Lady, bending to whisper, "They're our masters, John, look up to them."

John gaped at Ginger-hair. "Baron!" He found the notion of 'privilege' distasteful. But the pompous one was a fellow prisoner and seemed friendly. To show respect, the nobility were addressed differently. "What do I call you?"

The man stared back. "Oh, 'm'lord' will do. I am a Lord and I have a great mansion and estate." Looking down, he muttered, "Well, I had until they slung me inside, into that dump of a private asylum. I was stuck there for years." He turned away, raising his voice. "They told me I was getting out, the liars." He was booming now, and a wider audience – other patients and a white-coat – were showing interest. "They brought me here instead. Appalling. This is even worse!" The Baron got up from the chair. A big man, portly; he looked majestic.

John watched the Baron shamble away in the direction of the bog. The man was obviously having the same trouser waistband problem as he. So maybe social class didn't matter in here. One good thing about the place?

Then it struck him. Surely a true nobleman wouldn't be put in this dump – a public institution, a county asylum. Was 'm'lord' a con man, or just mad?

One afternoon, Sarge emerged from his office and yelled, "Airing Court!"

"Sir," Mullen replied, and set about lining up patients.

"Stay behind, Chisholm, you miserable wretch!" Sarge bawled.

John sprang to attention – an automatic response.

Sarge turned to stride back up the ward. "Bring him to my office, Mr Clark."

"Come," said the white-coat shaver, ushering him along to follow Sarge.

Standing outside the office, chaperoned by Clark and waiting for Sarge to invite them in, he wondered what this could be about. Maybe he'd get a beating.

He heard muttering, then the phone being slammed down, followed by something like a curse. "Come in!"

Clark opened the door, nudged him in, and stood erect. "Sir."

Sarge stood behind the desk. Eyes blazing from a flushed face, hands clenched into large beefy fists.

"Chisholm, you're a fucking high-fallutin' intellectual waste of space. Stand to attention!"

John bristled, but did his best to comply, still clutching his trousers.

"Why the hell would anybody want to see you, eh?"

"I don't know, Sir." Confusing. This man was surely crazy.

"Nor do I. The Lady High Almighty, our Medical Superintendent's sidekick, rang me about a visit. Now your visitor's come half an hour early – and will have to bloody wait." He banged his fist on the desk. "Clark, you dress this madman proper, take him down, stay with him, then bring him back to see me."

"Sir," replied Clark.

A visitor? His head was spinning. "Who – Sir?"

"Your missus, the stupid bitch."

Heather! He felt the adrenalin rush as Clark ushered him from the office.

18

Friday 11th May 1956 – in Aversham, then in Springwell.

Heather looked at the clock. Nine-thirty. Over three hours to go yet. Ringing Sam Newman had been the right move. He'd got her the visit. Frustrating having to wait so long for a visit she should have a right to; this was her sick husband.

A strident cry. Becky was awake. Fine – would help pass the time. She lifted the child. That special aroma! "Who's Mummy's girl then?"

She changed the nappy and nuzzled into Becky, who responded with a chuckle. "I'm going to see Daddy today. I'll tell him what a good girl you are."

Gently, she put Becky on the floor. Not crawling yet; more a half-hearted slithering. Could her precious child be backward?

She glanced at the clock. Five to ten. Still three hours! And he'd said something about maybe being late.

Becky had pulled herself to near the bloodstains. Must get these out. She picked Becky up. The child looked sleepy. Not surprising after all that crying last night. "Becky sleep," she murmured, and took the babe to the crib.

Back to the bloodstains. Armed with a scrubbing brush and warm soapy water, she sank to her knees and tackled the largest stain vigorously. The blotch was spreading! She should get a new carpet, but couldn't afford that. She stood up. The sight was macabre.

Washing her face of sweat and tears, a solution came. She'd put down the rug from upstairs – after the carpet dried.

She glanced at the clock. Half-past ten. What next? She'd done the housework, washed the nappies and hung them over the pulley.

She needed to unwind. Yes – *Gone with the Wind*. The characters had begun to live in her head. She extracted the bookmark and got into the story.

Gunfire? No, the door. Rubbing her eyes, she saw it was twenty-five past twelve. Heavens – Mr Newman? She was nowhere near ready. "Coming," she yelled, as she sprang up, charged to the front door and flung it open.

It was Elsie. "M'dear, I could take the bairn now."

"Thanks, Elsie. I'd fallen asleep. I'll get her."

With Becky gone, she dressed in haste – number one costume, high heels, perfume. Must look her best. No lipstick or face powder, as, early in their courting days, John said all that didn't enhance her 'amazing natural beauty'!

Newman arrived dead on time. Heather got into the front seat.

"You look great. You'll bowl him over."

She wished. John hadn't said anything like that for ages. "Thanks."

They drove off, faster than Heather was comfortable with, but at least she'd reach John quicker.

What state would John be in? Hopefully he'd be calmer, feeling the benefit of treatment. But Springwell was the asylum, and he'd be at risk from madmen. What would she say to him?

She realised suddenly she'd been asked a question and hadn't a clue what it was. "Sorry Mr Newman, I'm just so anxious about John."

"It's okay." His eyes were on the road. "I can't even remember my own question. It was just small talk." He laughed and she followed suit. She was warming to this helpful man. "Oh," he continued, "call me Sam – it's easier."

"Alright. Call me Heather."

They were at the forbidding gates. After the exasperating rituals, she was inside the Main Hall. Huh, 'mausoleum' would be a more apt description. She paced to and fro in the cheerless expanse. What could the delay be about? Eventually she sat on a chair near the entrance, while Newman stood over in another corner, talking to a nurse. The snatches she heard were about football, and she heard the two men laugh now and again.

At last, a door opposite was unlocked and two men – a gaunt, drab-looking man and a white-coated giant – emerged. John. Plus minder.

19

"These trousers should fit you, Chisholm," said Clark. And they did – round the waist. They were a bit short in the leg, but they matched the jacket. And he had braces.

"That's better, man." Clark stepped back, looking at him. "Can't have them falling down in front of your missus."

Why not? Might give Heather a laugh. "Where is she?"

"Downstairs in the Main Hall. That's where the visitors see you." Clark smiled. "No funny business. I'm a martial arts champ. And the boss fair crucifies anybody that gets feisty."

John wouldn't be trying anything.

Clark held up his bunch of keys and unlocked the door, then locked it behind them. As they went along the gloomy corridor, Clark added, "They don't let visitors on the wards, for their own safety. Visiting day's once a month. This is by special arrangement – and that'd be why the boss was so pissed off."

Clark halted, and unlocked a door to reveal a vast cheerless space. "The Main Hall," Clark said. "Let's find your missus."

Near the far corner, a woman rose from a chair. Heather, in her best costume.

"Mrs Chisholm?" asked Clark as they approached her. "I'm Mr Clark, a nurse on John's ward. I've been told to stay around during your visit."

John halted and stood beside the chair Clark motioned him to. He inhaled as he caught the aroma. Mesmerising. And a touch of evil – that's what he'd smelt the day they put him in here. He stared at her. She looked a bit startled.

Heather stepped forward, put her arms round his neck and pressed against him. Oh the allure of his beautiful wife – his arousal was immediate. He accepted the hug and squeezed her round the waist. That this moment could last! He felt a thrill at the kiss on the cheek, but hung back from reciprocating.

She drew back and sat down. He sat on the chair opposite her. Their knees were nearly touching. God, she was seductive. He wanted her.

"John," she said, "how are you?"

Well, he'd nearly died. And she put him in here. However... "Okay, Heather."

"Look John, I know you've been very ill." She was sighing? "I'm really sorry you're in here."

Was she apologising for getting him put into this madhouse, in collusion with that little toad? If ever he met that guy again... His head was exploding.

"I want you to come home again to me and Becky – after you've finished your treatment."

Sweet music. Would she rescue him? Nothing was clear. She had a lover? Yet she said she wanted him home. And he'd always loved her.

He heard a laugh. He glanced across and did a double-take. Over in another corner – that little smart-suited guy beside the white-coat. He looked at Heather. "How did you get out here?" He stood up.

"What?" She looked shocked and was flushing. "Mr Newman gave me a lift, John." She was standing now.

Clark moved closer. "Something wrong?"

You bet! "That mental man," John yelled. He pointed at Newman (now looking their way). "Her fancy man's come with her. They put me in here."

"What nonsense," she protested. "Mr Newman just gave me a lift. John, please listen. There's nothing going on. I love you and want you home – when you're well."

Nothing going on? He was sure there was and he wanted to beat up the mental man. Yet he couldn't decide whether to go for the toad.

He stood watching as the mental man followed the white-coat through an exit.

Heather seemed distant now – though he got the scent again as she moved closer to him. His head was emptying. "Go away," he said. Everyone was too close. He needed to be left alone, to have space.

Heather moved back. She was weeping – or was she laughing? Somehow it didn't matter. The whole scene was surreal, with some hidden force anaesthetising him. He stood, transfixed, as a white-coat unlocked the door for her to go out. She waved as she disappeared, and the door was locked again.

"C'mon Chisholm, let's go," said Clark, taking his arm.

He didn't like this, but let himself be steered by the other man back to the ward. They halted outside Sarge's office. Clark knocked on the door.

"Enter," barked Sarge, and John went in, with Clark at his elbow.

"Sir," said Clark. The parade-ground again.

"Did he behave himself, Mr Clark?"

"Yes, Sir."

"I can't be doing with teachers – and even less can I stand teachers' pets," Sarge ranted. "No more extra visits."

Well, who cared. Sarge moved round the desk and was right in his face.

Sewer breath. "A nice piece of skirt, I hear. Probably on the game by now." Sarge leered. "You'll never see her again, you pathetic scum."

This was torture, but he was deadened to it. Maybe he was pathetic. "No."

He felt a nudge. Was Clark trying to tell him something?

"And I won't have scum not respecting my authority," Sarge bawled, and, turning to answer the phone, added, "Get out – both of you."

Away from the office, Clark let go his arm and muttered, "For God's sake, remember to call him 'sir'."

He was taken to the airing court and added to a row of patients. Walking round in this army was okay. He was an automaton, anonymous, and nobody could get at him. His head throbbed, and it was like his brain was clogged. Images - of Heather and the mental man, of Becky with the spoonful of baby food, of the day Dave vanished, of Da on the floor legless, of Ma on her deathbed, of Sarge yelling - all came and went, like a nightmare with no focus.

He heard his name called. Sounded derisory. He looked up. Niven. Even that sadist couldn't penetrate his protective shield.

The guys next him were clutching their trousers' waistbands, but his were staying up. This surely was the nuthouse. There were two musts - survival and escape.

A downer awaited in the ward. Clark passed him the elephantine trousers. "Boss says you've to change back - so's you can't escape." Sarge had read his mind.

20

Friday 11ᵗʰ May 1956 – to and in Aversham.

En route home, Heather slouched in the seat. Within, a bubbling cauldron jostled her weariness.

"How're you doing, Heather?" Newman's eyes stayed on the road.

"How do you think! I do not want to talk about it, or anything else." If this stupid man hadn't stayed around chatting...

She closed her eyes. But images of John, wild-eyed and ranting, wouldn't let her snooze. What hurt most was his bitterness against her. How did he get this insane idea she was having an affair? And with Sam Newman!

Suddenly it struck her. Sam too was an innocent target – harangued over an affair he wasn't having. A man who was courteous and supportive. There had been no advances, even insinuations. Before she'd met John, there were guys who tried it on. John had taken good care of her since – until just before his fateful birthday. And now Sam was looking out for her.

The car was slowing to a halt. She sat up. They were outside her house.

"Thanks very much." She felt like kissing him to emphasise her gratitude – though that wouldn't have been right.

"Don't mention it." Was he blushing? "All part of the job."

Out of the car, she stood with the passenger door held open, looking in at Newman. "I'm sorry I snapped at you. And I'm sorry John was so –"

"Can I join you for a minute," he cut in, "on the pavement?"

"I suppose so." She stood up straight as he exited the car and limped round the bonnet to face her. He was going to try something – and she didn't know how she'd react. Right now, she could do with a hug!

"Look," he said, "there's no need to apologise to me." He glanced around and continued to keep his voice low. This man was aware of possible damage from gossiping tongues. "I get a lot worse than this in my job. And –" He paused, staring past her shoulder.

Heather followed his gaze. Number 86's curtain was twitching. "The Allens. An older couple, keep themselves to themselves – they're not usually nosey."

"Okay. I'll be brief. Don't blame yourself, Heather. Your husband's had a breakdown and probably feels the world's against him. And –" He paused again. The curtains were still. "I'm the man who got him into Springwell. He's bound to feel like I'm a villain. This may change once he's had enough treatment – though I guess that could be a long time yet." He smiled. "Meanwhile, look after yourself, get on with your life as best you can, and try to get friends and relatives on side with you."

She nodded, unable to find words. This man cared about how she'd cope.

He drew breath, looking thoughtful. "If you need help with childcare, how about a nursery, like The Windmill?" He shifted his feet. Maybe his leg was troubling him? His face stretched towards her. Eyeballing her, but this was no confrontation. He was handsome. "If you need my help again, get in touch and I'll do what I can."

With that, he returned to the driver's seat. No hug, but it was probably just as well. She still loved John. Her cheeks felt moist as the car pulled away. What a decent balanced man, despite his work with people having breakdowns. And there were so many questions he might be able to help with.

Today, though, she'd had enough.

She went over to Elsie's. Becky needed her, and she hungered for Becky.

The shop was closed. Early? She pressed the bell. Elsie appeared with Becky on one arm. "Heather m'dear, come on in."

"Becky," she whispered, taking her precious child into her arms and kissing her. "Thanks Elsie." She followed the older woman up the stairs to the living room. She sat down, dandling Becky on her knee, smiling and murmuring "Choo-choo-choo." Becky smiled back. Lovely. She buried her face into the babe's tummy, savouring the aroma, then looked at Elsie. "Has she been a good girl?"

"Aw, she's been perfect. Just like wee Ailsa would've been." Elsie's joy was tinged with sadness. After all these years, the pain of her loss was there. Maybe it never went away, but you found ways of coping. Could something similar apply to John?

Elsie was staring at her. "You didn't hear me, m'dear?"

"Sorry, I was miles away."

"You look fair worn, m'dear. A cuppa? And smoked haddock for tea?"

"Yes and yes, please." She wasn't hungry, but needed to keep her strength up.

She heard coughing. "Mattie?"

Elsie's face wrinkled up. "Yes, m'dear. He's not well – coughing and spluttering and fair boiling – so we closed the shop. He's having a lie-down. He'll not be joining us for tea. Though I might tempt him to a wee piece of fish."

Worrying news. Mattie – reliable and indestructible – was ill.

"I'm sorry," Heather said, as Elsie returned, bearing a tray with teapot and cups. "You must be worried." She stopped dandling Becky and the child snuggled into her.

Elsie laid the tray on the table and sat down opposite Heather and Becky. "It'll just be a cold." She paused, looking thoughtful. "It's a long time since he had anything like this. And then he'd work through, shake it off." She smiled. "We're a right pair of oldies now."

"You don't look old." Untrue. "What about the doctor?"

"Mattie won't hear of it. I'm giving him some old cough medicine I found in a cupboard. But, m'dear," Elsie said, pouring the tea. "Enough of that. How did you go on?"

"I want to tell you, but I might cry a lot."

"When you're upset m'dear, it's better to cry." Elsie stretched out her arms. "Here, I'll have the bairn."

Face awash, Heather surrendered Becky. "It all went wrong – horribly."

Elsie held out a hankie. "M'dear, use this."

She wiped her face. "John turned nasty when he saw Sam Newman. Shouted at Sam, and at me." She paused, dabbing with the hankie again.

"That must have been awful for you, m'dear."

"He thinks we're having an affair – and we're not." She was calming.

"Oh m'dear. Is that part of the sickness they're trying to cure?"

"No – but." Hang on, what *was* wrong with John? "Probably it is, Elsie. If so, their treatment's not working."

"But it's not been long, m'dear. He'll still be getting over the pneumonia."

A thought. Maybe it wasn't so hopeless.

Elsie squeezed her hand. "M'dear, I hope John gets better soon. He's always been polite and friendly with us, though we never saw much of him."

"Thanks Elsie."

"Take care of yourself and the bairn. And remember we're here to help out."

Back home that evening, with Becky asleep, Heather lay awake, her tired brain working overtime. Being with Elsie was comforting. The older woman was a brilliant listener – and Elsie had looked after Becky all afternoon.

That's why the shop was closed. They'd lost an afternoon's trade because of her. Customers could go elsewhere if they feared the shop might close suddenly. She mustn't put Elsie in that position – not while Mattie was ill.

She'd cope on her own, without their help. She needed to be independent. It would be useful, though, to go to her parents' again for a few days. They'd invited her to go and live there. While she didn't want that, a short break could let her gather strength and think of ways ahead. And there was unfinished business - about Mother's headaches, and the 'terrible thing' Granny mentioned. In the morning, she'd ask Elsie about using the shop phone again.

Her restless mind switched to the nightmare meeting with John. She'd been moved by how sad and forlorn he'd looked. Until he'd been alerted to Sam's presence - when he was transfigured. Enraged, hatred blazing from his eyes - and towards her, not just Sam.

John had changed into a hostile being she scarcely recognised. Yet this was *her* beloved John. Would this wholly unreasonable jealousy be cured by treatment? He'd until recently said he loved her, and shown it. Maybe their love affair was over?

Could the real love of John's life be his big brother? Someone he'd pined for - been obsessed with - all the time she'd known him. Now she was feeling jealous...

21

Tapping. On the front door. This early?

Heather's un-set alarm clock registered 12 noon. She must have got to sleep at last – a deep sleep. Heather leapt out of bed and glanced in the crib. Becky was asleep. There was that *tap-tap-tap* again. A creaking sound – the letterbox resisting an attempt to open it – and a voice, distorted and faint, saying, "Heather?"

She grabbed her dressing gown and scrambled downstairs. John? Newman? Not the postie? He'd have banged loudly – and he didn't call her Heather.

"Who is it?" She stood in the hallway, putting on her gown.

The letterbox creaked open. "It's me, m'dear. Elsie."

Had something happened to Mattie? She sprang to open the door. "Sorry Elsie. I overslept. Come in."

"I won't, m'dear. I've got a lass standing in at the shop. I wanted to check you were all right. Your bedroom curtains aren't drawn back."

"Thanks Elsie. I'm fine. How's Mattie?"

"He's determined to stay up, so he's in the back-shop – he doesn't like his bed – but he's coughing and sneezing and not himself."

"I'm sorry."

Elsie's face crinkled. "It's better you don't come over for a few days, m'dear. Becky – nor you – mustn't catch what he's got. Place'll be alive with germs. I might be getting a touch of it." Were those tears in Elsie's eyes?

"That makes sense to me, Elsie. Thanks for caring about us so much."

"It's all right, m'dear. I'd better get back."

"Tell Mattie I'm asking after him," she shouted to the retreating figure.

That ruled out the shop phone. But she must contact her parents. She'd get Becky dressed and go to the public phone-box.

Trekking to the nearest phone-box – a mile away, and some of the journey uphill – was the harder for having to push Becky's pram. The last time Heather went there – months ago (alone, with John baby-sitting), to ring her parents – the walk was okay.

The problem then was two teenage girls ignoring an angry queue. An elderly man at the front of the queue rapped on one of the glass panes and yelled, "Get a move on." One teen opened the door and screamed, "You dirty old man." The man flushed deep red and hung back.

She gave up and went away then. This time she must phone.

Now she could see the box. There was a woman in it. Green coat, grey-haired, standing erect, back turned.

She stopped a few feet short.

Moments later, the woman emerged, smiling. "Hello, Mrs Chisholm."

Mrs Allen, from number 86. "Hello, Mrs Allen. A nice day."

Mrs Allen looked into the pram and whispered, "Your Becky's asleep – so peaceful." It was pleasing that the elderly neighbour she'd rarely even seen remembered Becky's name. "Look," Mrs Allen continued, "I'm not in a hurry. I'd be happy to wait outside with Becky while you make your call."

A welcome offer. Leaving Becky in the pram outside the phone-box wouldn't be ideal. "Thanks, yes."

She went in, dialled her parents, and got an immediate response. Father. She pressed button A and heard the money drop. "Father, I'm ringing from a phone-box, so must be quick. Could Becky and I come again for a few days please?"

Silence. Maybe it wasn't okay. "Yes, Heather. When?"

"Would today be possible?"

"Yes. I could collect you in an hour or two."

"Thanks, Father. I'll be ready."

She re-joined Mrs Allen and Becky (who was still dozing). "Thanks, Mrs Allen. I'm Heather."

"I'm Moira. I'll walk with you - if you're going home."

"Yes, good. I'd love to hear more about you and your husband." She didn't want to tell her neighbour John was in the loony bin.

Moira talked readily about herself and her family. "We've been here thirty years - we're Brummies." That explained her accent. "We were in our thirties when we married and moved here... We've one son, in London - we rarely see him... We're retired civil servants - I was Ministry of Labour, Joey Social Security."

Especially interesting. They might know about employment rights and benefits. They rounded into Green Drive. "I'm talking too much. You must be bored," said Moira.

"No - I'm interested in what you're telling me." Though preoccupied with getting home - and a need to be ready for her parents - she'd been listening. Moira was friendly, and could maybe be trusted. Elsie and Mattie apart, she lacked friends here.

They were nearing number 86. "Will you come in for a drink, Heather?" The older woman was looking at her.

"Thanks, I'd love to, but I can't." She explained about her parents coming.

They were outside number 86. Moira touched her on the sleeve and they both stopped. "Look, Heather, I know it's been hard for you, with your husband away and ill. I was in Mattie's shop when you had a problem the other week. If there's any way Joey and I can help you, please don't shy off asking."

Moira sounded genuine, like she cared. "Thanks Moira." She paused, fighting back tears. "You know John's in hospital?"

"Yes, and I guess it's Springwell? I saw the DAO outside the house. It's a place any of us can go if we're too stressed and need treatment."

Heather nodded. "I'll see you after I'm home again." She wheeled the pram home. A new friend, who spoke positively about Springwell and recognised Sam!

Becky was still asleep. Good. She set about packing. Must greet the car from the pavement, otherwise Mother would come straight into the house.

22

When the Riley drew up, Father was alone. He wouldn't have come in anyway.

From the back seat, Heather asked, "How're you keeping, Father?"

"Fine." His stock reply. He'd surely lost some weight, but seemed fit enough.

"And Mother?"

"She's got a headache. She's resting." Father sounded casual about Mother's suffering. Yet they'd always seemed devoted to each other.

For the rest of the journey they didn't speak. She was occupied cooing and singing to Becky. When they got there, Mother was still in bed.

Father shouted "Heather's here." He turned to Heather. "Do go up."

She lifted Becky and went up to the darkened bedroom.

Mother lay propped up by a pillow. "Heather darling, and little Becky, how lovely to see you. But don't come near in case it's a bug."

"It's good to see you too, Mother. I'm sorry you're not well."

"Oh, I should be better by tomorrow. I'll stay here tonight."

"Sounds wise." A bit of role reversal – felt okay. "Can I get you anything?"

"No, my hero looks after me well. I'll say goodnight."

"Goodnight Mother. I hope you're better by tomorrow." Going downstairs, she wondered. It wasn't a work day for Mother, so what was this headache about? A bug?

"Poached egg on toast for tea, Heather?" Father shouted from the kitchen.

"Yes Father." She got Becky's tea ready.

Tea passed without conversation. Becky needed her attention, and Father sat eating in silence. Between spoonfuls for Becky, Heather devoured the poached egg on toast. Father had never been into cooking, but this was nice.

After the meal, Heather tapped into Father's financial expertise. "Standing orders don't cost you. Tell your bank manager about your situation. He should advise. And let us know if you need money. We're still not badly off."

"Thanks. But you said –"

"We've stopped going abroad." He smiled. "Travel's getting wearisome."

They were communicating pretty well, and here was an opening. "You know, I've never heard from you and Mother about your early days together."

"Another time, Heather." He yawned and rose. "I said I'd join your mother, and I must catch up on my sleep."

As she took her sleeping child upstairs, she had no inkling of how memorable and disturbing the morrow would be.

Sunday 13th May 1956 – in Bolsall.

Heather awoke to the smell of frying. It was eight-fifteen and time to rise. She donned her dressing gown, peeped into Becky's crib, then went downstairs.

"Darling." Mother, smartly dressed and transformed, stood beaming. "What will you have for breakfast?"

"Fried eggs please, Mother. It's good to see you up."

"I feel better. Whatever it was, I've shaken it off."

Mother rarely smiled like this. "Wonderful, Mother." She smiled back.

"How did you sleep, darling?"

"Well, thanks. Becky's still teething, but slept most of the time."

"Good. You had quite a scream when you were teething!" Mother laughed. "But you were a lovely baby, and much admired."

Mother was in top form. And Father sounded okay too, as he shouted from the kitchen, "Breakfast's ready."

"I'll get Becky down, Mother." She dashed upstairs and was greeted by a wail as she picked up her half-awake child. A cuddle, a nappy change and a clean pink dress later, she and Becky were down for breakfast.

"May I, Heather?" Mother took the spoon and, cooing gently, started feeding Becky the gooey stuff from the jar. This was a side to Mother she'd rarely glimpsed.

"Will you come to church with us, Heather?" Father asked.

It was Sunday. "I don't think so. Do women still have to wear hats?"

"I wear one," said Mother. "But you're younger, and nobody would think you lacked respect if you didn't."

She hadn't been to church for years. Now agnostic, she'd been baptised and, in her teens, confirmed in the Church of England. Maybe she should go and pray for John. Did that nurse hint at needing the Almighty's help? "Well," she hesitated.

"Oh do come, darling. Our friends would love to see you again – and our lovely grandchild."

That settled it. "Thanks, but no. I'm tired – might fall asleep and snore through the sermon." Mother's friends would cluster around and Mrs Snape would no doubt ask, in that loud posh voice, where her husband was. 'He's in the asylum, Mrs Snape, and I got him in there'. No, she would stay put.

Her parents didn't offer to take Becky. Too rusty on nappy-changing?

That evening, with Becky upstairs, she joined her parents in the living room for a post-meal cup of tea. Mother and Father huddled together on the settee, looking toward her as she sank into the armchair.

It was unusual to see them sitting like this, holding hands. Nice. Also, she and they were bonding (Bowlby's term) as fellow adults.

Father coughed. His expression had changed – he looked edgy. And Mother looked serious, almost stern. "Heather, there's something we need to tell you," Father began. He was holding Mother's hand, and she too was nodding. Their expressions vied in glumness. What catastrophe was this?

"Please understand that this is very difficult for us." Mother was pleading?

God, let them get a move on. "Yes. So?"

"I'll cut to the chase." A favourite saying of Father's in the old days. "You had an older brother who died before you were born."

The 'terrible thing' Granny mentioned all these years ago! "An older brother?"

Mother was almost shouting, pleading, as she told Heather for the first time. "Our Edward – we named him after the King." She was sobbing into a handkerchief supplied by Father, who put an arm round her.

Heather waited. This wasn't real. She couldn't find words.

Father continued with the revelation, in a low controlled voice she hadn't heard before. "Born in 1910, Edward was a fine outstanding scholar, about to study Classics at Oxford. Then –" He faltered, then regained control. "He was killed in a motorbike accident in the summer of 1928." The control went, and Father too was weeping, his chest heaving, all the while cuddling his sobbing wife.

A brother who died five years before she was born. Tragic. Why hadn't they told her? How hadn't she known? Eyes blurred, she remained silent, an intruder into private raw grief. She should leave the room, and she felt like fleeing. But she sat immobile, except for her face working to control the tears. She was a part of this grieving – for *her* brother, whose very existence she'd never been told about.

After a time – it felt like hours, but was probably only minutes – her parents regained some composure.

"Edward dying seemed like the end –" Mother choked off, dabbing her face with a large handkerchief.

"But life went on." Father's voice was cracking. "We tried to escape the torture by moving far from Edinburgh. I got the manager's job here in Aversham, and your granny moved in with us. Nobody here knew us or what had happened."

"We were devastated, darling. My head hasn't felt right since," Mother said.

"Why didn't you tell me?"

Father replied. "It was years before you came along. We, and Granny, thought it best not to say anything when you were little. I'd thrown myself into work and taken on a lot in this community; your mother was on a five-and-a-half day week."

They'd tried to forget, to escape their misery by blotting out his memory and not talking about him. "He was my brother. Why didn't you tell me?"

"We're so sorry, darling." Mother looked gaunt, exhausted.

"Maybe someday you can understand and forgive us," Father added.

There would be no answers tonight - maybe not ever. She'd had enough. She raised herself unsteadily. "I need my bed. Good night." She turned, ran up to the bedroom, where Becky lay sleeping, and quietly, firmly, closed the door.

Aspirins - one, two, three, stop. Maybe this would soften the raging within. She stretched out on the bed, banged her forehead against the pillow, then twisted to lie on her back, staring at the ceiling with unseeing eyes - until, mercifully, Becky's crying brought her back to the here and now.

23

Survive? John was regaining strength. Escape? He couldn't see a way.

Now his mind was blocked, like it wasn't his own. Over the next few dreary routine-laden days, waves of hopelessness kept coming to replace his fury and torment over his lovely Heather. She and Becky could manage better without a lunatic husband and father. He'd be in there forever and nobody would care. In fact, did he care? He might as well be dead.

Suicide? But how could he top himself anyway - imprisoned, closely guarded? With braces or a belt, he could have tried hanging; but he didn't even have shoelaces, and the sheets were too coarse and strong to do anything with. The windows had bars and were too near the ground anyway. Overdosing was out - with everything stashed in a locked medicine cupboard in the office - as was poisoning, with the bleach locked away. The cutlery was either rubber or too blunt to go through paper.

No. He'd decided against trying suicide. Yet at nights the thoughts kept coming and rolling around in his head. Suicide was a crime. Ridiculous. It was *his* life, and his choice whether to try ending it. And they could scarcely prosecute if you succeeded. Though technically, couldn't they do your family? And what if you botched it? Yes - even to attempt it was a crime.

And suicide was a mortal sin, condemning you to eternal damnation, old Father Murphy had said. You'd no right to kill any human that God had created. God would punish eternally anyone who acted to end their misery? Scary stuff, that didn't square with the central messages of Christianity, about love and compassion.

No, he would not kill himself. But somebody might kill him. Maclean's warning about 'the odd violent psycho' had been noted; though so far John hadn't seen much to worry about in his fellow patients.

He saw plenty glowering, heard a lot of groaning and grunting, and longish muttering and ranting (often into empty space, and ignored by the white-coats - unless directed at one of them). Tensions simmered between a few patients and sometimes these erupted into noisy skirmishes, whereupon the parties were speedily rendered unconscious. And each protagonist was taken to a cooler - yes, there was another adjacent to the one he'd been in. But no, if there were psycho patients (whatever that meant; maybe everybody locked in the bin was one), he hadn't seen behaviour he'd consider seriously threatening.

Not scary, though sometimes weird. Strangest was a guy, didn't look much older than himself, who stood babbling, face twitching, in the dayroom one evening.

He'd strained to follow the babble, but it sounded like nonsense verse. Then suddenly the man froze, silent and statuesque. Was this a game? The man was still, bent forward, his eyes staring ahead, like a figure in a tableau.

"Don't touch him." Clark now stood facing the man. He waved a hand in front of the man's eyes without producing a blink. "A catatonic stupor, I think. Is it, Sir?"

"Yes, Clark, that is correct." Sarge pushed past Clark, bawled an obscenity and pinched the man's arm - without response - then held up a large safety pin. "Now, we'll see if the patient's kidding."

Sarge yanked the man's trousers down and stabbed the buttock firmly through the long johns. Predictably savage. Amazingly, there was still no response, though the man's face seemed to redden. "Classic. Sort it, Clark." Sarge walked off, trailed by a white-coat.

"Get back," ordered Clark to the assembled patients. "Fairnie probably knows everything that's going on." From a tin in his pocket, Clark took out cotton wool and a piece of plaster, then looked round. "Chisholm, the man'll be okay. Best if you don't stand gawping."

He'd been mesmerised by the horror show. "Sorry." He moved away.

There was more menace among the white-coats. Sarge was an outstandingly sadistic bully, gratuitously shoving or kicking patients or grabbing them by the lapel and headbutting. With John, the assaults were verbal – sneering or taunting. Well, sticks and stones... Keep the head down – and someday the dark alley!

Though none of the white-coat underlings could begin to rival Sarge's brutality, John was cautious about them. Mullen and Clark and associates he'd thought were okay. Yet they too could behave a bit like camp guards in that war film where the captors looked nice guys but were ruthless killers. No – any white-coat could be menacing, as a player in this regime. But Sarge was a sadist, out to do him. Niven had shown similar form – good riddance from the ward.

He was getting to know one or two patients. Opposite at lunch yesterday, a small balding middle-aged man kept grimacing. Afterwards, in the dayroom, the man came to sit next him, tapped him on the forearm, and whispered in his ear, "Ssht. You mustn't tell anyone."

Mysterious, but he was to be the repository of something important and confidential. "I won't," he whispered back.

The man whispered, "I'm called George – my real name. But," he paused, glancing around, "I'm a famous science fiction author."

Gosh, he was in the company of the high and the mighty. First Ginger the lord, now George the best-selling author. John too glanced around. There was nobody near, though a distant white-coat seemed to be looking their way.

"Science fiction – sounds interesting." He didn't read science fiction and didn't know names of authors from that genre.

"My books are –" George sprang up from the chair, looked quickly around, then sat down and whispered into his ear. "I get my plots via rays from Jupiter."

John tried to digest this information. "Uh-huh."

George continued, "I've not told anyone my pen name, and nobody here knows of my writing."

Intriguing. "What is your pen name?"

George's face twitched, and he whispered, "Ssht. I cannot tell that to anyone, not even you."

"But how will I know I'm reading your books?"

George glanced around quickly. "You won't. And they mustn't know I'm famous, or the thought police will torture me. I know they suspect, as they all watch me closely and they've extracted energy from me." A white-coat was approaching. "Mum's the word." And with that, George moved away speedily.

They hadn't spoken since. But today after breakfast he saw George, finger on lips, winking at him conspiratorially.

The fellow patient he liked most was Ginger - 'm'lord' had settled for this name. John was pleased when they managed to pair up for the airing court.

"My estate's in Bedfordshire. I should be there now, instead of my little brother. He put me in the loony bin."

"Why? You don't seem mad."

"I'm not, but I did crack up. Thought I could rule the world and everything rocketed out of control. They stuck me in a private asylum - a palace compared to this dump. Manic-depressive, they said, and wouldn't let me out. Miserable runt said the money's running low and got me sent here. Much cheaper - huh!"

Ginger sounded more believable than George. Delusions of grandeur? He'd read about these when he'd looked up the book on schizophrenia. Ginger was surely crazy. His stories were so far-fetched.

"Before the war, I toured the capitals of Europe. I won and lost fortunes in the casinos. The women swarmed round, wanted money and a title." As they plodded along, John would lose track of the tales, which were told in a loud stage whisper. He could almost hear Da's periodic moan about those 'high and mighty wastrels, the curse of this country', and see Ma shaking her head, disagreeing. Ginger would prattle on, as if no audience was needed.

Sometimes Ginger probably did not have an audience. Though the tales were entertaining - reminiscent of *1001 Nights* - John tended to switch off into his inner world. Images and fleeting thoughts came and evaporated, like they were stolen. As though part of him wasn't there – oddly detached from himself and his surroundings. Dream-like, without dreams. Or more aptly, nightmarish.

One day he heard, "Carrot-top." Niven. An outstanding figure with his flaming mop of hair, Ginger didn't appear to notice. Certainly the whispered prattle didn't cease.

"Carrot-top, get your fat arse over here," bawled Niven.

Ginger ceased talking and swung to waddle towards Niven. John too stepped out of the column, and hung back, avoiding confrontation but ready to act if his friend was set upon.

"Do you know who I am, my man?" Ginger, majestic in facing the aggressor.

"You are a fucking piece of shite. Get your hair cut." Niven shoved Ginger, making him stumble. "Get back in your line. You too, Chisholm."

"Stupid man," Ginger muttered, as they resumed plodding round, then prattled on like nothing had happened. Maybe mad, but a great companion.

On the ward, there was no such incident. In fact, Sarge and his gang seemed to treat Ginger with respect – even had the guy in well-fitting clothes.

It blew up suddenly. John had noticed the trusty Mackay, a giant known as 'Kong' (after the legendary gorilla King Kong). A man who commanded respect among fellow patients, yet was clearly subservient to Sarge and his gang. A man who'd at first seemed capable only of growling, and soon proved verbally fluent and amiable. A man who ambled, yet moved at speed on his cutlery task. Not a man to provoke.

After tea, the white-coats lined them up in a queue – apparently randomly, in a long single file that began a few feet short of the hatch in the office and stretched as far as their dining area. This was strange. He started, as a voice immediately behind him boomed out, "What's this for?" Ginger – good question.

"Boss is doing medicines tonight," Clark said. "Wants it like this."

Sarge, standing by the office door, surveyed the line, then bawled, "Scum are ready. Open the hatch."

The procedure started, with Sarge barking out names. Clearly the queue was not a queue. It was a line-up that a patient left on hearing his name – to get medicine at the hatch.

"I say," observed Ginger loudly, "I'm fed up having to stand around like this!"

For a moment there was silence, then came a low-pitched command, unmistakably from Sarge. "Mackay, sort the bugger."

John reacted to a yelp behind him, to see Ginger on the ground moaning, and Kong's foot swinging lightning-fast into the body. There was another yelp, then silence. Kong's leg swung back – foot poised in the air.

The white-coats were standing by! He charged Kong, knocking the big man back a pace, and started wrestling. That unarmed combat stuff from the army was handy – and his strength was back. He held the giant in a lock, then felt himself grabbed – by white-coats (he saw the sleeves). With both arms pinned, he had to let go. He was driven backwards, then turned. The floor loomed.

"The legs." Sarge again.

A weight crashed onto his legs. He felt a sharp pain in the bum and then everything faded.

John came to in semi-darkness and silence. That smell. The cooler. His body wasn't right. Not aching all over, but not right. Maybe they'd put something noxious into him. He'd heard of medical experiments with humans, and Sarge didn't like him. He turned over on the mattress to lie face down. They'd spied on him before and they'd be doing it again.

A grating sound, and a shaft of light appeared. "Chisholm." An unfamiliar voice, clear yet hesitant. "We're coming in. Don't try anything." Some chance. He raised himself to face the incomers and lay propped by his elbows.

Two white-coats stood over him. "We've to give you

parahaldehyde," said the man. Broad Scots – hadn't heard him before. "Enough to give you the K.O."

He didn't know either of these guys. Aliens?

"We're the night shift." They'd read his thoughts. Spooky!

He warmed to the smell that meant sleep. "Right, give me the dope." He opened his mouth to receive the blessed liquid and gulped it all greedily. He was thirsty.

"You've to stay in the cooler a while yet."

His next question answered. His thoughts *were* being read. He drowsed off.

24

John struggled to open his eyes. His head was thudding. He was still in the cell. Somebody was shaking him. A white-coat.

"Wakey, Chisholm." Mullen. "You're going back on the ward. Now! I'm on duty in a minute." Glad to oblige, John stumbled out of the cell towards his bed, escorted by Mullen.

"No breakfast today – just a mug of water. And no medicine after." Weird. "Why?"

"I'll explain later," the retreating nurse yelled.

Mullen wasn't joking. After he'd been shaved, had his supervised wash, been to the bog and struggled into his wretched clothes, John was escorted to the dayroom to sit out breakfast. The mug held little water. He was being punished.

He sat, replaying last night's incident. He hadn't figured Kong for violent, but the guy must be a henchman of Sarge. And Ginger got a kicking – probably into unconsciousness.

Serious! And Ginger was his friend. He sprang from his chair, walked as quickly as his constraining anti-escape apparel would allow, scanned the after-breakfast medicines line-up and looked in the dormitory. No sign. Had they killed Ginger?

Joining the line for the airing court, he looked around again. No Ginger!

"Chisholm." Neck twisting out from Sarge's office, Mullen was shouting. "Stay in the dayroom."

Well, at least Niven and co. wouldn't get at him in the airing court. He sat down and watched his fellow patients leave the ward. A lone white-coat sentry remained, posted by the door of the dayroom.

Mullen came out of Sarge's office and shouted, "Bring Chisholm here."

He shuffled along with his white-coat minder. Sarge was going to bawl him out. Entering the office, he was confronted by Mullen, who sat in Sarge's chair. He looked around. No Sarge, thank goodness.

"Chisholm, boss said you've to start ECT today. The god ordered it for your schizophrenia. That's why you had no meal – they don't want you sicking all over."

"What do you mean, ECT?"

"It's electro-convulsive therapy. Shock treatment. Most patients have had it. But –" Mullen hesitated, "you've to get the all-clear on your physical first, and Doc Singh's coming to check you out."

Dodgy. They were going to mess him about with electricity. "But I –"

"Doctor'll be here any minute," Mullen cut in. "I'll start by taking your pulse. Hold out your arm and keep it still."

John did so and felt Mullen hold his wrist, searching for the pulse. "Patient's ready – over thirty, say 'when'." "When," came from behind – the other white-coat. Mullen – wary eyes boring through him – kept holding his wrist. This was like some kind of slow dance. Not a partner he'd have chosen. "Thirty," came from behind.

"Right," said Mullen, and let go of the arm. "Thirty-six. Good."

"A romantic numbers game?" He didn't expect an answer. This elaborate approach to pulse-taking must reflect their fear that he'd cut loose.

"You'll be having ECT this morning." Mullen swung round. "Ah, Dr Singh. The patient's pulse is seventy-two, normal."

The turbaned doctor had joined them. "Thank you, Mr Mullen. Good morning, Mr Chisholm. How are you feeling?"

This guy was at least civil. "Doctor, I don't want any shocking treatment."

"Ah, the consultant has ordered it to treat your mental condition. But you have been critically ill with the pneumonia. We must establish

131

whether you are physically fit again." Dr Singh gestured to a chair. "Please sit down and remove your upper clothing so that I can examine you."

John sat down and stripped to his waist. He felt the cold stethoscope as the doctor tapped his chest in several places, then did likewise to his back.

"Hmm, I detect murmurs." Turning to Mullen, the doctor said, "Treatment will be delayed for seven days, until next Monday. I will return then to examine the patient."

Mullen looked disappointed. "The boss, Mr Parker, said the patient'd be fit. He cut up rough last night and they put him in seclusion till I came on this morning. With his pulse being normal, I thought..." Mullen paused, looked unsure.

He cut up rough?

"But there are murmurs. There would be a risk I cannot sanction. You will note this and inform Mr Parker, please. I must go."

Well done, Doctor. They wouldn't be putting electricity through him – yet.

When Dr Singh left, Mullen turned to the white-coat. "Take him to court."

So John trudged round with an ache in his stomach where food should have been. He kept his eyes lowered when he heard Niven taunting. *Survive!*

After lunch, he asked Clark about Ginger. "He was hurt pretty bad, I heard. I think he's in Infirmary."

At least Ginger survived the kicking. Would he live, and come back? Funny. Their backgrounds were worlds apart, and he hardly knew the guy (who sounded mad). And the nobility reeked of unfair privilege. But his close affinity with this likeable and entertaining man was the nearest thing to a friendship in here.

25

The next morning Mullen was in charge again. John realised he hadn't seen or heard Sarge for two days. Whatever the reason, the brute's absence was a blessing – as Heather would have put it. Heather, his once-darling wife he'd have sacrificed anything for.

The hopelessness was worst at nights, when there weren't distractions. Thoughts of killing himself usually came then, but were stolen away. Sometimes he could think clearly, but much of the time his mind was blocked. Like an alien force invaded his head and swiped the thoughts and images.

There was little relief from the boredom and inner torment as one wretched day followed another. Occasional arguments and fights were quickly broken up, with men sent to the cooler. These were light diversions; and he didn't get involved.

The week passed and there was still no Sarge, or Ginger. The ward was less sinister without Sarge. Men were talking more to each other.

George the author came and whispered in his ear one day, "They've taken my energy and I can't write. Mum's the word."

He missed Ginger. Just the prattle was something.

Monday 4th June – in Springwell.

Mullen – still in charge – shouted "Chisholm, no breakfast," and had him sit in the dayroom until the doctor arrived. Electricity day?

Yes. John was summoned to the office, where Dr Singh listened to his chest and pronounced him fit to start ECT. He was escorted from the office by Clark and a fellow white-coat.

"Remember – the bog first," Mullen yelled after them.

"Sometimes patients wet themselves in the Shocker," said Clark.

This Shocker must be bad. But they called it treatment. Escorted to the bog, he peed as ordered to. He wouldn't be wetting himself!

He was taken along corridors into another room. Green-gowned men stood in a huddle. Aliens? There was a noise like buzzing or humming, and a funny smell.

"John Chisholm from Admissions, Doctor," said Clark.

"Right. Onto the table with him, on his back – head there." Doctor pointed.

This was the large table in front of him, that the green-gowns were standing round. "I can manage myself," he protested, shaking off the hands grabbing him. As he clambered up (struggling only with his trousers), he saw it. A machine. Yes, the noise came from there. He lay down on his back.

"Shoes." A different voice gave instructions now. His shoes were being removed. "Arms and legs." Each arm was stretched out. A number of hands were jostling him, adjusting him. "In position," a voice called.

He felt his wrists and ankles being clamped. And they were messing with his forehead – felt cold. A green-gown hovered above, peering into his face. "Open your mouth wide." He did so and the green-gown stuck something rubbery between his teeth. "Ready for action, Sir," said the green-gown.

Somebody was putting clamps on his head. Then – *phht*.

The helter-skelter ride was bumpy, shaking him as he whizzed round. Catapulted into the air, he hung onto a cloud. The angry fairground threatened to re-claim him, but the cloud whisked him away, then crumbled. Falling at speed, he saw dark mountainous waves.

He hadn't drowned. His mouth was dry and his head throbbed, with a ringing in his ears. Trying to think hurt his head, which surely had the insides sucked out. Sleep beckoned.

"Wakey." His shoulder was being patted. He made to raise his hand, but it wouldn't move – like it was tied. No point in struggling. His back ached. He made to turn onto his side, but he couldn't. He was in chains.

"Chisholm." The voice sounded familiar and intrusive. He tried again to turn over. Where was he? He opened his right eye to a white ceiling. Someone was tapping his shoulder. "Are you awake?" He opened both eyes. An ugly face stared into him and through him. It looked familiar. He tried to sit up, but some force held him down. The bed was hurting his back.

"You're attached to a trolley." They'd read his thoughts. A trolley? "It's for your safety, in case you fall off." Off his trolley – that rang a bell. "You're awake enough – I'll free you."

He grunted. Hands were messing with his body.

"I'll help you down," said the familiar-looking white-coat.

He was standing, with his head throbbing and vision blurred. His arm was being gripped by the white-coat.

"You can go to your bed for an hour," the white-coat said. Okay, but where was he? He walked on jellied legs with his companion until a bed confronted him. "Take off your jacket and trousers and get into bed," said the white-coat.

John did so, and sank his head into the pillow.

Monday 4ᵗʰ June – Monday 2ⁿᵈ July – in Springwell.

John had survived the electrical treatment. But two days later Mullen said another dose awaited. No use protesting that he'd had the electrics. Mullen laughed. "This is only the beginning."

And indeed, every couple of days or so he was given a dose of the Shocker. He might get onto the shortlist for zombie of the year – moving from breakfast to the airing court, trudging round, to lunch, to the airing court again... The electrical punishment was unremitting. He was forgetting things, especially names.

"Twelve doses in the four weeks," Mullen said at bedtime one day.

"And now you've had number twelve. Tomorrow, my son, you see the consultant."

The 'my son', which John initially resented as patronising (though the man was surely old enough to be his father), had come to be reasonably welcome. 'My son' signalled Mullen was in a good mood, and more disposed to talk.

"The consultant?" John queried.

"Yes, the consultant psychiatrist – the mind doctor we call 'the god'."

This was vaguely disturbing. "Why 'the god'?"

"That should speak for itself." And Mullen walked away.

Next day after breakfast, John was summoned to the office. He stood blinking, figuring out the scene in front of him. A white-coat on either side jerked him up to stand more erect as he eyed the small bird-like figure bowed over the desk. Familiar and sinister. The god?

"John Chisholm, Sir." Mullen was seated, flanking the god.

"Hmm, he's had twelve doses." The god looked round at Mullen. "Has he been a good boy, Mr Mullen?"

"Yes Sir. No further incidents. And we didn't start treatment until he'd fully recovered from pneumonia."

The god nodded and turned to stare across the desk. More torture? "The patient looks more settled, less hostile."

His thought, *I could wring your neck*, was simply dream-like. The grip tightened on his right elbow.

"Yes, Sir," came from Mullen.

The god was studying the papers on the desk. With a sweep, he closed the folder and looked up. "Do you still hate your wife?"

His wife? He remained silent, struggling with jumbled thoughts.

"Continue the treatment and review in one month." The god rose, waving his hand in dismissal.

He stumbled off with his escorts. Amid apathy and jumbled images burned a fire, deep within his being. Punishments would not extinguish this. Nay, they would fuel and strengthen it. Today, *survival*. Tomorrow, *escape*.

A Prologue to Part Two

Tuesday 20th September 1932 – in middle Scotland.

Aunt Jean – his beloved Auntie – was dead. Seventeen-year-old James Braid Macdonald could not then have known how pervasive her influence would be over his life's path. But for his aunt's sacrificial love and suffering, he would not enter psychiatry; nor would he, decades later, encounter Springwell Mental Hospital.

Back to this miserable day. In the still cool of the asylum's darkened room, young Jamie stood, his lanky frame bent over his auntie's frail shrunken figure, willing her through his blurred vision to breathe and sit up.

But that wasn't going to happen. Gently stroking her icy cold face, Jamie mused in sad reflection.

He shuddered to think of her dying within this wretched place, in God knows what misery, a prisoner amid demented ravings on that locked ward. He hadn't, though, actually seen her die.

Not like when Mum died. He'd been there, with her. The day after his eighth birthday, Mum had served up his porridge. She twisted round from the kitchen sink, said "Jamie, what do you –" Her face went absent and, clutching her bosom, she dropped to the floor. Curled up like she was asleep.

For a moment, Jamie thought it might be a game. Mum, a star in amateur dramatics – 'until you came along' – would sometimes engage him in impromptu melodrama. That is, when she was in a good mood.

When she was weepy, she'd invite him to a cuddle as they looked at the grainy photograph of herself with the young soldier – "Your dad, killed at Cambrai when you were a wee bairn... you know, he had braw dark curls and a freckled face, just like you." She'd go on to tell him stories about his dad. "He was daft on golf. When you were born, we named you after a famous Scottish golfer."

But no. This had not been melodrama. The limpness of her body and the colour of her face signalled tragedy. The ambulance man's "No pulse; she's dead," confirmed his fears. As the neighbour led him away from the body, numbness was ceding to desolation at the loss of his mum and best pal.

That was when Aunt Jean came to his rescue. Mum's sister, she took a train from Edinburgh to St Andrews the same day she got his neighbour's phone call. She stayed with him, in support and comforting, when needed – at his side through the misery of the funeral, while he remained a 'brave boy' and didn't cry (in public). Uncle Frank came to 'sort out the business end', then returned to Edinburgh.

Auntie stayed on – taking him some schooldays for a 'treat' lunch at nearby Macarthur's Café, showing interest in his homework, encouraging him in his football (later, rugby) and golf. At Easter she took him to her house 'for a wee break'.

One day, she asked how he'd feel about her and Uncle Frank adopting him. "We've no bairns and can't have any. We love you and we'd like to come and stay with you, Jamie. This house and what's in it would always be yours." He said 'yes' immediately. They sold their house, put nearly all the money into a bank account in his name and joined him at home. And she did a great job, as a sweet loving 'second mum', for more than half his life.

Now, holding Auntie's cold lifeless hand, he wept silently. At least in death she looked peaceful. But what a tragic end, in this asylum and surely in torment.

For years, she'd been depressed, and often her mood was deeply melancholy. He spent hours talking with her, trying to lift her spirits – sometimes feeling his effort was useless, other times encouraged by "Jamie, these wee chats are a help."

She would scream at Uncle Frank, a mild-mannered man, and bang things around. Poor Uncle Frank would look bewildered and retreat into pipe-smoking.

But she never screamed at 'ma Jamie'. When most deeply depressed, she was fidgety and restless, kept sighing, and mumbling "Sorry, I should end all this."

Her mutterings alarmed him. His best efforts to pull her out of this didn't work. Uncle Frank got the doctor in and she was taken to an asylum miles away.

He'd protested. That was the loony bin. But the doctor explained she needed to go there to help her nerves, or she might die. "And, laddie, it's called a mental hospital now – not the loony bin or an asylum."

He got on okay with Uncle Frank these awful few weeks. They didn't speak much to each other, but shared the household tasks. He buckled down to his homework and kept up the rugby and golf. In everything he did, he could hear Auntie's gentle firm voice. "Jamie, stick at it. You'll do it."

Last month (the third of Auntie's stay in the mental place) he'd insisted on accompanying Uncle Frank on the bus for the monthly visit.

"It's no place for youngsters." Uncle Frank addressed him like he was still eight. "She's being looked after." Uncle Frank lit his pipe.

"Uncle Frank, I'm coming along." He had good news he must tell Auntie.

So to the loony bin he went. Feeling unwelcome at the forbidding locked front door, he trailed his uncle and their escort – staying well behind them, gaping at dingy smelly corridors. He'd stopped as a door off the corridor opened in front of him and a brown-coated woman wheeled out a trolley bearing laundry. He craned his neck, to glimpse inside a world of madness – of haunted-looking women staring his way, against a cacophony of wailing and shouting. Oh God, was his precious Auntie caged in here? The door slammed and keys jangled as it was locked.

Their escort halted outside a door with a sign saying 'female visitors', unlocked it and showed them inside. "Wait here please." It was vast, gloomy, cold. He couldn't see Auntie among the faces.

"They bring her in from the ward," said Uncle Frank.

"Why can't we go there to see her?"

"Don't know. We might get attacked by loonies, I suppose."

A hunched figure in drab clothing was shuffling towards them, escorted by a woman in a white coat. The white-coated escort helped the old woman sit down.

No! His beloved Auntie looked twenty years older, with her wrinkled face set in a mask of despair. Uncle Frank kissed her on the forehead, and stepped away.

"Auntie, it's me, Jamie."

She didn't respond. He bent forward to kiss her and she turned her face away. Trying to cuddle her produced a grunt and her shrinking into the chair.

Taking her hand and squeezing it didn't work either. She didn't return the squeeze, and withdrew her hand. She kept sighing, rubbing her hands together, and her eyes moved restlessly. She wasn't really looking at or communicating with him or Uncle Frank.

He must, though, tell her his news. He grasped her hand (firmly this time), and leaned over to speak into her ear. She shrank away from him, but he persisted. This news would be important for her to know – about the career direction she'd passionately encouraged. "Auntie, I will be going to Edinburgh to train as a doctor."

He fancied he felt a slight squeeze of his hand. But when she looked his way, her eyes reflected only misery. What hellish nightmare world was she in?

He wanted to rescue her from this terrible place, but was powerless to do so.

"Time's up." The white-coated woman was back, helping Auntie stand.

"What's wrong with my aunt, and what treatment is she having?" he asked.

"I think she's depressed. I'm only an attendant."

"I want to see a psychiatrist about my aunt." He didn't mean to shout.

He persisted, and eventually (with Uncle Frank) saw a white-coated elderly man with a careworn face. "She has involutional melancholia – a profound depression which affects mostly women in their middle and later years."

"Is there a cure? And what treatment's she having?"

"There's no cure, or effective treatment. And because of the risk of suicide – she's very agitated – we're keeping her under heavy sedation."

Why wasn't there a cure? The suicide stuff was scary, and he'd felt inclined to stay in that crazy place to watch over Auntie.

Now she'd died in there. An inquest would follow, and he wanted to know exactly what had happened. Could she have committed suicide? Had they killed her with too much 'heavy sedation'? His beloved aunt had been in torment.

In his final moments with her, he took her hand, and closing his eyes, said the Lord's Prayer (as she had done with him that day Mum died). Then he gripped her hand more firmly and, bending to look her in the face, uttered loudly a vow. "I, James Braid Macdonald, will dedicate myself to helping people who suffer mental torment."

He felt a tap on his elbow. The attendant whispered, "Aye. It's time to go, laddie." He'd forgotten about his escort's presence.

"Aye." So what if the woman heard his vow; and probably thought he was mad? In fact, he'd like to tell the world about his resolve. He squeezed his aunt's lifeless hand and whispered, "Thanks, Auntie. Good-bye." He brushed his eyes and kissed her on the cheek for the last time.

He straightened his shoulders. "Thanks," he said to his escort, and followed her along gloomy corridors to short of the massive front door.

She stopped and faced him. "Good-bye laddie. You remember what you promised your aunt." Aye, he'd remember.

"Lachy, can you take over?" she said to a large white-coated man.

Trailing his beefy escort (silent but key-jangling), he strode down the path towards the iron gates between high walls. One day, he vowed, I will change all this.

Part Two

HOPE

26

Now Heather was grieving for the newcomer to her life, the dead brother she'd never known. Edward – uncle to Becky, and brother-in-law to John.

A brother she was almost getting to know. Having ended their silence, her parents kept talking about him – his shyness, his love of rambling, his prowess at cricket, his dedication to study, his likes and dislikes, his delight in that motorcycle (and how they rued buying it). Mother would talk, then suddenly go speechless and weep. Father would talk until he couldn't carry on.

Heather listened, asked the odd question, and found herself choking as her eyes blurred. The stirrings inside her were momentous, almost overwhelming. In their disjointed harrowing chatter, her parents communicated with more warmth and honesty than she'd thought them capable of.

They should have told her. If her parents hadn't moved, she'd have heard from neighbours and friends. And she'd have visited the tell-tale family gravestone (of which she'd now seen a photo, showing Edward's name at the bottom).

From psychology classes on her Social Studies course, she'd learned about the concept of unresolved grief, and been touched by case studies of people thought to be stuck in their grieving and unable to get on with their lives. It hadn't occurred to her this might happen in her own family.

Of course, her parents had got on with their lives. They'd dealt with tragedy in their own way, throwing themselves into work and

Bolsall high society. It sounded like they'd bottled up their grief and managed their feelings in a 'stiff upper lip' tradition. When they moved, they'd even kept the photos of him locked in a drawer. "We were too upset, seeing him all the time," said Father.

"We loved him so much," said Mother. "We're sorry we didn't tell you earlier."

"Why didn't you?" Something impelled her to keep asking.

"It wasn't just that we'd get upset," said Father. "We'd started again with you, and when you were young we thought it better not to confuse and trouble you."

Her parents had certainly been protective of her; they had indeed treated her like a child, up until she'd left home. "And I'm not confused or troubled now?"

"We were so afraid we might lose you," Mother said. "We were lucky to have Granny helping out."

"And life went on," Father added. "We were all busy, and we agreed not to say anything about your having had a brother. We thought it might unsettle you."

This was going round in circles. "Why did you tell me now?"

"You asked me what 'terrible thing' Granny was talking about. I spoke with your mother and we decided to tell you," said Father.

"We always meant to tell you, sometime in your teens," added Mother. "But there was never a good time, what with your exams and so on."

"I didn't have exams all the time."

"I know. But your teens were difficult for you, darling," Mother countered.

True, things had been tough for ages after Granny died. In Year Three at grammar school, she'd withdrawn into herself and feigned sickness to avoid classes.

"We know we should have told you. I'm glad we have now," said Father.

There was no point in pursuing this. Her parents felt bad about having kept this secret from her, and were apologising. "I'm glad too."

Howls from upstairs signalled that Becky was awake. "I must go." At the foot of the stairs, she paused and, looking back at two haggard elderly faces, added, "Thanks."

Tuesday 15th – Friday 25th May 1956 – in Bolsall, then to Aversham.

Heather's chats with her parents continued. Daytimes, she saw a lot of Father, who accompanied her on morning walks with Becky. He was warming to the role of granddad. And he'd answer questions about her dead brother.

Late afternoons, Mother would join them – still looking tired at first and reaching for aspirins, but rallying over tea and staying up to talk about Edward.

Evenings, Heather examined old photos and listened carefully to her parents' comments. Sometimes she was moved to laughter, sometimes tears. She wanted to find out all she could about her brother. And the more she learned about him, the greater her sense of loss.

Anger at her parents was dissolving. The keeping of the secret was largely (though, she suspected, not wholly) to protect her, a vulnerable teenager.

How she wished she'd known Edward. Though 'never interested in girls', he'd surely have been there for his sister in her troubled teens. And now, she'd have been in touch to gain solace.

Her parents had been crushed by losing the child they doted on. And their openness now about their sadly hurt feelings was welcome – almost embarrassing at first, but moving in the revelation of their humanity. On Sunday, she felt like going with them to church and praying for Edward's soul as well as for John. But she didn't see that would help. And inhibitions about searching questions were too strong.

A roller-coaster time with her parents. Now she must get on with life back home. She wanted to ensure Becky's welfare (and her own).

That evening, she asked about Mother's headaches. "They started after Edward died," said Mother. "They've never really gone away. Talking with you this past few days has helped."

"I'm glad."

"Darling, I've never told you this. You're a good listener."

"Thanks." Mother praising her? Within her now was a fuzzy kind of warmth towards Mother.

In the night she lay awake, imagining Edward and what he was like. Before she drifted off, it struck her. She had this in common with John – a big brother (also a caring one) who died tragically.

Home beckoned. She must face up to living without John.

Next morning her farewells were hugs, fond and tearful – with Mother after breakfast, then with Father outside her house. Brushing her cheeks, she lifted Becky and waved at the retreating car.

27

Friday 25th May 1956 – in Aversham.

Heather unlocked the front door. Home again. Well, almost. The door opened a couple of inches, then stuck. Maybe the house didn't want her back?

She didn't relish the idea of entering the cold, John-less house, its happy memories overlain by the recent horror. But it was home. And something was jamming this door. Yet the hallway floor was just lino. A body? Ridiculous – but no! Could John be lying there – discharged home?

Braced, hands shaking, she bent down and peered through the letterbox. She could see the lino by the stairwell, but that was a few feet in. She couldn't see what was directly behind, obstructing.

She tensed and, with an energy charge fuelled by anxiety, heaved against the door. It gave way and she sprawled into the doorway.

Brown envelopes. A relief – although they'd be bad news, asking for payment of bills. John's duty to open these would now fall to her.

Sure enough, one was for electricity, another for gas, another for water. At least they were bills, not reminders. And John's pay was due at the end of each month. For now, she and Becky would be covered. Thank goodness for the joint account and a chequebook she could use.

Where was the chequebook? Did he have it on him when he was taken to Springwell? He normally kept it in the small bureau that was his desk, in the corner of their living room. Happily, the drawers were unlocked.

She found the chequebook straight away. About half used. In the same drawer, she spied an important-looking document headed 'Aversham Education Department Terms and Conditions of Contract'.

Compulsory reading – to clarify about John's employment and pay – though not right now.

She rummaged through his drawers, in case there was anything else she might need. Something she'd never done. And in the bottom left drawer, she found treasure.

It was a large, faded brown envelope with something scribbled on it. She lifted the envelope out. The scribble, in John's handwriting, said 'personal'. What was 'personal'? She removed the contents. Then she sat gaping, fascinated, and aware of a powerful sadness.

The banner headline from the faded newspaper cutting was 'Boy drowned on school trip'. Mid-page was a photo of the boy, a smiling lad in school uniform who could have been John as he looked then. Except that it was his big brother.

John had often told her about Dave's drowning. He wasn't there to see it, never knew how it happened, and picked up contrasting versions from Dave's pals and the local paper. This news cutting blamed 'the pupil's rash behaviour'. While the pals' accounts varied in detail, all had Dave as an innocent victim of sloppy non-supervision by teachers. His parents wouldn't talk about it with him.

He'd not seen Dave's body and wasn't allowed to the funeral or the inquest. He'd read in the papers of the 'death by misadventure' verdict, and the school and teachers being exonerated. "A cover-up," John told her. "Dave wasn't irresponsible and wouldn't do a daft thing like they alleged."

In their early days together, he'd always got worked up talking about it. She'd listened sympathetically, moved by the tragedy. But he'd gone on about it so often that she'd long ago tired of listening and switched off. It was ancient history and he should be getting on with his life. She'd resented his obsession and started to believe that Dave was the real love of his life.

What selfishness! She'd felt jealous of his love for Dave? Her love, longing and grief for a dead brother that she'd never met were real enough. But her pain could scarcely be compared with John's at the loss of his big brother, lifelong companion and best mate.

Now she could understand and identify fully with John's agony. The brother he idolised had deserted him – forever. And 'drowned' wasn't enough explanation. The pain would surely always be with him.

Brotherly love. The love between her and John was different, with a vital sexual attraction, overlapping with brotherly love only in the tender bonding.

She still couldn't help a jealousy pang. What happened to the undying love for her that John used to proclaim in his words and behaviour?

Dave's death had clearly been the biggest tragedy of John's life. But not the only one, she was reminded as she peered at the next item – a small black and white photo of a youngish couple. The rugged smiling features of the man looked like an older version of John. The woman – smaller, homely and plump – was also smiling. They held hands and looked happy. His parents, who died before she met John.

Another photo of the couple showed the man in a collarless shirt with sleeves rolled up, the woman in a long-sleeved dress – each with their hands on the shoulders of the two children standing in front of them. The couple were older and looked proud of their young offspring.

She used the magnifying glass to get a closer look at the children's faces. They could have been taken for twins, but one, her John, must be a few inches smaller. He had a cheeky grin. Dave's expression was more serious, thoughtful. The brothers looked around the middle and upper ends of primary school.

The photo must have been taken not long before the pit accident. John had mentioned about his da coming home with an old Kodak box camera and getting the next-door neighbour to take a family photo. Said he regretted not having that camera – a childhood memento, and something to picture the three of them now. "Ma sold it to help us survive after Da died."

The family in the photos looked so like she'd imagined. Of course – a memory catch-up! Soon after Becky's birth, John showed her the photos. She'd given them a disinterested glance and he'd put them in his pocket. Oh, to have that moment back!

She wiped her wet cheeks with her sleeve and closed the drawer. Enough. She'd get on with housework before Becky awoke.

All through the chores, she thought of the heroic child John shouldering his burden. She'd known from Social Studies that mining communities were no strangers to tragedy and hardship. When she expressed amazement at how he and his ma coped, John shrugged. "When bad things happened, we'd all look out for each other."

But he'd had more than the proverbial bucketful. Not just Dave's drowning, but his da's calamitous accident and, after two years' struggle, death. ("Got home from school to find Ma weeping over his body... massive crowd at the funeral..."). And his ma, who took on three jobs to keep them alive, dropping dead soon after John started at Uni. ("Brain haemorrhage, they said, but sheer overwork caused it...").

She marvelled at how he took on the extra paper round, passed the eleven-plus, won a university bursary and got a first. She'd married a special guy. Maybe he had been driven over the edge? If so, the treatment should help. Anyway, she'd stand by him, and one day soon get him back from that place.

A soft moaning signalled Becky's waking. Her lovely child – *their* lovely child. She lifted her infant and nuzzled her aromatic midriff. Becky must not suffer the kind of early hardships that beset John.

She'd contact The Windmill Nursery. Now. It was only three streets away.

Heather wanted to sing and dance down the path from the old stone building. But, with a sleeping infant in a pushchair, she settled for walking quietly.

At last, she saw a positive way ahead. Becky would have a free place at the nursery from Monday. And she would go in with Becky to start a four-day-a-week job as a nursery assistant. Matron's offer was a welcome surprise.

The pay wasn't great, but the cash would help. She'd see Becky at nursery and could check on her infant's progress. And she'd have a focus outside her woes, doing work that interested her. Surely this would work out!

28

Heather stretched out on the settee. Good to have Fridays off. Work at the Nursery was hard. And it was fun. The toughest part was caring for other infants with Becky around. Nappy-changing was a chore, but good for communicating with the children. The fun came when the children played, sang, or listened to simple rhymes and stories. And being with other infants would be good for Becky. The only downer had come on day one, when an older girl made Becky cry.

The nursery nurse she worked with ('I'm Gemma, and I've passed my NNEB") was around the same age as she. Bossy, though nice enough, Gemma took turns looking out for Becky, in nappy-changing and playing. A real plus was Matron, who was pleasant and encouraging.

So it had been a sound move. She was suited to the work, and it was useful to have cash at the end of the week.

A couple of days ago, she'd called at the shop to ask after Mattie. Elsie said he wasn't right yet, but he'd insisted on getting up and serving in the shop. He still had the cough, but the doctor said he wasn't infectious.

Also she got from Moira much-needed advice on claiming benefits and the position on John's sick pay and employment rights. The news wasn't all great, as scrutiny of John's teaching contract indicated he could be sacked.

But at least she was clearer about her situation and more in control. A deep longing for John, and worry over how he was faring in that awful place, nudged her towards trying to contact him again.

Now, on her day off from The Windmill and free from Becky, she'd do something about getting to see him. Elsie had said it was again safe for her to use the phone.

In the back-shop, Elsie greeted her with a teapot. "A cuppa, m'dear?"

"Thanks Elsie. Could I use your phone?"

"Of course, m'dear. You'll want to do it in private?"

"No, I just want to find out how John is. I'll wait till I've drunk the tea. I need something to fortify me."

She sat down at the table opposite Elsie. This steaming mug was just the job.

"We're all right for a wee chat to catch up over the tea," Elsie said.

"How's Mattie?" She kept her voice low.

Elsie leaned forward. "He wheezes a bit, but the cough's near gone away."

"Good. I thought he looked better."

"Tell me m'dear, how's Becky – and the nursery?" Elsie leaned back again.

She told Elsie. "I suppose it's kept my mind off the troubles with John."

"Good, m'dear. So you'll try to find out how John is?"

"Yes, and I'm not sure whether to ring Sam Newman – the mental man, who said to get in touch if I needed help – or to ring Springwell directly."

"Hmm. What's stopping you asking for Mr Newman's help, m'dear?"

Good question. "He's very busy. And John doesn't like him." Aware her cheeks were warm, she continued, "And I've a feeling he fancies me."

"Are you drawn to him, m'dear?"

"Well, yes. Though I do love John." Her face must be afire.

"M'dear, you can always be honest with me, and I'll keep any secret. So you're afraid you might depend on him too much?"

"Yes, and I trust you, Elsie."

"M'dear, we'll do all we can for you and the bairn." Elsie was smiling now. "What about ringing Springwell?"

"Their switchboard treat me like a hostile alien." She drained her mug. "But your tea's fortified me. Springwell – look out! And," she smiled, "If I'm not satisfied, I'll contact Mr Newman."

"Sounds sensible, m'dear." Elsie rose. "Use the phone when you're ready. I'm joining Mattie, but I'll come back to ask how you got on."

Friday 1st June 1956 – in Springwell.

Back from lunch, and with all patients despatched to the airing court, Charge Nurse Parker sat hunched at his desk, reading a paper and sipping tea. He twitched at the sound of the external phone. Rare to get anything through to the ward. Last time it was Sandra, his second bitch of a wife, asking for money. He snatched the receiver.

"Parker."

"Mr Parker, I have a woman enquiring after her husband. She sounds really worked up." The irritating Welsh whine of Switchboard Jones – a right drip.

"So?" He'd better things to do than answer the phone about patients.

"Well it's a Mrs Heather Chisholm, about John Chisholm. You remember the fuss when he nearly pegged it and the Medical Superintendent granted a special visit."

Heather Chisholm – the wife of that snotty madman teacher he'd be starting on an ECT career. 'A stunner', Clark had said.

"Are you still there, Sir?"

"Of course I'm still here," he snapped. "Put her through."

"Hello," came a woman's voice, "I'm Mrs Heather Chisholm, wondering how my husband John is and when I can visit him again."

"Mrs Chisholm – might I call you Heather? – I'm Charge Nurse Anthony Parker, head of the Admissions Ward. I take a special interest in John's care. I'm afraid the news about his mental state is not good.

156

He's very disturbed. Sadly, your last visit set him back. The paranoid delusions are murderous and centre on you."

There was silence at the other end, then a squeal. "No!"

He'd keep up his charming façade. ("A right lady-killer," his first wife said). "Heather, this must be terrible news, but it's better if I'm honest with you."

"Yes, thanks. It's a dreadful shock."

Shock – yes, electric in fact. "I assure you Heather, I and my team are doing all we can to help John. You could of course come out on next visiting day, but I have to advise strongly against a visit at this stage."

"So you're saying I shouldn't come to see him?" She sounded weepy. He wouldn't mind giving her one. That would help her forget her loony husband.

"Yes – for John's sake. Look, I know how upsetting this must be for you."

Silence again, then, "Yes. It is."

"I wouldn't be saying this if it wasn't important. I'm sorry you're upset, and I wish I could be there to comfort you in person, Heather. I really care about John's mental health and we're doing our best. Do you believe me?"

"Yes."

"Look Heather, this is unusual, but if you want, I'll ring you periodically to let you know how he is. The only thing is that I'll need your phone number."

"Thanks. The problem is that I have to use the shop phone across the road, but they're my friends and I don't think they'll mind. Let me check."

He hung on. Damn Chisholm, not having a phone. He could've got off with this bird.

"It's all right. You can leave a message any time. Here's the number."

He noted it down. He could feel the stirrings, the excitement of the chase.

Heather sat down on Elsie's sofa, forcing herself to take deep breaths. This was horrible. Her John was murderous, with delusions centring on her. She remembered from abnormal psychology (the most intriguing subject on Social Studies) about delusions – fixed ideas that were false.

"All right, m'dear?" Elsie had come in, and joined her on the sofa.

"No, Elsie." She could hardly get the words out.

"I'll make us another cuppa, m'dear."

"Thanks, no. I'll have to go soon for Becky." She needed to offload now though. Nearly choking, she told Elsie about her phone call.

"M'dear, you must feel very sad."

Her eyes were moist. "Yes. The only good thing is that Charge Nurse Parker sounds caring and genuine, and he says he's doing all he can to help John."

"That's something, m'dear. We'll let you know if he rings."

"Thanks again, Elsie." She dabbed her eyes and stood up. "I'm off to get Becky from nursery." She turned and rushed out through the shop.

29

Peering at the bathroom mirror, Charge Nurse Anthony Parker shaved round his moustache. At least that was still ginger. His sideburns were greying, along with his hair.

As a kid he'd had a red mop. 'Red' they'd called him – which was okay, until one day a big lad pointed at him and shouted, "Redhead, he's a girl!" He gave that shit a pasting. He said they could call him 'Reddy' – which he translated into 'Ready'. Ready implied action. That was him, a man of action.

He couldn't stick disobedience. Discipline was the key, right through his life. As a kid it was rough, but his dad's tough approach to discipline got him, a young-un with a hell of a temper, to comply. Not that he had to do anything wrong to get a thrashing. When his dad was drunk or in a rage, 'Ant' (as his dad called him – and he hated the name) copped it.

Damn, he'd cut his lip. It was thinking about his dad. He dabbed the wound with cotton wool. The thrashings were from his dad's massive paw, and nearly always on the bum. Never on the face. He ached like hell and swore revenge some day. As a nipper, he howled, but as he got older, he took it all without crying.

The Great War was great for him alright, as his military policeman dad was away a lot. His mum was okay at first, but after his dad was blown up somewhere, she began tippling. Pathetic bitch got fonder of the bottle than of him, her only kid.

'Big boys don't cry' served him well in the orphanage. 'Care', they called it – laughable. There were some evil bastards, but he learned to survive. Being big for his age helped, and he was a scrapper. Soon even the biggest kids treated him with respect.

The internal phone rang. He glanced at his watch. Who the hell would ring him at six-thirty a.m.? He wasn't on duty till seven. The curse of living in.

He lifted the receiver and growled, "Parker."

"The Chief."

He could feel the blood pumping, the adrenalin of anticipation. "Sir."

"Report to me seven a.m., instead of the ward. I'll see it's covered." Chief Male Nurse Hallman didn't waste words. Another ex-army man strong on discipline.

"Will do, Sir." This would be about the promotion. Since leaving the army, his mental nursing career had been spectacular. Joined up at Springwell as an attendant and – with his size and military police background – proved ideal for the job. He was up to sorting out loonies, keeping them under control and locked away to protect the sane folk outside. He went to the lectures and found he was good at exams. Attendants were re-named nurses, and he was soon a staff nurse (and deputy charge). Then last year came promotion to a key post, as Charge Nurse on the Admissions Ward. And the Chief had mentioned, over a drink the other evening, an assistant chief vacancy coming up, with Porter retiring.

The next step. He'd then be in with a shout when the Chief went, early next year. As Assistant Chief, he'd prove his worth.

Shaving finished, he put on shirt and tie, then his blazer. At six forty-five, he looked in the mirror. He brushed back his well-oiled thinning hair and straightened his shoulders. Immaculate, he marched off to this further step in his destiny.

At seven-fifteen, he emerged from the Chief's office. He marched back to his room and fished the whisky bottle out from his underwear drawer.

Parker sat sipping the bottle, re-playing. The Chief had greeted him real

160

friendly. Standing, the man shook hands (a bit premature, as they hadn't even talked about the assistant chief job yet – but maybe he wouldn't need a formal interview). "Ready – sit down." The Chief sat down himself. Then – *bang*! The Chief brought his beefy fist crashing onto the desk. "There's a problem, Ready."

Confusing. Maybe he was too old for the job – but surely not. "Sir?"

"In fact, Ready" – the Chief was looking fierce – "a bloody great headache."

Was the Chief making fun? "Sir." Or maybe he wanted help. "Can I help?"

"It's too late for that," the Chief snorted. "Our friend the Baron's had his ribs kicked in – on your watch – and you wonder now if you can help?"

Jesus Christ! A fuss over a patient? Of course he hadn't meant the ape to break bones – just duff the conceited little sod up a bit. "Sir, it was another patient that went wild, assaulted him."

The Chief didn't seem to hear this. "A nobleman, whose incarceration brings Springwell repute and dosh – I told you to look out for him, and you bloody well let him get beaten up," he thundered. "His slimy colonel brother's been on to the Med Super and I've been given a right sore ear."

"But –"

"No buts. You're suspended on full pay, pending an inquiry."

With that, he was dismissed from the room. No handshake.

Whisky – the old medicine. His dad used to boast about being reared with a nip in the gruel. Now he, Ready Parker, had drained this whole bottle. He hurled the empty at the blank wall facing him. Like a mine or a bomb – splinters all over the place!

A hell of a shock, that telling-off was. But he was a survivor, always came through. Gawd, he would burst. He pulled himself out of the chair and staggered across the splinters to the bog. Just in time to stop peeing his pants. That was better. He tugged the chain and sat down on the bog – too early.

But the cold water gave him a thrill. He chuckled, then roared, as he slithered onto the bathroom floor. Suspended – getting paid for doing nothing. Bugger Springwell. Up the Red Lion! And he lapsed into oblivion.

30

Monday 2nd – Monday 30th July 1956 – in Springwell.

The Shocker was now part of John's life. The blasting and battering didn't seem so bad. White-coats told him what to do and he complied. Each day, it was the same routine – meals, trudges round the airing courts, that welcome smelly medicine to help him sleep. Sometimes he remembered names, other times not. Images of people and incidents were fuzzy. These neither bothered nor interested him much – like he was anaesthetised.

Every few days, he was treated to a variation from the routine. He was jostled into readiness for a hygiene ritual. They called it 'bathing' ("The 'a' as in 'bath' – in case you get the wrong idea," said Mullen). With fellow patients, he was lined up in single file, marched out of the ward to a large area with baths in it, stripped naked and (overseen by a white-coat and a brown-coat) ordered to stand waiting.

When his turn came, he was nudged to sit in a bath of water. Being sponged while sitting in cold water wasn't a great experience. It was better when they gave him the sponge. At least the ritual ended quickly. They'd pass him a towel, with an order to dry himself pronto.

Somehow, all this didn't seem too mortifying. He didn't protest. Even when one sadistic white-coat sponged his genitals and bum roughly, then rubbed them dry. Even when he was told to get into water where pieces of shit floated.

Through this and the other routines and rituals, however humiliating, he obeyed the orders. He survived.

Sarge was back. The brute stamped out of the office, barked a command and went back in again. A white-coat came over. "Chisholm, I've to get you into the office to see the consultant psychiatrist, the god."

John shuffled along beside the white-coat. The psychiatrist, the god? He'd a bad feeling about this. He could see Sarge (one name he hadn't forgotten) sitting in the office. The white-coat stopped outside the door and knocked. "Bring him in," he heard, and felt his elbow gripped as he was propelled inside.

"Chisholm, Sir." The white-coat stood to attention.

"Yes, Mr Clark. I know this son of a witch." Sarge stood leering. "He's the creature with that nice whore of a wife. I'll be giving her one soon."

"Sir." Clark was unsmiling.

Sarge laughed. "Not that he'll ever be able to."

The door opened. "Mr Parker, good day." The turbaned man.

What was his name?

"Mr Chisholm, you may remember me. I am Dr Singh."

His thoughts were being read? But he'd a good feeling about this man.

"Sir, I expected –" Sarge had turned to face the doctor.

"Yes, I too expected my superior back today. But sadly he is still unwell and I am instructed to act in his place. May I use your seat, Mr Parker?"

"Yes Sir." Sarge stepped back. "The file is on the desk."

"Thank you." The doctor sat down and studied the file.

John could feel Clark relaxing the grip on his elbow. The doctor frowned at something, then looked up at Sarge. "He has had a lot of ECT in a short time. Have you observed any effects?"

"Sir, this has curbed his violent behaviour. Isn't that so, Mr Clark?" Sarge was standing at ease.

"Sir," said Clark.

The doctor glanced from one to the other, then looked at John. "How are you feeling, Mr Chisholm?"

"Dazed."

"I am not surprised," said the doctor. "You have had twenty-four ECT doses this past two months – which is a lot. One short-term effect is on the memory."

Spot on, Doctor. I've already forgotten your name.

"How is your mood now – are you still depressed?"

Well he wasn't great, but he wasn't bent on doing himself in. And he was sure he had been. "Not as much."

Sarge coughed. "Chisholm, address the doctor as 'Sir'," he barked.

"No." The quietly-spoken doctor had shouted? "Thank you, Mr Parker, but I do not wish to be called 'Sir'. Mr Chisholm and you and your staff may, if you wish, call me Dr Singh or simply 'Doctor'." The doctor smiled, looking at Sarge, whose face had reddened. "I do apologise if I shouted just now. I wish both patients and staff to communicate with me without such an unnecessary barrier."

He heard Clark shuffle, and felt his elbow shake. Could the man be giggling?

"So you are not as depressed, Mr Chisholm. That at least is good. ECT is often useful for depression, though we usually give fewer doses. ECT will cease. Now."

"But –" began Sarge.

"No more ECT, I said." Thank God – an end to the electrical torture. The doctor wrote something on the file, then looked up.

"Yes – Doctor." Sarge spat this out slowly, with emphasis.

"Mr Chisholm, I know your diagnosis. I wish to check what disturbances you have been having in your mind. Do you hear voices that you cannot account for?"

"No."

"Your wife, Heather. Do you still believe she is having an affair?"

Wife – Heather. Yes, he could picture his beautiful wife, those soft brown eyes gazing up at him. "I'm not sure, can't think."

"Try to relax, Mr Chisholm, and think. You believed your wife was having an affair with a man. Can you recall why you thought this?"

Sarge cleared his throat very audibly. "Sir, Doctor –."

"Ssh, Mr Parker," said the doctor. "Can you remember, Mr Chisholm?"

He struggled to think. It began to come back. "She was distant, like she didn't want to know me."

"I see. And have you control of your thoughts?"

"What do you mean?"

"Do you ever feel your thoughts are being read, or stolen?"

Bang on. "Yes."

"Can you give me an example?"

He struggled to recall. Fog swirled in his head. "No."

"Thank you, Mr Chisholm." The doctor made a note on the file, and looked up again. "I am prescribing you new medication. Chlorpromazine is quite a recent drug which has proved helpful to many people who suffer similar disturbance. It is more commonly known as Largactil."

Surely an improvement on electrical torture. "Thanks."

"Also, I am taking you off paraldehyde. Largactil is one of what we term the tranquillisers and will provide enough sedation. I will put you on a low dosage, as you do not appear to manifest some of the worse symptoms of schizophrenia, and this will reduce the possibility of side-effects."

The doctor glanced at Sarge, who was coughing. "You are not choking, Mr Parker?"

"Sir – Doctor." The reply sounded laboured.

The doctor looked back at John and smiled. "Either I or the consultant will review in one month. Before you go, is there anything you wish to ask me?"

Of course. "When can I get out?"

"I cannot say. You are detained and will be here many months while we treat you for your breakdown."

A breakdown – awaiting a restart. Sounded too simple.

The doctor turned to Sarge (whose impassive face was an unusual red, flecked with purple). "I have finished with Mr Chisholm. What activity will he return to?"

Sarge stood erect. "He will be escorted to the airing court – Doctor." This sounded like the announcing of a sentence. "Mr Clark – take the patient there."

"Sir." The grip on his elbow tightened and he was escorted out.

Parker slammed the door behind the doctor, the high-and-mighty that looked and spoke funny. A fucking nerve this turban-and-beard, a lowly registrar, had, swaggering into his office, telling him – the charge nurse, and boss of Admissions – to say 'doctor' instead of 'sir'. Insulting bugger. Should be sent back to where he belonged. They'd got above themselves, should never have been given independence. He walked round his desk, swearing. The god would be back soon and he, Ready Parker, would complain about this 'doctor'.

And the namby-pamby way this 'doctor' treated the patient! Taking the hooligan off the Shocker, when it was serving its purpose. This teacher snob, nutty as a fruitcake, was trouble, and one patient he'd vowed would suffer when he got back from suspension.

Mrs C, Heather, was juicy by all accounts. Ages since he had a woman. The last one was that student nurse Aileen – gone now, thank God. Threatened to report him, the silly bitch. She asked for it, and no way could she have proved anything.

Greying hair needn't be a problem. It gave him that mature distinguished look. The 'foul breath' that Aileen said disgusted her wasn't a problem either. Chlorophyll tablets sorted that for special occasions. He still knew how to charm a girl and give her a good time. With a 'softly softly' approach, he'd have it off with Mrs C. She should be hungry for it by now, unless she had a fancy man. And he would teach that teacher, give him every detail of what he did to her.

Friday was her day off. He'd ring, tell her about hubby and try to meet up. Ready the lady-killer. Yes, but he'd have to go careful. An affair with a patient meant the sack; an affair with a patient's wife could be dodgy too, if anyone found out.

Maybe the suspension hadn't done any harm. The Chief had investigated, and recommended he be reinstated with immediate effect. Hallman was okay – coming in for a whisky one night and telling him he'd be in the clear. But the Med Super had insisted the Management Committee must decide – to try and shut up that bloody colonel brother. He'd never liked colonels, but they had to be obeyed. By the time the Committee – a load of figureheads that knew nothing about loonies – met, weeks had passed. It was last Friday evening and the Chief had come straight round to confirm. Over a whisky, the boss agreed he would start duty Sunday at seven a.m.

Not that the waiting was all bad. Being paid for doing nothing was all right, and the Red Lion was okay, with Flowers Keg Bitter and the darts.

And that stuck-up toff was in Infirmary. Good riddance.

He sat down at his desk. Without a stain on his record, he was back. Boss of Admissions – the best job in nursing, apart from up the hierarchy. The Chief, over last Friday's whisky, had confirmed he was in line for the assistant chief job when Porter went. And the Chief added with a wink, "Ready, you'll remember I'm going too next year." His career was on track.

31

Tuesday 31ˢᵗ July 1956 – in Aversham, then Springwell.

Sam Newman sat at his desk, blowing smoke rings. Life wasn't so great now. Ella was in a bad spell, staying in her wheelchair, negative and accusatory. She'd been pretty upbeat for weeks; and he couldn't think of anything that triggered this downturn. She'd never be the Ella he married.

And Helen was walking out with another Woolworth employee – a man the same age as himself. Sam believed the guy was after one thing only.

At work he was now 'senior', with an extra increment – and theoretically his workload would be reduced. Huh! The first problem was having to share his room – they'd crammed another desk in, facing his – with a raw newcomer DAO. Maybe he could put up with that, but scarcely with a non-smoker who kept sniffing and coughed all over the desks when Sam lit up.

And he hadn't been involved in the interviewing. The MOH and the Chief Admin Officer, with the Health Committee Chairman, had constituted the interviewing panel. Newman had asked the MOH if he could be involved, but was told he needed all the time for his job. He wasn't even consulted. And when he objected to room-sharing, the Chief Admin told him there was nowhere else. On complaining to the boss, he was told, "It will help Carter learn the ropes."

Mary, in on the interviews taking notes, gave him the low-down. They'd interviewed two men. The one in his fifties was an ex-relieving officer under the Poor Law, and the young man a civil service clerk. The older man had some experience working with 'mental folk', and

Mary liked him ("reminded me of my dad"). The young man wore a three-piece suit and 'talked smart'. She didn't like him. But sadly the panel – including, critically, the boss – did.

Newman hadn't warmed to his opinionated new colleague. And inducting him was burdensome. Carter talked too much and didn't listen enough. It would be ages before this rookie could be let loose independently into complex situations.

Last week the pressure heightened to near unbearable – particularly with a couple of sleep-wrecking emergencies. This week was no better, and last night he'd been out to a middle-of-the-night 'domestic'. Neither party was mad – though after two hours' peacekeeping, he'd happily have whisked both off to Springwell.

It should make sense for him to teach his colleague know-how, but this guy was raw and totally unsuitable. Taking Carter on visits was a drag, though at least then the rookie obeyed the order to "Keep your mouth shut and stay in the background."

Today, though, his new colleague was at Springwell for the morning, sitting in lectures with student nurses as part of being inducted. The room was blissfully devoid of idle chatter. He sat back, yawning and enjoying the smoke.

He found himself daydreaming again about Heather Chisholm. Maybe she still loved her loony husband. But he'd sensed a growing bond with her, and it had taken superhuman self-control to hang back from grabbing her when they last parted. She was beautiful, naively seductive – and vulnerable, needing help.

It was some weeks since he took her to Springwell. Visiting her – a wife distraught at her mad hubby being in a nigh-inaccessible loony bin – would just about be legit. Last he heard, hubby was given ECT big time and she hadn't been to visit again. Odds were the poor sod would be in forever, but she didn't have to know that.

Nothing had come in. Still short of nine-thirty, and he didn't have the inhibiting presence of that fool. He stubbed out his fag. He'd ring the shop to check Mrs C was at home.

He got the number from his diary and reached towards the phone, then paused. That damn circular last week from the Chief Admin about making only urgent phone calls in the morning, when rates were dearest. He couldn't ignore a memo from the boss's right-hand man. And he did not want to broadcast this visit.

He left a message with Mary – "Out on a visit, back soon" – then drove to 90 Green Drive. There was no reply.

Over at the shop, Mattie told him, "Mrs Chisholm works at the nursery where the bairn is."

Mattie's wife emerged from the back-shop. "Come in here, Sir."

He didn't want a conversation. "Thanks, I won't. I'm busy. It's a flying visit to ask how Mrs Chisholm's coping while her husband's in Springwell."

Those eyes, compassionate but searching. "I'll tell her you called, Sir. She'll be sorry to have missed you."

He mustn't give any clue he was attracted to Heather. "Tell her she does not need to contact me. I'm hard to catch anyway." He drew breath. The woman was half-smiling, as though she'd guessed the real reason for his visit. Damn, he never was any good at acting. "And I'll be in touch only if there's anything she needs to know." Was it hot in here?

"Thank you, Mr Newman."

She remembered his name. "Must dash. 'Bye." He turned and exited the shop as fast as his limp allowed. He'd better hold back on this for a while.

32

Thursday 2nd August 1956 – in Aversham.

On Tuesday evening, Heather had got two messages via Elsie. Mr Newman called to ask how she was. Nice of him, and she felt a tug towards the man. Though Elsie voiced caution. "I think he might like you, m'dear, just a little too much."

And that afternoon, Charge Nurse Parker had rung suggesting she meet him on Friday evening to discuss John's condition. He'd be happy to call at her house, sometime after seven p.m. "Sounded a nice gentleman, m'dear, caring for John. And thoughtful, as he said it might be better if he came to your house – easier for you, with having the baby to look after, and there'd be privacy for him to tell you about John. Said he'd ring back for your answer on Thursday between one and two p.m."

She agonised over whether to accept. She wanted to hear from someone so involved in caring for John. But how much could she trust a total stranger? Why did he suggest meeting, rather than asking her to ring? Was it because he really cared? Or was he trying to date her? Or was it a mix of both? She was too cautious. What was the harm in the man coming to the house with news she craved?

Elsie offered to have Becky. But in the event, she didn't need Elsie's help.

Lacklustre and clingy all week, Becky had been hot and running a temperature overnight. This morning the doctor said it could be measles (though there wasn't a rash) and prescribed penicillin.

A faint tapping? On the door? Yes. "Come in, Elsie." A welcome visit. She wanted to speak to her friend, but daren't risk leaving Becky alone – or taking her out of the 'constant room temperature' the doctor advised.

172

"Just a quick call to ask how Becky is, m'dear."

She told Elsie what the doctor said and led her to where Becky was asleep. "Poor wee soul," Elsie said. "You must be worried sick."

"I am, Elsie."

"Anything I can do?"

Yes, she'd nearly forgotten. "Could you ring the nursery, let them know Becky's ill and that I can't come in?"

"Yes, m'dear. Anything more?"

"Oh, tell Charge Nurse Parker if he rings - thanks, and sorry, but my child's ill. And ask him how John is."

"Yes, m'dear. I'll come over later to see if you need anything."

She'd wait over the weekend to see how Becky was, and she'd ask her parents for more help. The nursery wage wasn't great, but was vital now, as another wretched brown envelope had signalled an end to John's employment. Her parents could cover the rent. She and Becky would not be homeless.

Friday 3rd August 1956 – in Springwell.

Parker leaned back in his armchair, sipping whisky. It had been a long day. He'd worked a double shift. Yesterday's news about Mrs C's blasted child being ill meant he'd be at a loose end after the early shift finished at 2pm. They were a man down, with Mullen off, and he'd stayed on as Charge, rather than let that shit Niven stand in. He'd made sure the Chief knew. This would not harm his promotion prospects!

The day was capped by the news that the dandy nobleman had recovered from the kicking and would, from Sunday, grace the Admissions Ward with his presence. He'd have to see this prick was wrapped in cotton wool.

He switched on the wireless. Home Service - boring. Light Programme - rubbish. He turned the wireless off. He'd make the Red Lion before closing.

A loud knock on the door. Who the hell was this, disturbing him?

He rose quietly, unlocked the door and flung it open to confront the intruder. The Chief!

"Thought I'd pay you a visit, Ready, rather than you coming to the office."

"Sir. Come in." This must be about the assistant chief job. "Join me in a whisky, Sir?" He beckoned to the other armchair.

"Yes, Ready." The Chief looked distracted as he sat down.

He poured a large whisky and passed it to the Chief. Was the man's hand shaking as he took the glass? "Sir."

The Chief took a gulp, then set the glass down. "I needed that, Ready. I've just seen the Med Super and come straight from his office." He paused.

Had the Med Super agreed on the assistant chief job? "Sir."

The Chief took another gulp. "The Baron's brother was told about the transfer back to Admissions. The bastard demanded that the nobleman should not be on any ward you're in charge of. And the boss has damn well caved in."

What! Bloody colonels! "Sir, I –"

"I'm moving you, from Sunday, to Refractory." The Chief drained his glass.

The Factory, taking care of bad boys. Okay he could do that, but this was a demotion. And who the hell was this colonel to dictate to Springwell? "But Sir –"

The Chief rose. "This is not demoshun. Could help with th'assistant chief job – broaden experience."

Aha! He'd never been Charge on Refractory.

"Ready, friend, gotta go." The Chief made for the door.

Parker leapt up and opened the door. "Sir." The Chief exited without turning.

174

33

Friday 3rd August 1956 on – in Aversham.

Heather thought the coughing and sneezing and fever that tormented her child would never end. Was Becky going to die? If so, she'd want to as well. John might not need her any more. Murderous, the charge nurse said. She didn't want to think about that.

At last a red rash came and, soon after, the coughing and sneezing seemed to trouble less. The fever subsided and, with Becky fully alert, the cheeky smiles returned. The red rash gave way to brown spots.

The proverbial turning of the corner. Heather, inspired, took to singing nursery rhymes and reading stories to Becky, till they both fell asleep.

At other times, she got on with housework – humming the Elvis hits, listening to the wireless, losing herself in a Dickens novel, or reading snatches from women's magazines Elsie brought for her.

But she kept thinking about John and mourning her loss. Evenings, she could sit for hours ruminating. She tried to divert her thinking into the happier memories of their time together. His sense of fun – and the dry humour similar to hers – hadn't been evident for a long time now.

That wonderful sunny day by Lake Windermere, on a trip the Students' Union organised. She was dawdling along, holding hands with John. Lightning-fast, he swung to kneel in front of her and, clinging to her hand, gazed up – his eyes shining and blond hair chaotic from the wind. "Heather Sloan, will you marry me?"

He was fooling – they hadn't been courting five minutes. She screwed her face up like she smelt dog shit. "John Chisholm, I'll not be marrying a lowlife."

His blue eyes stared earnestly. "That's it! What I really love about you. You're so discerning."

"Unlike you."

"Sure – I guess I'd only ever go for a lowlife."

"Kick him in the goolies, Heather." Her friend Amy. They had an audience!

"Yes or no, Heather?"

"What do you think?"

"Lowlifes don't think. Hey – this is doing for my knees. Yes or no?"

Maybe he wasn't kidding about the knees. "Okay. Arise, Sir Lancelot."

He remained kneeling, and the grip on her hand tightened. "Okay yes, or okay no?"

She extended her other hand. "Okay yes, you fool!"

They laughed and hugged, cheered by their fellow students. Her happiest day?

A story she read in one of Elsie's mags featured a woman spurned by her husband, and her dilemmas when pursued by two other men. This, she'd thought, could be uncannily like her situation. But she didn't want to think such a ridiculous thing – that Sam Newman or Charge Nurse Parker might be wooing her.

Tap tap? The door. Elsie. "Won't come in m'dear. How's Becky?"

"She's nearly better thanks, Elsie."

"That's a relief, m'dear. Oh, and when Charge Nurse Parker rang, I told him about Becky being ill. Mr Parker said he was very sorry to hear that and to pass on his best wishes for a speedy recovery."

"Thanks Elsie. Did he say how John is?"

"No m'dear. Said he could only tell you, as it was confidential, and even with you he couldn't say over the phone. He said he'll ring soon to ask after Becky and whether he can meet to tell you about John." Elsie paused. "He sounds a real good-hearted man, m'dear. And if he comes of an evening, I'll be happy to come and sit with Becky."

Nice offer. Swept away lingering hesitations about Mr Parker visiting.

Friday 21ˢᵗ September 1956 – in Aversham.

Heather glanced at the clock. Six-fifteen – just over an hour to go, and she was still coaxing Becky to eat. She was using all her wiles, talking and singing while surreptitiously shovelling in the odd spoonful. Dollops of food were on the carpet. She just could not stop her hand from trembling.

Abandoning the effort, she changed Becky's nappy and put the child down to sleep. She'd ignore the bawling. She must get the mess off the carpet.

On her knees, rubbing with a cloth, she left a big wet patch. It might dry before her visitor came. Six-thirty – better get ready! She dashed upstairs and changed into her costume, then looked in the mirror. Her hair was still in curlers! She started taking them out. Careful, she shouldn't rush it. Lucky it was her day off, and she'd had time to wash and dry her hair.

Curlers out, she combed her hair. But she couldn't ignore the yelling any more. She went and picked Becky up. That aroma – again! She changed the nappy and sang lullabies until, thankfully, Becky's eyes closed.

She rushed back to finish combing her hair, then brushed it.

Just on seven. She looked in the wardrobe mirror. Fine. Should she put the wireless on? No, she might not hear him knock.

The other evening, Elsie had come over. "Won't come inside, m'dear. That nice Mr Parker from Springwell rang. Asked how you were and whether he could visit this Friday evening at seven-thirty, to tell you about John. He'll ring back Thursday for an answer."

She'd done the agonising. "Tell him 'yes thanks'."

"Yes m'dear. I'm afraid Mattie's started fair coughing up again – so it's best to stay away from the back-shop and me for now, in case Becky catches something."

That had been a downer. Elsie could not help with Becky for Parker's visit.

However, things had worked out. She'd decided to tell Moira about the charge nurse's offer. "It's unusual," Moira said, "though it sounds genuine. Look, I'd be happy to come over when he visits and stay with Becky in her bedroom."

"That would be good, Moira. Thanks."

They'd agreed Moira would call at around twenty to eight. Heather wanted a few minutes alone with her visitor first.

So now, a quarter past seven, Charge Nurse Parker was nearly due. She fiddled with the cushions on the settee, still not sure she'd done the right thing.

Two thunderous raps on the front door! She ran to open it, and suppressed a gasp. The man filled the doorway. He was smiling. "Mrs Chisholm - Heather? Charge Nurse Parker, boss of Admissions."

He was early. She took his extended hand to shake it. Did he squeeze her hand - or was it a friendly handshake? "Pleased to meet you. Come in." She led the way into the lounge and motioned to the armchair. He sprawled into it.

"Would you like a cup of tea, Charge Nurse Parker, or some lemon squash?"

"Thanks, Heather. I'm parched. I'll go for the lemon squash, please." He was still smiling. "And you needn't call me Charge Nurse Parker - though I assure you I am. Ready's the name - for 'Ready for action'."

"Yes, eh, Ready." She went to the kitchen, poured a glass of squash and brought it to the nesting table beside the armchair.

The man stood by the sideboard, looking at something. At the photo she'd taken from the bureau. "Is that John's family when he was young?" He pointed.

"Yes, with his brother and parents." She paused, aware she was blushing. This intruded into her very private domain. She was being churlish though. The charge nurse was showing his concern for John.

"Now can you tell me who's who?" The man was holding the

photo, peering at it, and she'd have to move close to examine it. Where was Moira?

She moved alongside him. Nice smell – was it hair oil? "John's on your left. The other boy's his brother who drowned aged ten." She drew back. "Do sit down."

The man propped the photo back on the sideboard, sank into the armchair and drained the squash. "Thanks, Heather. I needed that. Haven't stopped all day." He put down the glass and sighed. "How sad, the brother drowning. In his few sane moments, John's talked about this."

A loud knocking. "Excuse me." She went to the door. "Moira, come in."

Back in the living room, she performed introductions. The man beamed and, lifting his gigantic frame to tower over them, squeezed Moira's hand.

"Moira's come to look after Becky while we talk."

"Good, because I couldn't say anything about John in your friend's presence." He looked towards Moira. "In my profession, we swear an oath of confidentiality."

"Becky's asleep through there, at the other end of the living room, Moira." She pointed to a door that was slightly ajar.

"Thanks, I'll go through. Good-bye, Mr Parker," said Moira, and left them.

Mr Parker sank back into the chair. He nodded towards the bedroom door, still a fraction open. "Can we close that?"

"It might waken Becky, as it doesn't shut easily. Anyway, I'm sure what we talk about wouldn't interest Moira." Heather sat down on the settee.

"Your friend must not hear what I have to say. I could face the sack if she did. I'm telling you about John in the strictest confidence."

This man was trusting her. Putting his career on the line. "Well…"

"It's all right." He'd lowered his voice. He stood up. No – he was leaving? "If I may, I'll join you on the settee, so I can keep my voice very low," he whispered.

He was staying, thank goodness. "Yes, that seems sensible." She moved across to ensure he had enough room.

He tiptoed over and she felt him sink into the settee beside her. His vast bulk meant he was almost touching her. She moved her legs towards her end of the settee. This skirt was shorter than she'd realised.

He leaned against her, whispering into her ear. There was a whiff of something sweet on his breath. "What I have to tell you isn't good news, Heather. John's condition is worse, despite all our efforts."

"You said on the phone he was murderous," she whispered back.

"I'm afraid that's the case. And I despair of him ever changing."

She twisted round to look at him. His expression was grave.

"This must be upsetting, Heather. It's all right if you cry."

She drew her sleeve across her eyes. A long weep was overdue.

"The problem is that with his paranoid delusions - which will be lifelong - he has strange unshakable ideas that you are an evil force needing to be extinguished."

Her worst fears. She could hear John shouting at her, and see him picking up the breadknife. Tears were now streaming down her face. She used her sleeve again.

"There now, Heather," he said. She felt his comforting arm across her back, his large hand drawing her in towards him. Nice. A rock. "You need a good cry."

Yes. Her world was shattering. And she needed a good cuddle - which this decent man was giving her. She could feel her bare leg being warmed by his trousered one. She heard a soft whisper, "There now, Heather." Her knee was being patted. All felt okay; comforting.

A loud bawling erupted. Becky. "I must go. Excuse me." She leapt off the settee, wiped her eyes with her sleeve, and rushed through to her wailing child.

"I don't know what happened," said Moira, standing by the crib.

"It's okay. I'll change her nappy and settle her. It'll take some time. Can you thank Mr Parker for calling and tell him I hope to see him again soon?"

"Yes." Moira went back into the living room, leaving the door ajar.

Heather sang lullabies till Becky dozed off, then returned to the living room.

"Mr Parker's gone," Moira said. "I gave him your message and talked to him while he lingered. I asked him about his job and said my husband knows a man that works in Springwell's Admin."

"Thanks Moira. I was in tears - the news about John was so bad."

"I'm sorry to hear that."

"In fact he was starting to comfort me - put an arm round me."

"I suspected as much. I heard a little of your conversation."

Had Moira listened throughout? Maybe, but her friend wouldn't waken Becky deliberately. Would she? "I was distraught, Moira. I'm glad you were there."

"What did you think of him?"

"There was something scary about him at first - just his bulk, I guess - but he's been very kind to me. And he's taking a special interest in John."

"Yes, Heather. He might be entirely genuine. But I should go carefully. He struck me as evasive, and I do wonder why he wanted to meet you. Remember, I'm your friend, and if you want me to help again like this, just say."

"Thanks again, Moira."

The older woman gave her a hug. "Take care, Heather." On the doorstep, Moira turned to face her. "And my hubby could ask his cousin Rob - he's a clerk on Admin - if he knows anything about Mr Parker?"

Fortuitous - and an idea! She mustn't antagonise the man caring for John. But she'd like to know more about him - be sure he was for real. "Maybe..."

"I promise it wouldn't get back to Mr P. Rob's very discreet. He mightn't know - and it could be a while before we see him. But I'd let you know of anything."

"Okay then. Thanks Moira." She waved her friend good-bye.

Left alone with Becky, she moped and wept, abandoned and hated by the love of her life, her hero - her poor mad murderous husband.

34

John was now seeing Dr Singh for periodic check-ups (the god, thank goodness, still being off sick, according to Mullen). And each time he could report improvements in how he felt.

At their last meeting, he'd asked about discharge.

"No, your treatment will continue here for some time."

"But I feel well and I'd be okay at home. And I doubt my wife's having an affair. I got to feeling certain, but I could be wrong. Anyway, I could hardly blame her – the way I was."

"However, it is still early in your treatment, Mr Chisholm." The doctor coughed. "And I am only a psychiatric registrar, without authority to discharge patients. Legally you are detained under an order, for review next April. Only a consultant could vary this if he thought fit."

A downer! The god would never set him free. Much of his thinking was about Heather – the great times they'd had, and the way he'd treated her. She couldn't be blamed for not visiting. He'd made it clear he didn't want her to. He must have been sick. If only he could get home to her and Becky. How were they managing? He must achieve the impossible. *Escape.*

One thing making life tolerable was the continuing unexplained absence of Sarge. While Mullen didn't rate that highly on caring, he was fair on the whole and didn't engage in torment and sadistic threat.

However, this was offset by Niven's return. "I've got a promotion from Infirmary to come and make your lives hell – you and your carrot-top mate," the bully said, confronting John on the airing court one day. And back on the ward, Clark confirmed this. "We both passed our exams for staff nurse. I leave here tomorrow for another ward as deputy charge, and you'll have Tommy Niven regular as staff."

The one outstandingly good thing was Ginger's reappearance. "There was a huge fuss when they brought me down from the infirmary. Nurse Mullen and another man – said he was the Medical Superintendent, the boss – were there. This boss asked me how I felt about Kong, and did I want him off the ward? I like Kong and we always got on. I'm sure he was just obeying that beast Parker." He laughed. "They got Kong into the office then and talked to him. Poor fellow, I never saw him look scared before. The upshot is that he's now my bodyguard." Certainly Kong never seemed far from Ginger, and was the third person on their airing court walks.

On the airing court, Ginger soon became talkative again, and John was transported into different worlds. Okay, the tales were fantasy, but who cared – they were interesting. Ginger should be an author.

The white-coats clearly thought Ginger was special and treated him with respect. Except for Niven, who was unfortunately now on the ward daily. The man was a bully – but a sly one, as the swearing, threats and shoving didn't seem to happen when the Charge or other white-coats were nearby.

Surely escape wasn't impossible – or was it? Today, in a rare moment of silence with Ginger on their airing court walk, he voiced his recurring daydream. "We patients rise up en masse and overpower the staff. We put on uniforms, take the keys, lock the staff in, and walk out."

Ginger's response was unexpectedly robust. "Not bloody likely. Can you imagine these men working together on a plan? No, old boy, we'd all be rounded up, given electric shocks and doped unconscious. And they'd slice our brains open, before consigning us to an eternity of torture in this prison."

Nice to hear Ginger back to his eloquent best! This portrayal of a bleak outcome was probably accurate. But he wasn't giving up on the idea.

Over lunch John heard bangs. Thunder – and lightning. Mullen unlocked the outside door, and, a few seconds later, shut and re-locked it.

"No airing court this afternoon. It's flooded," Mullen announced. "You can stay in the dayroom or go lie on your beds." He turned and went back to the office.

What to do next? John wondered. Not lie on his bed; he felt like exercise. He looked around the dayroom. A group huddled near the entrance to it – Jimmy, George, Paranoid Pat, Alf, Ginger and Kong. John wandered over to them.

There was no white-coat anywhere within earshot. Maybe he could raise the question of escape.

The ward door rattled. A white-coat – Niven – came in and slammed the door behind him, locking it then jangling the keys.

"What's your problem?" growled Pat.

Niven ignored him and went towards the office, where Mullen could be seen at his desk.

"They're the mad ones," said Jimmy. "They should be the patients."

"What I wouldn't do for a fag," said Alf.

"How about murder?" asked Pat, nodding towards the office.

"I don't want to be clapped in the cooler," said Alf.

"This air's poison," said Pat. "That bastard Nosey Parker took me over – I felt it right through my body. That fucker Niven's got me too."

Sarge's nickname could be spoken aloud now he was gone. Before, it was rarely even whispered. A derogatory play on the man's name that John wouldn't be using. No, the man would, for him, always be Sarge. An unspoken nickname that existed only in his own head.

The office door opened and Niven stomped out. "Chisholm," he shouted.

What now?

"Boss says you're on the dirty laundry."

"Again?" he muttered. Fourth week running. The laundry stank.

"Yes Chisholm, you shit. Again! Mr Macleod's gonna take you."

Good news. Browncoat Mac, a man about his own age, was great company on the dirty laundry a couple of weeks back. "John, call me Mac. I'm a ward orderly, which means I'm a dogsbody. But I'm paid and I walk away at the end of my shifts. You guys cooped up here – you're the ones I feel for."

A man in the patients' corner? Indeed, Mac had encouraged him to talk about himself, and seemed genuinely interested.

Now Mac was walking towards him and appeared to be grinning. A sudden clatter indicated a fight breaking out in the dormitory. Mac switched direction and ran to help sort things.

"I want to kill these white-coat bastards Niven and Nosey," said Pat.

"Okay, kill them and let's get out of here," said George.

They were moving onto the topic John wanted to explore. Not much hope – but if they didn't talk about escape, their chances were zero. "I don't agree with killing." He kept his voice low, looking at the rumpus still going on in the dormitory. "How about we knock them out, truss and gag them?" The idea of murdering anyone – even an evil guy like Niven (or Sarge) – was anathema. He'd too much respect for people; besides which, swinging on the gallows in public disgrace wouldn't be his chosen means of expiring. "But this place must be like Fort Knox."

"One man," Alf came in, "who's dead now, got away. I never knew how it happened, but Slinky said he could make keys out of coins and sardine tin-openers – and that being a trusty helped him do it." Alf started a fit of coughing.

Interesting. Escape had happened before. Alf had been here the longest, "A trusty for decades 'til I crossed Parker and got slung in the cooler." A Passchendale survivor, Alf had come in with shellshock, "Though they gave it a fancy name – neurasthenia. I've been sane near all the years in here, but I still get nightmares." Alf's word should be reliable.

Nobody spoke. All looked interested. John listened as Alf, throat cleared, continued the tale. "Poor Slinky stayed out thirteen days and thought he was free."

"What do you mean?"

There was a hint of a smile on Alf's gnarled face. "Well, if you stay out fourteen days you're legally free. Slinky got the sums wrong. Stayed

185

holed up somewhere; then on the thirteenth day, walked down the High Street and got stopped by a copper that started asking questions. Slinky ran for it - with the copper hollering to stop - was tripped up and caught. They brought him back in a straitjacket."

That was a tragedy for poor Slinky. And a pity the man died; a key would have been handy. But maybe there was another way - if they acted together.

"There's an alarm in the office," said Jimmy. "So we'd have to overpower the Charge first." This was gathering steam.

John glanced around. No white-coat was overseeing. The group had fallen silent. Maybe the others were luxuriating in the idea of taking out Sarge, or Niven!

Watching the struggle in the dormitory, he had a thought. "How about a diversion? Somebody starts a fight, draws the white-coats, and we take over the office."

"Sounds good," Jimmy agreed.

"I could beat up two white-coats at once," said Kong.

Useful. Kong had resented being put in the cooler after the Ginger incident, then being demoted by Sarge from the cutlery job and not reinstated by Mullen. Though back to being more amiable as Ginger's bodyguard, the mighty man could still give the impression of a sulking volcano - and surely had the will as well as the strength to take out a couple of white-coats.

Enough for now. "So we *can* get out. We'll plan again soon."

"Hear hear!" said Ginger, quietly. A change of tune from an hour or two back. "We should not be incarcerated like pigs." A glimpse of Ginger the orator. "I should be on my estate."

The dormitory row had ended. Mac was coming over for John. The plotters dispersed. But for that memorable few minutes, hope was re-kindled. The genies were starting to believe there could be a way out of the bottle.

35

The 'dirty laundry' was a euphemism for a heap of stinking excrement-encrusted and urine-soaked long-john underwear and pyjamas. "I get an extra penny for doing this," said Mac, turning the tap to let water into the pile in the huge washtub. "Great reward! And they're too mean even to provide gloves." He put a cupful of soap powder in, then another. "I wish to god they'd put the lot straight in the machine."

John had his sleeves rolled up, ready to start tackling the mess. "But then you wouldn't have heard my fascinating story."

Mac grinned and handed him a washboard. "Let's go."

They set about their distasteful task, scrubbing to tackle the worst stains.

"You know," said Mac, pausing. "I was on the Factory last week. Nosey's Charge there now."

John stopped scrubbing. "Just hope we don't get him back."

"Hope not," said Mac. "But if you do, for God's sake don't insult him. Months ago I saw a man - cocky little guy, new to Springwell - get shirty when Parker pushed him. 'Nosey Parker,' the man shouts. Parker lifts him by the lapels, curses him, headbutts him and whirls him round. The guy keeps yelling 'Nosey Parker' till a couple of nurses put him out and take him to the cooler." Mac paused.

"The little guy had some guts."

Mac frowned. "Aye, but the tale has a sad end. Weeks later I saw the guy in the Annex, where they put the older patients who're no bother. Looked zonked - just sat there staring. The Charge said Parker had got the god to prescribe a leucotomy, which means they sliced the poor guy's brain."

A scary tale. "Some treatment!"

"Aye. Anyway, on Refractory Parker's with the hard men. Nosey's always treated me like shite, but I didn't see a lot of him. He'd stay in his office, letting the other nurses do the dirty work and sort out the fights. Maybe he was scared. I could smell murder there."

"How did you cope?"

"Och, all right. Worst I got was a black eye in one shindig. It wasn't so bad for me, being an orderly. I guess the patients didn't see me as Authority. And between chores I could talk with them, and listen to their stories." Mac would be good at that – helping guys feel respected. "And there's more staff on that ward. They expect trouble. I think they invite it."

Mac resumed scrubbing and John did likewise. The Factory was clearly a place to avoid, especially with Sarge the boss there.

Uppermost in his mind was still the matter of escape. He could trust this man – well, to an extent. Could any staff here really be trusted? "Has anybody ever escaped from here?"

"I haven't heard them talk about it. All I hear about is how we must, on pain of being sacked, keep locking up after us. We get these keys when we come on duty and hand them in when we finish the shift." Mac paused, filthy underpants in hand. "But I've only been here a few months – and I'm part-time."

"You're part-time?" It wasn't a good idea to stay too long on the escape theme.

"Aye. Didn't I tell you? I'm a student at the university and I only work Sunday Monday Tuesday back-shifts, that is from two p.m. until ten."

So Mac wouldn't be one of the 'in crowd'. There was a fair chance he could be trusted.

They resumed sifting and scrubbing.

"Stand back. Better change the water." Mac let the sludge out down the drain and poured fresh water in.

"How come you're working here?"

"A psychiatrist from here came to the uni's Psychological Society to give a talk on Mental Illness. Said there could be a ward orderly job part-time if I wanted. I went out to see the Chief Male Nurse, a dour old guy who lectured me on keys and took me on. I was interested and needed the extra cash."

"What are you studying?"

"Psychology and philosophy. Final year. In fact, I'll have to leave here soon." What a downer. "Need to get the head into these books. Have to get a good degree; I want to be a clinical psychologist."

"Hope you make it," said John. He'd heard of clinical psychologists, who saw people with mental problems individually. He would have been better off seeing one of them than a psychiatrist. And Mac listened well, with a great bedside manner.

"We'll see. The girlfriend's taking up too much time just now." Mac smiled. "You know, I left school wanting to be a psychiatrist and found out then you have to train as a doctor first. It was years too late, as I'd dropped science early in secondary school."

A pity. Mac would have been a damned sight better than any he'd met.

The tub re-filled and each resumed their task. Soon there were a couple of piles, ready for the two mangles.

Mac broke the silence as they each set about a mangle. "I know you're a teacher, with a history degree. Do you think you'll go back to teaching?"

"Some chance! I don't think I'll ever get away from here."

"Is that why you mentioned escape?"

Okay – he'd trust the guy. "Yes. Maybe there was something wrong with me, but there isn't now. I don't see them letting me out."

"I'd help you if I could, but they're so tight with the keys I can't see any hope of copying them." Mac sighed. "And the place is guarded like a prison."

The man was definitely in his corner. But Mac's observations reinforced his belief that only a brilliantly planned escape could stand a chance of success.

As they hung the clothes to dry, Mac said, "I'll tell you a wee story."

"Go on."

"In St Andrews, where I grew up, the castle has the darkest, scariest place. It's called the bottle dungeon, because it's cut into the rock in the shape of a massive bottle, with a neck at the top that's big enough to let a man in. It's deep and was used in mediaeval times for guys who'd offended by way of politics or religion. Not just any guy, but somebody important – like an enemy nobleman – that mustn't ever get away." Mac coughed.

"How did they get a prisoner in and out? And food and drink?"

"I'm not sure exactly, but I gather they used ropes. Anyway, you can imagine it. Stuck in the bottom of a rock bottle, with smooth walls, on your own in the dark. Escape was impossible."

He could imagine. Made the padded cell sound like grand luxury. There would be no way out. "Yes."

Mac chuckled. "But one man did escape."

"How?"

"His loving sister was lowered in to visit. After she'd gone, they discovered next mealtime that she was still there. They'd swapped clothes and he'd hoofed it – a free man."

"Brilliant."

"What I'm saying is, don't give up hope."

"Thanks. I won't."

As they walked back into the ward, a thought struck him. "Presumably they let the sister go, as she was innocent."

"Can't remember for sure – but I think they were peeved, took a hard line and kept her in there."

A sad ending. But sometimes ingenuity could achieve the impossible.

That night, John lay thinking of the conversations and his fellow conspirators. Yes, that's what they were – conspirators, who'd floated a few embryonic ideas about escaping. Maybe a core group, who could work on a strategy?

All seemed motivated, and that tale about Slinky helped with the hope of getting out and staying there. Ginger could be useful, in that he clearly had influence with the white-coats. And he could be trusted to keep the plotting secret, as could George and Alf. Kong too - a man of few words, discarded as a trusty.

Jimmy and Paranoid Pat, he didn't know so well. Jimmy, a quiet well-spoken man, should be fine. A man who "faked insanity to dodge National Service, got certified, banged up, then found I couldn't get out," would be an asset.

About Paranoid Pat, he wasn't so sure. A wiry man with a grim expression who often ranted in a low voice, "I'm paranoid, but I don't lie," (and hence the nickname), Pat would obey the inevitable 'shut up', then stand glowering. The man could be a bit weird. First time they'd met, John's nod of greeting had Pat edging away - staring, suspicious, hostile.

Pat had strange ideas. Weeks later, trudging round the airing court, Pat whispered corner-of-the-mouth, "The white-coats are aliens."

"Pat - you say aliens?"

Pat then told a sad tale - punctuated with the habitual rants. "I'm a science teacher... lunchtime I get a message... aliens are going to invade my classroom lab... I run back there, barricade myself in... I grab a bunsen burner and hide behind a desk... aliens in police uniform and white coats break in... I scorch one of them and hear yelling... come round a prisoner of white-coat aliens."

There would be a problem if Pat did try to kill Niven - popular though the sentiment was. More importantly, could the guy work on and stick to an agreed plan? Intelligent, hated white-coats, and surely wouldn't blab to anyone - so? Yes. Pat should be okay in the group.

As soon as chance permitted, he'd try to get them working together on a plan. He saw how they could get out of the ward - and the detail, timing etc. would be vital. But once in the corridor, what then?

36

Moira was at the door. "Heather, I've something from Rob."

Seated with a cup of tea, Moira came out with it. "Mr Parker's not on the same ward as John."

This Heather did not believe. When she'd rung to ask about John, she was put through to this Charge Nurse on the Admissions Ward. So she knew Mr Parker was, as he said, boss of Admissions. "Well, I know that –" She paused. "Unless –"

"One of them moved." Moira had followed her line of thinking. "Parker was on Admissions, where John's a patient, but he hasn't been there since early August."

If this was true...! "How does this cousin know?"

"Sorry Heather, I can't tell you exactly, but Rob gets information and statistics from all over Springwell. He writes some of it up for the Hospital Secretary and the Management Committee."

Rob could still be mistaken. "So where does Rob say Mr Parker is now?"

"He's charge nurse on another ward they call the Refractory."

When was it she rang and spoke with Parker? Before Becky had measles. Yes, early June. She drained her cup. "Another cup, Moira?" She was pouring into the saucers. "Sorry."

"It's a shock for you. Rob's thoroughly reliable. I got him to double check."

"Thanks Moira." She fumbled in her handbag and located the aspirins. "I need a couple." The picture of John being murderous and hating her mightn't be true.

192

"I think Mr P's a scoundrel." Moira paused.

She felt like confronting Mr P. The agony he'd put her through – and the trust she'd placed in him! She stood up and took a deep breath. "I hope he rots in Hell. And Moira, I'd never let on how I came by this information – to anyone, him included if our paths ever cross."

Moira rose to exit, stopped and turned in the doorway. "Heather, be careful. This pretence and visiting – I'm sure he's been trying to get you into bed."

Ugh. Dirty old man. But Moira was probably right.

That night, Heather barely slept. Becky waking once was a welcome diversion from her turbulent thoughts. She must find out how John really was, and get out to see him again. Near dawn, she decided. It was time to ring Sam Newman!

Tuesday 16th October 1956 – in Aversham.

Sam Newman sat in his office with his feet on the desk, blowing smoke rings. He'd about run himself into the ground. Work pressures were unrelenting. Having Carter as a colleague was like having a wayward child dumped on you. The man's slick appearance and fast talking were more suited to a salesman than a DAO.

He'd insisted Carter come on night call-outs, but mostly he got no reply to his phoning. Then the man started turning up, and yawned throughout – every time. In a confrontation with an angry paranoid husband threatening to get physical, Carter exited fast, leaving Sam to appease the man and tackle the family situation. "Thought I'd only make things worse," was the excuse. And for once, Carter got it right.

It had been a relief when Carter said he was emigrating to Canada, "Where the future lies. I applied months ago, didn't hear, and assumed they didn't want me."

Thank God Canada wanted the bumptious one – as the MOH

clearly did too. "Carter smartens the department's image," the boss had responded to Newman's complaint about the man.

Last Friday, due notice was served and Sam no longer had the burden of carrying the useless one. And at last he had the room to himself.

Mary had told him the job was being re-advertised, with a 'previous applicants need not re-apply'. She'd been asked to ring the ex-relieving officer, and the man was still interested. "You'll like this one," she said.

He hoped Mary's judgment on this man was as accurate as her misgivings about Carter. With that work background, meeting folk in potentially hostile situations should be familiar ground for the guy.

The MOH had agreed to him being in on the interview (subject to his not being needed for a call-out). The Health Committee Chairman and the Chief Admin. Officer would be there, with the MOH – and Mary taking notes.

At home, Ella had been going through a rough patch for ages. Her sulks and suspicions meant that home was unwelcoming. At least Helen had broken off with that ne'er-do-well. She didn't seem happy either, though.

The phone rang. He snatched the receiver. "Newman."

A woman. "Mr Newman – Sam. I need help." She sounded edgy.

"Heather?"

"Yes, Heather Chisholm."

"Good to hear from you." An understatement. Ages since he saw her – he'd been so damned busy – but in his quieter moments, he kept seeing those soulful eyes gazing at him. She was alluring, unattainable. "I'll help if I can."

"I wonder if, when you're out at Springwell, you can ask how John is, check which ward he's on, and find out when I might visit?"

"Surely will do and get back to you. It might be a day or two, but I'll be in touch." He clarified when she'd be at home. "I called some weeks ago, with news of your husband, and left a message with your shop friend. Did it reach you?"

"Yes. Thanks. I appreciated that."

"When I get the info, I'll pop round. Right?"

"Yes, I'd welcome that."

Great. He wanted to see that friendly voluptuous woman again.

That evening, a chance came. A GP rang. "Mr Newman, can you visit a man who's gone round the bend. The wife's distraught. She came back from a break with her mum to find him acting crazy. Says he's not dangerous. I'll join you there."

Newman was greeted by the stressed-looking wife. "He's normally quiet, a peaceful man. But now he's restless, like he's possessed, speaking doggerel, singing, and pacing round the room. He wouldn't look at me. Then he went to his study – he's a university lecturer. Can you hear him?"

Clattering and singing? "Yes." Newman knocked on the study door and it swung open. A small man with staring eyes addressed him in nonsense rhyming, then set off round the study, chanting.

He tried to engage the man, following him round, but to no avail. The guy sounded perky though unintelligible; but in his eyes was vacant misery.

The GP arrived, and asked, "What's the score?"

"Manic. No way he'll come voluntarily. Urgency order?"

Newman followed the van to Springwell. There he got news about Chisholm from Charge Nurse Mullen and noted the date of next visiting.

Wednesday 17th October 1956 – in Aversham.

Heather yawned. Another sleepless night. Not problems with Becky; night-times were long and invited ruminating. That evil Parker. Was John murderous? Did he hate her?

She prepared Becky's food, and sat smiling as, spoon in hand, the infant managed to find her mouth with much of it. How sad John couldn't see this.

195

Someone was knocking on the door. This early! "Who is it?" she yelled.

"Sam Newman."

She rushed to the door and there he was, briefcase in hand. "Sam."

"Thought I'd catch you before the nursery. Last night I spoke with Charge Nurse Mullen on Admissions. Your husband's had treatment and seems less disturbed. He's certified and there till next April at least. Visiting's on Saturday 27th."

Next April! But even that was a lot better than the hopeless picture given by Parker. "Thanks for finding out - and so quickly."

"I'll call for you around 1.30 on Saturday and take you there. Unless I'm out on an emergency, and if so I'll ring the shop." He was fidgety, like a spring poised.

A tempting offer. It was so much easier by car, but she wanted to visit independently. "Sam, I want to try going by bus."

"Okay. I thought it would be easier for you. But I suppose I messed up last time." He sounded hurt.

"No, you didn't. John was unreasonably jealous. You're a good friend."

He smiled. "I try to be, Heather. Must fly." He was edging away. "Get back to me if you change your mind about the lift. I'll pop in after to ask how you got on."

She watched as he limped quickly to his car and started the engine, then waved him off. He'd put himself out to help and responded to her immediately, though he must be busy. He reminded her of someone. Clark Gable? Yes - a mini version. Again, she wondered if Sam was married.

37

Monday 15th October 1956 – in Springwell.

In the last few days, Alf had vanished.

On the dirty laundry with Mac, John learned of Alf's fate. "I spotted Alf in the Annex. Men don't come back from there, so I guess you've seen the last of your friend here."

A shame – and a blow for the planning! Alf would have been useful. "Sorry to hear it."

"He's a hardy veteran that knows this place well. I expect you'll miss him."

Was that a wink? "Yes."

Washboard at the ready, John looked at the pile as Mac poured water into the tub. "This stinks worse than just shit and piss. Maybe there's sick in it as well." He turned away, inhaled deeply, then, holding his breath, set to work scrubbing.

"You've got a point." Mac threw more soap powder in. "That should help."

The powder fumes made John cough, but the stench was more bearable. As they scrubbed on the washboards, it was Mac who raised the subject.

"You were thinking of escape."

He trusted Mac fully. "It's hellish trying to plan in there. No privacy."

"Hmm." Mac paused. "You need to divert the staff."

"Trouble is – how?"

"Dunno. Somebody fakes a fit, or cuts up rough?" He turned to face John and grinned. "I think you've a wee gang. I saw you the other week when it was thunder; and after our blether, I had a guess. But don't worry. Nobody else would cotton on."

The smile vanished and he looked intently at John. "And I'm trusting you, John Chisholm, never - I mean never ever - to say anything about our wee chats."

"My lips are sealed with glue."

"Aye. It wouldn't just be getting the sack. 'Aiding and abetting a patient to escape' - as they call it - is a crime. You can be jailed or get a hefty fine."

"What! Scandalous!" Forget civil liberties.

"Agreed. But it's the law. So I need you to keep quiet about me - forever."

"Don't worry, Mac. All this I take to the grave."

There was another area he needed help on. "We know the ward, but not the grounds - apart from the airing court."

"Aye, don't go to the court." Mac turned, looking around. "Just making sure - you'll remember those wartime posters 'walls have ears'." He lowered his voice to a whisper. "Look." He fumbled in his pocket, brought out a pencil and notebook and began sketching. "Here's the layout. Memorise it. I won't give it you, in case some daft nurse spots it and figures. You want the route that staff take. The night shift come in via the Main Hall, and staff going off duty leave by another door." He tore out the page and, keeping hold between thumb and finger, laid it flat on the draining board. "See."

John studied the map, and noted the door to exit by, the driveway, the main gate. Handy - he'd been concerned about bumping into night staff coming on duty and being recognised. "Thanks. Got it," he whispered.

"Just outside the exit door on your right, there's a wee niche that should be big enough for you all to shelter in when you come out." Mac added a cross to the sketch.

Mac scrunched the paper and put it in his trouser pocket. "The other thing is the drill for giving in keys and checking out."

He'd assumed they couldn't simply walk out. He listened carefully as Mac described the scenario and procedures. "Okay, I can visualise that."

"Right, let's scrub."

Walking back to the ward after they'd completed their task, Mac gave the bad news. "Tomorrow's my last day. Academia needs me."

"Sorry." He struggled for words. This guy was a fellow spirit.

"Aye, I'll miss the wee chats." Mac looked thoughtful. "But my going might give me a chance tomorrow to divert the nurses. In the evening I'll plan to go into the office, tell the charge how good it's been working here and start a bit of farewell blethering. I'll try to get one more nurse drawn in. Maybe you could distract any others? And you might have a chance to talk with your wee gang."

"Thanks. I'll work on that."

"I'm saying good-bye now in case the nurse bloodhounds sniff anything."

"Okay, farewell. Viva the dirty laundry."

Mac laughed and clapped him on the shoulder. "Viva the dirty laundry."

Tuesday 16th October 1956.

Ginger would be the best to divert attention. On the airing court in the afternoon, John whispered to his friend, "Escape plan - just listen." And as they lumbered round - Kong the third man, on the outside and a pace behind - Ginger did exactly that.

"Fine, old boy."

After dinner, the cutlery counting and the medicines handout, John got the small band of plotters together in the dayroom. *Now Mac, do your stuff.*

He watched Mac enter Mullen's office and engage the charge nurse in conversation. Two other white-coats stood talking. One disappeared in response to a shout from the office. The other was strolling this way.

He whispered in Ginger's ear. "Could you distract him?"

Ginger waddled off unhesitatingly. "I say, my man, can you help me?"

The way clear, John quickly outlined the plan to the others. On a signal from him, they'd act one evening after dinner, late, when it was dark, and preferably when the ward was short on white-coats.

Jimmy said "I'd be happy to lead outside the ward. I can imagine the route."

Jimmy would be the best guy to improvise if anything tricky arose. "Fine."

He'd have liked more time to rehearse the ritual for handing in the keys and leaving, but at least he told the others what was involved.

"Right. You all okay with this?" John glanced round the faces. George and Kong nodded; Pat looked blank and grunted. "In the next few days I'll try to speak with each of you individually and go over it again." He could see how whispered talking on a one-to-one basis could be managed, though they'd have to watch out.

The odds would be against them. But it could work, and he was desperate to escape. Staying out the fourteen days would be a problem. He couldn't go home. But he had friends from uni he'd kept in touch with. Two lived within a few miles, and each would be a good bet for shelter and ready cash.

Tuesday 23rd October 1956.

All had been briefed on the plan. And this evening looked ideal. Niven presided over dinner, with only two white-coat assistants. Mullen was down with flu. Ginger had heard Niven say so, "With expletives I would not care to repeat."

John could see Niven stretching his legs in the office. One white-coat was by the office; the other stood by the dayroom – hovering and watching.

Any minute now it would be bedtime. Each of the plotters had followed his lead in giving the agreed sign – clenching both fists by their sides. They were ready.

One white-coat went into the office, then came out and yelled "Into your beds, all of you." The inmates began shuffling towards their beds.

Time for action! Ginger waddled quickly to his bed (now, since he'd returned from Infirmary, opposite the office), flung back the bedclothes, then boomed, "I say, can I have a word, Sir?"

Great melodrama from Ginger, the one patient they didn't ignore. The white-coat stood to attention, then sidled across to the bed. The distraction was working.

John walked speedily to the office and tapped on the door. "Who's this?" bawled Niven. John stayed in the doorway.

"What the hell - you bloody shift it from here, Chisholm." Niven bounded forth and lifted him by the lapels.

He heard a rumpus. Kong? As Niven pushed him out of the doorway - still holding him by the lapels, shaking him and cursing - John saw the white-coat speed away from Ginger and down the ward. Meanwhile, Jimmy and Pat slid into the office.

John felt the blow to his face. Niven headbutting, with a head like granite! He feigned sinking towards the floor, and, once free, delivered a perfect uppercut. Niven dropped like a stone. The joy of this moment!

Jimmy said, "Alarm's disabled and the phones are off."

Pat was kicking Niven. John yelled, "Stop!"

Pat stopped mid-kick. "Why?"

"Mustn't kill him."

"That's right, old boy," said Ginger. "You'll swing." Pat moved away.

John knelt beside the motionless Niven. A strong, regular pulse. He removed the belt with the keys and handed it to Jimmy. Then he ran down the ward.

Kong had subdued the two white-coats - and George held both sets of keys, with belts attached. The white-coats lay inert. The big man was grinning. "Sorted them."

John crouched beside the white-coats. Each had a strong pulse. Phew. "Get them into the office," he yelled, then sprinted back up the ward.

"What's all this?" a hoarse voice croaked. The trusty Snoddie, in one of the huddles of patients stood gaping.

An elementary complication he hadn't foreseen. "We're trying to escape. Anyone fancy joining us?" Impracticable – but he had to say something!

Nobody spoke – thank God. Most were probably in shock.

Jimmy added, "All of you – please don't do anything except go to your beds. You will not be blamed for this, as they'll know we did it."

For a minute that seemed like hours, Snoddie and a few others stood as though poised for action. Then, grunting and mumbling, they made for their beds.

John started dragging Niven into the office. "Get the white-coats in here and strip them to their underpants," he shouted.

Soon there were several heaps – white coats, suit jackets, trousers, belts (with keys attached), shirts, socks, shoes – augmented (*thanks for the tip-off, Mac!*) from an unlocked cupboard. After sorting and swapping, all the escapers were transformed into staff – though some of the garments were ill-fitting. The most useful find in the cupboard was the stash of four greatcoats. One was so huge that only Kong could wear it, and the other three went to Ginger, Pat and Jimmy. He and George, bringing up the rear, would manage with reasonably well-fitting suits. A couple of peaked caps came in handy, especially as one fitted Ginger!

No perfect fits, and some of their outfits were incomplete – but hopefully all should be passable in the dark. There was however a major (unforeseen) snag – a shortage of keys! Only three sets! One per pair exiting – for Jimmy, Ginger and himself. Plus another Pat found locked within the cupboard – and attached to his belt. And on Niven was a separate, smaller, set. John passed them to Kong. He himself would have to rely on distraction, to let George slip out.

The white-coats were all showing signs of coming round, with grunts and moaning. Jimmy and Pat tore up a couple of their (patients') shirts to truss and gag the three. John checked the gags to ensure the men could breathe properly.

So far, all was okay. Except that the three white-coats had taken a beating, which was something he hadn't intended. He should have foreseen this; the pent-up rage exploding.

He glanced at the office clock. "It's too early. Let's wait till it's nearer the shift change."

An age passed. "Let's go."

Jimmy shot to the ward door, unlocked it and tiptoed out into the corridor. Pat and George followed, then Ginger shadowed by Kong. Last out, John locked the door.

There was no sign of anyone in the corridor. But they'd better not dally. The night shift weren't due yet; and the possibility of somebody arriving early had been one of the hitches foreseen. Another had been someone going off early. But no, the corridor was empty. They moved silently, keeping the same order.

They reached the exit door. Here John went to the front, unlocked the door and stepped outside. Yes, the dark niche on the right was as Mac described. They could huddle there until it was right to go for the main gate. He motioned the others towards the niche as they appeared, then locked the door and joined them.

"Great place for hide-and-seek," Jimmy whispered.

The air smelt good. Amidst the raised adrenalin and excitement, John was calm, clinical. So far, fine.

They'd agreed to go in pairs – Jimmy and Pat, then Ginger and Kong, then George and him. All must blend in with night-shift leavers. Timing could be critical.

Keeping an eye on the exit route, he whispered with George to outline how he planned to deal with handing in their keys. The group remained silent.

"Now – good luck."

Jimmy and Pat set off, and a few paces after, Ginger and Kong. Then it was time for him, and he nudged George. By now other greatcoats and suits – some chattering – were making for the exit.

George and he filtered in. Their luck ran out. The great-coated giant immediately in front, looked round. Sarge. The audible gasp and "Chisholm!" told John he was rumbled.

Blast! But the others could still be okay. Yelling "Can't catch me," he ran towards the wall at the far side. He glanced backwards. Sarge and at least one other were pursuing. He'd give them a run – he could sprint fast. Taking up rugby league at uni, playing at Wakefield on the wing, had not only earned useful cash but toughened him up. He darted round Sarge and his mate, back towards the leavers. He wanted to draw more of them.

"Stop the bugger – he's a patient," he heard. Dark figures were leaving the queue and running his way. He turned and headed back in Sarge's direction. He ran at Sarge and side-stepped round – delighting at the roar as he palmed the brute in the face – then jinxed away from another greatcoat and headed for the wall again. He heard puffing and swearing behind him, and risked a glance. Several were giving chase. He halted short of the wall, gasping. He was pretty unfit. They were circling round, to trap him. He dashed through a gap, then ducked and weaved to go another direction. But someone trip-tackled him, and, sprawling on the ground, he felt the impact of bodies pinioning him. Hopefully the others had escaped.

"Gotcha, Chisholm." He recognised Sarge's triumphant growl. The adrenalin rush over, he lay panting. He heard in the cacophony, "How the hell did he get off the ward?" He was done for. "Hold him steady," the voice commanded. Strong hands obeyed. His bum stung. Everything faded.

38

Wednesday 17ᵗʰ October 1956 – in Springwell.

Dr James Braid Macdonald heard the door slam behind him and keys jangling as his escort locked up. He really wanted this job – a challenge at a backwoods place.

"Follow me please, Sir."

He walked in solemn procession – one white-coated companion leading and another tagging at the rear – across the vast gloomy space towards a door in the far corner. A platoon formation. The plodding on the wooden floor sounded funereal. Fittingly atmospheric. The man in front unlocked a door and held it open.

Macdonald stepped into a dimly-lit passageway and waited while his companion locked the door behind them. This was like a gateway to Hell. Along the dreary corridor (with its stone-flagged floor and walls too dark a brown), they trudged in single file. How many sad tales could these walls tell? There was nothing remotely charming about the sinister pathways. So far, everything was reminiscent of that asylum where they'd imprisoned Auntie.

They reached another solid-looking door. The nurse leading the way unlocked it and held it open for him and his other, much older, escort to pass through. This corridor was a lot brighter, the walls painted cream and the floor carpeted (in institutional brown, predictably, but at least it was carpet). He heard the door shut behind him, and keys jangling, as the door was re-locked. He glanced backward. His 'lead' escort had gone.

"This is a bit brighter," he said to his remaining escort, now alongside him.

"Yes, Sir. It needs to be because this is our administrative block."

Shocking, but not unexpected. "Ah."

"I'll take you to the waiting-room, Sir."

"Thank you, Mr Porter. You're Assistant Chief Male Nurse?"

"Yes, Sir, but I retires next month. Near forty years, I been here – ten of these Assistant Chief to Mr Hallman. He runs a tight ship, but he'll not be here much longer neither. Don't know what'll happen then."

What indeed? Change? "Well, all the best for your retirement, Mr Porter."

"Thank you, Sir." Porter stopped outside a door in the corridor. "If you'll wait in here please, with the other gentlemen. It's the ante-room to our boardroom."

Inside the room, Macdonald stood for a moment, looking around. Bigger than he'd have expected for an ante-room. Along the opposite wall, three grey-suited men sat in a row of armchairs, which were spaced well apart – two on each side of another door.

"Good day," he said, glancing along the row. One man – white-haired with a weather-beaten wrinkled face – looked up at him; the other two sat with their heads bowed. He heard grunting, presumably in response. "Jamie Macdonald. I'm afraid my train from up north was very delayed." More grunting ensued and the weather-beaten one gave a cough, maybe clearing his throat. The other two carried on staring at the floor. All three looked old – a good ten to twenty years older than he.

"Dr Macdonald, I'm Liam Kenney." The weather-beaten face now crinkled into a half smile.

He sank into the armchair next to Kenney.

This guy at least seemed human. "Where are you from, Dr Kenney?"

"I'm Deputy here. I'm near retirement age, but I was persuaded to throw my hat in the ring."

"Well, you must feel you've earned the job."

206

Kenney leaned over to whisper. "I don't want it. Too much time on admin, not enough on clinical. But I'll feel obliged to take it if I'm offered."

"I'm sorry to have missed the tour round." True. The two-hour delay had been a damn nuisance.

"You didn't miss anything. The boss planned to show everyone round, but cried off sick and cancelled. Normally I'd stand in - but well, I'm a candidate."

No wonder the others looked grumpy - assuming they arrived on time. "How long -" He started as the door beside him opened and an elderly woman appeared.

"Gentlemen, I am Miss Bewlay, Secretary to the Medical Superintendent." She paused, then resumed in her shrill commanding voice. "Dr Kenney, you will be interviewed first." She held the door open while Kenney sprang to his feet and walked through.

The door shut, he was closeted with two morose companions and his own thoughts. He recalled Auntie's tormented look in that asylum, and the vow he took over her lifeless body. The six-year medical slog at Edinburgh had been okay, except for pathology in year four, when he had to re-sit. He hated corpses.

The reason he didn't stay in Edinburgh? Simply Gill, the only woman on his course. "I have to go home, Jamie." He saw her anguish as she chose between her madly-in-love boyfriend and her widowed terminally ill mother. No contest. And he didn't regret following her to Manchester for his three-year psychiatry training. Life was good. He was set on the field he'd dedicated to and courting the girl he loved.

It was sad that Gill's mum died a few weeks before the wedding. And the other cloud was Adolf Hitler, with his gang of Nazis.

He leaned forward and glanced again at his two fellow candidates. Each was greying, hunched forward, and staring at the floor. They were almost statuesque. He curbed an impulse to laugh. Could they have fought in the War? Surely they'd been too old for active service - and could even have fought in the Great War.

Maybe it was being an only child and having a vivid imagination.

Reminiscing was for him a relaxation, a winding down from busy high-stress times. Happy or sad, memories served as affirmation and reinforced his learning from experience.

A year into the War he'd completed his Diploma in Psychological Medicine, married Gill, and joined the Royal Army Medical Corps. In France, he worked long hours, seeing folk with conflict-related breakdowns – not only shellshock, but also other hellish inner torments triggered by the war and separation from loved ones.

Sometimes he was sure he'd helped; sometimes he knew he hadn't – as with those two soldiers who committed suicide. He resisted army pressures to speed getting soldiers back to the front line. Where the soldiers wanted to get back, and he thought they were up to it psychologically – fine. But otherwise he ensured they got not only treatment, but the time they needed for rehabilitation.

A tough induction to psychiatric practice. The haunted faces, the harrowing tales, were still there in flashbacks. Sometimes he'd felt on the verge of sanity, and turned to a nightly whisky to help him sleep. But he survived, kept afloat by letters from Gill and those too-rare leaves with her, by his memories of Auntie – and by the whisky. He raged at God often. Sessions with the chaplains brought him back to worship and prayer. But through France and beyond, the nightly whisky got larger.

The door beside him opened. Liam Kenney emerged, looking unflustered, and, bending over, said in a whisper, "I've blown it, Macdonald. Good luck." Kenney straightened, and exited by the door back to the corridor.

Kenney seemed a nice guy. At a guess, conscientious.

"Doctor Hastings, will you come with me please." Miss Bewlay spoke as one expecting to be obeyed, and held the door open. As though electrified, the man in the furthest armchair leapt up and, with military bearing and searching eyes that stared angrily, marched past Miss Bewlay to the boardroom.

Left alone in monastic silence, with a companion who wasn't one (the man sat with eyes fixed on the floor), Macdonald continued reflecting.

He'd craved going back to civvy street, but that wasn't all roses. Early on the nightmares were so bad that he slept downstairs to let Gill have an undisturbed night. He got a clinical/teaching registrar post in Manchester University's Psychiatry Department.

It was not where he wanted to end up. But the quieter life of academia suited him for a time, and allowed him to address his growing alcohol problem. With support from Gill and the local Alcoholics Anonymous, he'd tackled this head-on and gone teetotal. It was years since he'd felt an inclination for a nightly soporific.

Then at a conference came a big moment – meeting Macdonald Bell, the boss at Dingleton Hospital in Melrose. What a guy, enthused by the idea of unlocking the wards – and branded crazy by the old guard, who predicted chaos and carnage.

When the consultant post came up there, he'd gone for it, with Gill's 100% support. She wound down with the practice in Hyde, stayed till the house was sold, and got part-time work in Melrose.

The door opened and Miss Bewlay entered. Hastings couldn't have been in for long. "Doctor Macdonald, please come with me."

He rose and stopped. "Excuse me. Dr Hastings?"

"His interview is over. He was escorted out by another exit."

He straightened his tie, insisted that Miss Bewlay precede him, and took a deep breath. Yes, he did want this job.

39

Waking up in a padded cell wasn't a shock for John. Trying to escape, and slugging three white-coats on the way, wouldn't have charmed the regime. He was a villain, surely to be punished and detained. The only question was what other sanctions or punishments might follow. The gallows? Beheading?

The hatch grated, letting in a shaft of light. A face?

"Chisholm!"

Even in his semi-drugged state, the sound struck a chill. Sarge? He lay looking up at the face. "Who's asking?"

"Who do you bloody think? I'm the boss here on Refractory, and I'm keeping you locked in this cell all day."

Bad news. Nothing he could do about it.

"You've been a right fucker. I'll see you gets your comeuppance tomorrow."

Predictable from Sarge. His punishment couldn't be any worse than before. Or could it? When three of Sarge's henchmen came in to give him the expected chemical knockout, he offered no resistance.

Thursday 25th October 1956 – Night-time.

John was in bed at last after his first full day in the Factory. It was hard to sleep. The dormitory lighting was brighter than on Admissions. At either end of the dormitory were white-coats, in pairs. At least Sarge wasn't around. Another white-coat sat in the office.

He'd survived, unscathed. But the atmosphere was menacing. And Sarge's presence daytime ensured he would be a prime target for bullying.

There was another dimension. Some of the patients here were the proverbial hard men, the tough guys. Micky, a scowling massive middle-aged man who'd sat jostling him at breakfast, claimed to be from Broadmoor. "I'm not the only Broadie here – there's three other lads."

He'd heard that Broadmoor housed the violent criminally insane. Micky and his fellow ex-inmates there had obviously been deemed fit for an ordinary asylum – but the guys must have had form. Micky reckoned he'd been in Broadmoor over twenty years. "Strangled me girlfriend. The bitch took over my mind and the voice told me to kill her. I'm from these parts, and they moved me to this dump so's me old mam could come and see me."

And so many white-coats! Their ratio to patients must be double anything he'd seen on Admissions. Apart from Sarge, he didn't recognise any of them. Some looked tough and mean. Could be contextual – violence breeding violence.

Again, looks could be deceptive. Clark, who'd looked a bully, was quite a caring guy, with a sense of humour. In contrast, Niven and Sarge, as well as looking the part, vied with each other in bullying credentials.

Shouting and heavy footsteps indicated a scuffle opposite the end of his bed. He sat up to look. A man, struggling and yelling, was being frogmarched by two white-coats. "Shut the fuck up," he heard somebody bawl. And indeed the yelling stopped after two more white-coats arrived. A limp body was carried by two white-coats into a padded cell. "A right bugger that," one of the white-coats said loudly.

"Shut up," came from the next bed. The two white-coats carried on talking as they went down the dormitory; one went into the Charge's office. There was silence, apart from muttering in the next bed and bronchitic coughing further along.

He slid down into the bed and sank into reflection.

So far, Sarge hadn't singled him out for the dire punishment promised, or even for humiliation. That could be to do with the large number of patients on the ward – or maybe the fights had kept him off the radar. In three incidents, violence had flared, and one escalated into a brawl, with several patients and white-coats getting stuck in. The scrapping patients were knocked out and put into cells. He'd managed to stay clear of trouble each time.

There were seven cells. And, soon before lunch, he'd seen patients being escorted – one-by-one – into each of these. There was no discernible reason for this.

"Screws' lunchtime," Micky growled loudly. And indeed the cell occupants were released when the white-coats got back to strength.

Friday 26th October 1956

After breakfast, John spied George. He'd willed the others to escape while he drew the hunters. But he felt bucked at seeing a fellow non-escaper.

George conveyed in whispers what had happened. "When they recognised you, I surrendered. A fiend twisted my arm up my back." George peered around. "They must know I'm a famous author and it would be bad to let me escape. Kong fought the white-coats and Ginger yelled 'Unhand me.' I didn't see Pat or Jimmy."

Maybe they'd escaped. But Ginger must be captive somewhere in this dump.

And as John lined up to go outside, he heard the ward door being unlocked. In came a party of white-coats bearing a stretcher with a body on it. Sarge emerged from his office and inspected the still figure.

Another victim. This was presumably how he himself entered Springwell.

"Caught the bugger," bawled Sarge, turning to address the patients. "A lesson. You try to escape, we'll catch you – and we'll cut your balls off."

Not literally. But with Sarge...? Must be either Paranoid Pat or Jimmy.

"Like Moloney here," Sarge continued, then said to the white-coats holding the stretcher, "Throw the bugger into cell one, till I'm ready to deal with him."

It was Pat. At least the guy presumably had a day or two's freedom.

On the airing court, John's nearest companion was a strange fellow who kept muttering with head down. Sounded like a diatribe, with "Fuckin' cunts" audible now and again. "Hello, I'm John," and "what's your name?" didn't seem to register.

He missed Ginger and the dazzling tales. Where could his friend be? On Admissions, or in a cell? Maybe Ginger escaped punishment? Could his friend be a nobleman? No. But maybe not crazy. A good actor who fooled the white-coats?

And what of the stalwart bodyguard Kong?

Abandonment, estrangement? Feeling isolated, even in company. Was this how John Clare the poet used to feel? A century ago, the man was writing from a county asylum in Northampton - imprisoned decades before dying there. Maybe he, John Chisholm, would die in this madhouse. At least he wasn't in a cell on his own.

Heather, love of his life. Did she still love him? Did she have a lover - or had he imagined it? Anyway could he blame her? Would he ever see her or Becky again?

Deep sadness - again like John Clare. How did the poem go?

'I am! Yet what I am who cares or knows.
My friends forsake me like a memory lost,
I am the self-consumer of my woes.'

Yes, the man was a great communicator. One of the hardest things was to relay feelings so expertly. Some gift! He envied Clare for having the means to write in that asylum. No hope in this one.

At lunchtime, they trooped inside. In the dayroom, awaiting the meal, two white-coats were overseeing, stationed at opposite ends of the room. He walked towards the one nearer him. He'd try asking about Ginger (hopefully a well-known character in the institution).

Tumbling, the white-coat shouted - felled by a grey battering-ram.

213

Micky, yelling curses, was now astride and thumping the limp figure.

Diving, John grabbed Micky at the shoulders, to prise the fiend off the inert white-coat. Something smashed into his face and he blacked out.

It hurt to breathe, and he could smell something – powerful medicine? His head was splitting. "John." A voice – friendly, familiar. Yes. But who was this, and where was he? Could he have died? "John Chisholm." An Irish brogue, gentle. He tried opening his eyes. The blurred figure was a white-coat.

"You've been hurt and you're coming to on Infirmary."

He felt like a steamroller had done him. "Who...?"

"We've met before. Charge Macnamara. Remember?"

He struggled to think, but had a good feeling about this guy.

"You were knocked unconscious and badly concussed, to be sure."

His tired battered brain couldn't help him remember. "What –?"

"You took a hammering. Doc Burn's been in to see you and you're under him for now. We gave you x-rays and your skull's okay, but your nose is broken. You've no other fractures, though your body's like an artwork gone crazy. We're monitoring for internal injuries." Macnamara paused. "How are you feeling?"

"Terrible." True. But at least he'd escaped Sarge's clutches.

"Right now John, you need to rest. Mr Maclean has something that'll help."

He closed his eyes, then felt a familiar, very welcome, sting in the arm.

Tuesday 30th October 1956.

Talking with Macnamara a couple of days ago had helped John remember. He began to recall trying to escape, and waking in a cell on Refractory. He got a sore head though, when he'd tried to think what happened to land him in Infirmary. Macnamara advised against trying to remember till he felt better physically.

214

Waking early in the morning, he was now clear about the whole series of events, including the attack. His memory was okay and his head felt better. He was recovering. And at least the attack headed off Sarge's torture.

Macnamara came and sat down on his bed. "How're you doing, John?"

"Better than I was."

"Fine. Can you tell me about the incident that led to you being injured?"

John told him – omitting mention of Micky by name. He wasn't a snitch. Macnamara was looking at him, listening.

"So you're saying you intervened to help the nurse being attacked?"

Strange, the Charge's reply. Sounded as though the man didn't believe him. "Yes. Is something wrong?"

The Charge scratched his head. "Well, the detail doesn't square with what I was told. But maybe I picked it up wrongly from Charge Nurse Parker."

Sarge! "I'd like to know what Mr Parker said."

Macnamara stroked his chin. "Sure you've a right to know how Mr Parker's account differs from yours. Mr Parker seemed to think you instigated the attack."

"Rubbish! I saw the white-coat being attacked and thought he might be killed. I pulled his attacker off and was wrestling with him, when someone or something knocked me out." He leaned towards Macnamara. "I swear to God that's what happened. I don't know why the nurse was attacked, but it was a brutal assault." He paused. "Do you believe me?"

"You sound an honest man, John. And a hero. Maybe I picked it up wrong. I'm happy to have a word with Mr Parker to give your account."

"I'd appreciate that. He'll never listen to me."

"Whatever – your stories differ."

"What happened to the nurse?"

"Nearly died, they told me. To be sure, the man's down in the local hospital, recovering, but not saying much yet about what happened."

"I'm glad the nurse's recovering." He didn't know the man, but the idea of dying from so vicious an onslaught was terrible. Micky had shown Broadmoor form.

Macnamara smiled. "Doc Burn's coming to check on you later this evening. Though you're much better, sure you'll be here with us a while. We have to be certain you get your strength back fully. Make sense?" He cocked his head.

There was no wink. But this Charge Nurse was surely protective as well as caring. An extended stay here would be no bad thing. "Yes. Total sense."

Tuesday 13th November 1956 – in Springwell.

Able to walk without discomfort, John went down the ward. In passing, he glanced across at a new patient who'd arrived a couple of hours earlier. With his bandaged head propped by a pillow, the man looked dazed. Badly injured? But it wasn't Ginger, or anyone else he knew.

Later in the morning, he heard a deep roar, then, after a pause, loud whining. The noises came from the new patient with the bandaged head. A white-coat shouted, "Ssht man, that's a terrible racket."

Not a great way to treat somebody that was hurt. The whining continued. However, the white-coat was now at the man's bedside, speaking softly but audibly. "It must hurt. I'll ask Staff if there's anything more to help the pain."

Maclean responded, coming out of the office with the white-coat and muttering something. The white-coat returned with screens and placed them around the bed. An improvement since his first spell in Infirmary, John noted – recognition of a patient's need for privacy. He heard more talking and suddenly the whining ceased.

In the afternoon, Doc Burn, accompanied by Macnamara, came to see him. "You're fit, Chisholm. You'll be discharged from here tomorrow." And the doc walked off down the ward, accompanied by the Charge.

That was it then. He must face Sarge in the Factory. He repeated to himself, "Survive and escape." The latter was nigh impossible, but he must keep hope alive.

Macnamara reappeared. "Back to Refractory tomorrow, I'm afraid. I'd have liked you to go elsewhere – but it's not my call."

"Thanks. I'll be okay." He smiled, though he would certainly not be okay.

Macnamara stood up. "I'll see you tomorrow before you go."

Something was nagging at him. "The new patient two beds down..."

"You'd know Mackay – a fellow escaper."

"Kong!"

"Surely is."

"What's happened?"

"They took the poor man to the General the other day for a leucotomy operation, and brought him back to this ward for recovery. Once the wound's healed, I guess Kong'll be for the Annex."

Bad news. Browncoat Mac talked of patients on the Annex 'being like vegetables, after punishment by leucotomy'. "Why did Kong have an operation?"

"I really don't know. The op is brain surgery that should be used only as a last resort to relieve unbearable tension. You might want to go over and say hello later." The Charge turned away, then stepped back. "But it's soon after the op, and Kong might not even recognise you."

Terrible. John couldn't believe the operation helped Kong in any way. Ginger! "Do you know what's happened to Ginger – the Baron?"

"Yes. Went back to Admissions after the failed escape."

Great news. "Is Ginger a real baron?"

"Sure, the man's in *Who's Who*. There's brackets round his name – a consequence of being detained in here."

Ginger was for real, not mad. If they could keep a sane nobleman locked up, what hope was there for anyone else?

A roar was followed by whining. He sprang out of bed and went to Kong's bedside. He peered at the bandaged head, whence came the noise. "Kong," he said, "hello Kong, it's John." The man looked at him and roared – a low guttural bellow – then started whining again. "Kong, it's John, your friend." The man roared again. The eyes were staring, not seeming to recognise, the face devoid of expression. And dribbles of saliva ran down the big man's chin.

Next morning, John tried talking to Kong again. The expressionless face stared through him. No longer the mighty Kong.

He asked Macnamara, "Will Kong recover?"

"I can't say, for sure."

But he knew from Browncoat Mac the terrible things that operation could do to a man.

40

Heather put Becky down to sleep and the babe nodded off. Good-bye to teething? She put on Elvis's latest record, '*Love Me Tender*', and settled with her book.

Knocking on the door? Yes. She switched on the hallway light.

"Who is it?"

"Sam Newman."

She unlocked the door and threw it open. "Come in, Sam." He looked grave.

"Thanks. I have news." He entered and sat down at the table.

She sat down opposite. "About John?"

"Yes. Oh, it's not to say he's ill or anything." His expression was more relaxed. "But you'll not be allowed to visit tomorrow, I'm afraid."

"What! Why?"

"Well, apparently John tried to escape and didn't make it."

"Escape... and didn't make it?" She forced a deep breath.

"So they tell me."

"Goodness. Is he hurt?"

"They said he's okay. They've transferred him to the Refractory Ward."

"Refractory Ward?" Rang a bell. Moira said Parker was Charge Nurse there!

"Yes." He shifted in the chair, looking at the table. "It's for patients that give them trouble."

"Are you sure he's been moved?" She took another deep breath.

"Yes. I got the story today, after Springwell rang and asked me to take back a patient who'd escaped and walked into a police station. And," he looked up at her, "I'm afraid John's not now allowed visitors. I'm sorry, Heather. That's all I'm told."

Her eyes were misting. She rose. "Cup of tea, Sam?"

"That'd be welcome, thanks. It's been a long day."

In the kitchen she put the kettle on and got out cups and saucers. John must have been desperate. Were they punishing him, and if so how? Moira said Refractory was for violent patients. Would he be attacked there? Would he ever get out? She spooned in tea and poured boiling water into the teapot, jerkily. "Ouch!"

"What's up?" Sam was on his feet, coming toward her.

Her forefinger stung and was reddening. She laid down the kettle and put the lid on the teapot. "It's okay. I poured hot water on my finger."

He was at her side. "Cold water." He turned the tap on. "Keep your finger under it for a few minutes. I'll take the teapot and cups through."

"Thanks." Stupid, missing the teapot. A decent man, Sam – caring and unselfish. She turned to watch as he carried the tea from the kitchen.

Her finger was numbed from the soaking. She turned off the tap, returned to the living room and sat at the table facing Sam.

"How's the finger?"

"Okay. Thanks for the first-aid tip." She reached for the teapot, started pouring the tea and put some in the saucer. "For you. Sorry."

"No problem. You've had a shock." He stretched across, lifted the saucer and tilted the tea into his cup. "Nice music. I'm an Elvis fan too."

Another good thing about Sam. "I'm crazy about his music. John's not so..."

"No. Look, I'm sorry about John. Have you other family?"

"Yes, my parents, but they live a distance away."

"No sisters or brothers?"

"No. Except...Well, I had a brother. Edward."

As she started to tell the tale, she sensed an impending deluge. Too late. Her face was streaming. She sat back and accepted Sam's handkerchief. "Sorry. I'm all right now. It's just – with John, and then talking about Edward..." She stopped again, dabbing her face. She must look a mess.

Sam was peering at her. "You sure you're okay?"

"I will be." She passed the hankie back, and managed a smile. "I won't bore you with the rest of my tale. Anyway, I don't feel like talking about it just now."

"You're not boring me. And any time you want to tell me, I'll want to listen – to the full story." He drained his cup and rose.

"Thanks for all your help, Sam." She followed him towards the door.

He stopped and turned, so that she nearly bumped into him. "I'll keep an ear open about John when I'm at Springwell, and let you know of any change about visiting."

"Thanks."

"You're certainly going through it, Heather. Now, don't take this the wrong way. You look like you need a hug. And I'm happy to give you one. No strings."

She stepped forward into his outstretched arms and they hugged. She clung on. His arms were protective, holding her gently, now clasping her to him. Arousing – something she hadn't felt for ages. But... She withdrew.

He looked flushed as he stepped away. "That feel better?"

"Yes. I'm good."

He opened the door. "'Bye. Take care. See you soon."

"Thanks Sam."

Closing the door, she wondered again. Is he married? She returned to the table and sat a few minutes, replaying what had just happened. She could still feel the comfort of Sam's arms around her, and smell his Brylcreem. When did she last feel aroused like that?

Enough. She picked up her book and tried to read. But images of Sam and imaginings of John being tortured kept coming. She put the Elvis album on to re-play. But somehow that didn't feel right and she switched it off again.

Through the night, waking from dozing, it was Sam's presence she could sense. And her finger throbbed. She got up and took two aspirins. Becky was asleep. Why wouldn't the babe wake up crying, needing Mum's comforting?

Newman bounced over the pavement, hardly aware of his leg that dragged. The hug had transported him into a world he hadn't thought he'd experience again – that of long-ago passion and primitive urges. Heather was even more beautiful and sensuous than Ella in her youth.

41

John knew it would happen. The taunting resumed. Taken by a white-coat into the office on Refractory, he was greeted by Sarge.

He'd never seen Sarge grinning hugely like this. What delight was in store?

"You won't ever leave here, Chisholm. You're lucky though, because your misery will end. I'm getting you a leucotomy. We'll slice your brain – assuming we can find one. It's how we silence troublemakers – and it gives them peace of mind." Sarge bellowed with laughter.

"Like you did to Kong, you bastard!" A mistake maybe, but he'd nothing to lose.

He offered no fight as he was hoisted by the lapels and shaken. "You call me that again and it will be the last thing you say," Sarge roared, green eyes bulging from his purple-red face. "And when you dare to address me again, you remember to say 'Charge Nurse Parker, Sir'. You are scum! I will see you get your come-uppance, Chisholm, this Monday morning's ward round."

Released from Sarge's clutches (how he'd missed that uplifting sewer breath), he had a question. "Charge Nurse Parker, Sir, may I ask –?"

"You may not!" Sarge bawled, and nodded to the white-coat standing erect and poised. "Take this abomination to the airing court."

Trudging round, John could think only of Sarge's leucotomy threat. Mac told him a leucotomy "Not only changes but damn well extinguishes a guy's personality." To punish troublemakers! And crucifying, compared with the electric shock stuff. The Shocker was a battering – that he'd about recovered from – but "A leucotomy," Mac had said, "can mean living death for life." Could it erase his treasury of memories?

A scandal, anyone undergoing such horrors in the name of treatment! He'd be better off in prison, serving his sentence without 'treatment' and then being freed.

Friday 16ᵗʰ – Saturday 17ᵗʰ November 1956 – in Springwell.

John woke early and lay seething. Kong had joined the unhappy band, de-humanised in the guise of treatment! And now he himself was to be rendered a bona fide zombie.

Monstrous injustice – an abuse of power to silence and suppress. Like the way officialdom dealt with Da after the accident; though this was probably worse.

Yes, he and his folks had experienced injustice. Hurt that was the downside of being human. It hadn't felt good – but maybe the anger helped fuel the single-mindedness with which he pursued his studies and his career.

He recalled his awakening in early days at uni, to realms of gross injustice he hadn't known. A psychology essay on homosexuality alerted him to how the law and policy discriminated in a way that must violate human rights. While his strongly heterosexual self couldn't figure how guys would want sex with each other, it must be wrong that doing so could earn them a generous break in prison. And mark them as candidates for psychiatric shock treatment!

And talking for the first time with non-white guys gave him insights into the prejudice, sometimes open abuse, that they encountered. Like the sign 'No blacks or coloureds' outside the odd boarding-house, the 'N-word' whispered or spoken aloud, stuff through the letter-box, a message on the house wall... While John had read about and admired Gandhi's non-violent stances against discrimination, he hadn't been aware of racist practices in the UK.

His course essays had reflected sadness and anger at suffering caused by racism and homophobia. But what he faced here – a deliberate assault intended to reduce him to a vegetable – was as cruel as anything. And in the name of treatment!

Stirrings on the ward. He'd better get up.

He was on red alert for Micky. Vengeance would be a powerful motivator for the ex-Broadmoor man; and the last thing he'd recalled about that incident was hate staring from Micky's eyes. A scary mad beast!

In a fair fight, he'd beat Micky. But was there such a thing in here? The likelihood was an onslaught that would surprise him. Micky might even recruit his ex-Broadmoor pals to help in the bashing.

There were a lot of patients on this ward, and an army of white-coats. He searched patients' faces, without seeing Micky's. Maybe still in a cell?

He did, though, find Paranoid Pat, standing, head bowed, in a corner of the dayroom. "Pat – it's John," he said.

Pat didn't look up, and whispered corner-of-the-mouth, "I know."

Strange. But on Refractory everything was. "Why're you whispering?"

"Buggers'll be watching us."

Good point. Co-conspirators, surely facing mega torture. "They caught you."

"Surrendered myself – though they still gave me the K.O. to get me here. No money or fags. And I've some business with Nosey."

A white-coat was heading their direction. Pat slouched away.

In the night, John lay wondering. What did 'some business with Nosey' mean? A deal with the almighty Charge Nurse Parker? Impossible. Or an assault? No hope there. Pat was a wiry fellow, but even catching Sarge off guard he'd be squashed.

Yet Pat 'didn't lie'? Intriguing.

In the morning John asked a white-coat about Micky.

"Sent back to Broadmoor."

So that threat had gone. But in this cauldron, he couldn't ever relax.

After breakfast a tumultuous brawl drew in the white-coated army. He spied Pat and went over to whisper "What about your business with Nosey, Pat?"

"Nosey's gonna see the god Monday, get my brain sliced."

So that was it. The dreaded leucotomy. "I'm on the same hit list, Pat."

Pat glanced across the ward. The fight hadn't finished. "I'll kill Nosey."

"You've no chance."

For the first time, he saw a smile on Pat's face. "Maybe I have."

"Oh?"

"I've a wee blade. Got it outside, put it up my bum, then hid it in here."

He didn't ask where. This was just Pat's madness!

But after the meal that evening, John heard a loud growl – 'Nosey Parker', from along the ward – then a wild-animal howl of fury. He turned to watch.

Sarge, red-faced and cursing, had lifted Pat by the lapels. High. Back went the head and the stiff upper torso for a harder-than-usual headbutt. Then the incredible happened. Pat's hand swept across Sarge's exposed neck, and the brute dropped to the floor, blood spurting from the wound.

42

Friday 16th November 1956 – in Aversham.

Hunched over his desk, losing the battle to catch up with paperwork, Newman kept yawning. Work had been consuming, and home more demanding of his presence, with both his wife and daughter pretty depressed and relationships in the household increasingly fragile. The days had flown without him asking about Chisholm and visiting. But now he had what he needed to justify calling on Heather.

The phone had wakened him around four a.m. He'd thought the GP was panicking. "A Mrs Black's rung. Her husband Sid went mad. Got out of bed, stood raving, and then chucked a bible through the bedroom window."

"So he shattered the glass?"

"No, he opened the window first."

"Is he violent?"

"No, but his wife's afraid he might kick off."

Probably a domestic. "I'll go later in the morning."

"No. I need you to go now! I told her you'd be there."

So he'd gone. As well he had. Entering via an unlocked door, after knocking went unanswered, he heard a scream. The wife? He found her - staring, wide-eyed - in the kitchen doorway.

"Sam Newman, Mental Health. Your doctor asked me to call." He followed her stare. A night-capped man stood by the back door, breadknife in hand. "Sid Black?"

The man nodded. "The Devil's in that bible. Tilly don't believe me. She mustn't go out the back."

227

"Sid, that's our family bible. I'm going out." She took a step, and screamed.

Sid had raised the knife, waving it. "I can't let you, Tilly."

"Stay back here, Tilly," Sam cut in. "Sid, how do you know the Devil's there?"

"The master told me. You welfare mysteria won't believe it. Go away."

Deluded – sounded paranoid schizophrenic.

A good hour and a half later, Sid had dropped the knife and, muttering, slumped into a chair.

Newman had summoned the police and followed the van to Springwell. He'd arrived there just as men came in for the early shift. The business of certifying completed, he'd got from Jock Mackenzie the date of next visiting, and the okay to phone Refractory. He wanted news of Chisholm.

Charge Parker responded, "That murdering bastard. No visits – ever!" Then Parker's tone softened with, "Give my regards to Mrs C." And the line went dead.

How did Parker know Heather?

The important thing was that he had a valid, pressing reason to call on Heather. He'd go this evening, when the child would be in bed.

He yawned, and lit another fag. He could feel the adrenalin buzz. He'd see the woman he lusted after. The sensuous memory of that hug, where she clung to him, ranked with his all-time highs. She'd been about ready to give herself to him.

Career suicide, an affair could be. But in any case how much longer could he stand this job? Impossible sometimes! The action with patients was okay. The rubbish pay, being forever on call and short on sleep, weren't exactly plus factors. And support? He was 'Senior' to a non-existent team.

Enough daydreaming. Must get on. This paperwork was doing for his head.

Ringing. The internal. He lifted the receiver, and held it away from his ear. Mary. "Boss wants to see you. Now."

He limped up to the MOH's office and knocked on the door.

The boss sat at his desk. "Sir, you want to –"

"Yes, sit down. We interview for Carter's successor next week, on Thursday, six o'clock. If you're free, be there. We've two candidates – Grayson from last time, and Jonathan Little, Springwell's Assistant Chief Male Nurse. Little comes with sound qualifications and excellent references. His is a late application, but it is very welcome. He's obviously outstanding. I met him at Springwell. A nice young man, and highly intelligent." The MOH stood up.

He hadn't met Little, but the grapevine around Springwell told him the man was having a breakdown and being given a brilliant reference to try to get rid – to a DAO job somewhere, anywhere. He too rose. He'd say something. "Sir –"

"Newman, I have pressing matters to address."

What was the point? Chances were he'd be landed with another useless DAO to wet-nurse. He exited the room.

Newman knocked softly on the door of number 90. It was seven-thirty – Becky could still be awake. A light went on in the hallway. "Who is it?" he heard.

"Sam," he whispered through the letterbox.

The door opened. Heather. "Come in, Sam."

He entered and stood there, briefcase in hand. Expecting a hug. Daft. He followed Heather to the living room and sat down at the table opposite her. Elvis's 'Love Me Tender' was playing. "Nice music."

"Yes, I play it a lot. Tea?" Those soft brown eyes were appealing, wooing him.

"Thanks." She rose. That figure!

He looked at the records on the table and started sorting through them. 'Heartbreak Hotel', 'Hound Dog'…

"I'll try not to burn my finger this time." She was shouting from the kitchen.

He got up and went to join her. "You'd better not." He stood in the doorway, admiring her. "How is your finger?"

"It's healed."

"Let me see." He advanced into the kitchen.

She held out a hand. "There."

He examined her finger, then kissed her hand. She was gazing at him invitingly. Next, she was clinging to him. They stood hugging while the kettle boiled. He kissed her on the lips. Intoxicating, to have her body meshed with his. A familiar stiffening below and full arousal. Heaven.

But she was withdrawing. Her face was flushed. "The kettle." She wriggled away and switched off the gas. "I'll get the tea, Sam."

Damn that kettle. "Right." He went back to the table and sat down.

She came with the tea, sat down and poured it into the cups. Her aim was amazingly true. She must have regained her cool. She stood up. "Let's have another Elvis." She picked one up from the table.

Sam heard the strains of 'Hound Dog'. "Elvis is King," he mused aloud. And was 'ain't nothing but a hound dog' a message for him, a man still aroused?

"Why did you call, Sam?"

"I've been to Springwell. Next visiting day's on Saturday 24th, but the Charge Nurse on Refractory, Parker, said John's still not allowed visitors, I'm afraid."

She looked glum, upset. He was aching to hug her again. But she rose, went to the sideboard and got out a tissue. "They're punishing John."

"Could be. Parker said your husband hated you. 'Murderous' was the term he used."

She was stroking her chin. "I see."

"Oh, he said he knows you, and to convey his warmest regards."

"He visited the house once ages ago, to tell me about John."

She sounded evasive. Had Parker had a hug, or more? "Sorry about John."

"Thanks Sam, you've been very kind." She stroked her chin again. "Won't your wife be wondering where you are?"

He forced a smile. "Wife? I've no such problem."

"Really? Well, I'd like to hear more about you, Sam, if you have time. I notice you're limping."

An invitation. He'd talk about anything but family. "A war wound. An enemy plane strafed us at Dunkirk, and my leg got in the way of bullets."

"Gosh, at Dunkirk – you were nearly killed."

"Yes." He'd been terrified. A cold sweat was breaking on his forehead.

He felt his hand being squeezed. Heather had stretched her arm across. "Are you okay?" She looked concerned.

"I'm fine. Thanks." He squeezed her hand back, and she withdrew it. "It's harder than I thought to talk about Dunkirk." He managed a smile.

"Your work must be stressful, Sam. Are you ever threatened, or attacked?"

"Threatened? Yes. Attacked? Rarely, though I'd a close call last year. I suddenly found myself helpless in the air over a stairway banister three floors up, held aloft by this giant enraged at the mention of Springwell. Luckily the guy started to howl and weep, and grounded me on the safe side of the banister." He pulled out a hankie and wiped his brow.

She looked impressed. "Gosh, Sam!"

He glanced at his watch. Nearly nine-thirty. Better go, otherwise he'd meet a barrage from Ella, and probably Helen, who moped around the house these evenings. "I hadn't realised it was so late. I'm on call. I'll tell you more another day."

He rose, picked up the briefcase and went towards the door. He turned in the doorway. She was standing back. Keeping her distance? He'd ask. "A hug?"

She smiled, but didn't move. "I think one's enough for this evening, Sam."

Teasing him? "You're right, Heather. I'll call when I get more news of your husband." He went out onto the pavement.

She was at the door. "Thanks again, Sam."

He got in the car and revved up. Ella's suspicions were now spot on.

43

The god was back. Escorted by two white-coats, John stood watching the shiny pate of the bird-like man bowed over a file and drumming fingers on the desk.

He knew the sentence. There was no Sarge around, only Deputy Jackson. But he'd been told earlier by a harassed-looking Jackson, "The boss has written in your file that you need a leucotomy, and what he says goes with the god."

The god looked up, beaming while he adjusted his specs. "A pleasure to meet you again, Chisholm."

"What a charmingly evil snake you are."

This seemed to go unnoticed. "I see Mr Parker suggested a leucotomy, and I would concur with that." The god was frowning now, looking down at the file. "Hmm. But meanwhile you will restart ECT, then I shall review."

Phew – no leucotomy. He could survive ECT. But 'meanwhile'? Ominous?

The god snapped the file shut and pushed it toward Jackson. "Madness," he muttered. "Three doses a week from tomorrow for four weeks, then review – unless I get this ludicrous ruling overturned before then."

"Sir." Jackson took the file.

"Next patient," the god commanded.

No great prospect, having ECT again. At least John knew the drill. The problem would be his memory. But after the last battering, he'd eventually been able to remember. Maybe his brain hadn't suffered permanently.

He'd pondered a lot about Heather and Becky. It was hard to imagine how convinced he'd been that Heather was having an affair. She had been ice-cool towards him. But the post-natal depression could have been prolonged.

She did seem pally with the mental man. Maybe by now they'd teamed up.

He could hardly blame her – with a loony husband locked away, probably for life. And he was surely a nightmare to live with, before they took him to this dump.

Two white-coats approached. "We're off to the circus, Chisholm." And so began his next set of encounters with the Shocker.

44

Friday 23rd – Sunday 25th November 1956 – to and in Springwell.

The Edinburgh train puffed towards Birmingham New Street and drew to a halt outside. Its driver awaited the signal. Its stout-hearted engine hissed loudly.

Jamie Macdonald opened his eyes. It had been restful to drowse en route. He could feel a buzz. A change of train and a bus journey and he'd be there.

The offer of the job as Springwell's medical superintendent had come two days after he got home. He'd read the letter aloud, and Gill rushed to embrace him. He replied to accept, from 1st February 1957. This allowed time for him to wind up at Dingleton, and for recruiting his consultant successor.

Soon after, he'd received a welcome note from Liam Kenney. Kenney's boss, off sick and past retirement age, was to leave at the end of October. Kenney would act up for three months, and wondered if Dr Macdonald and his wife would care to spend a weekend as guests to familiarise themselves with Springwell.

The only decisions were when, and whether Gill would come. In her fourth month of pregnancy with what would be their first child, and struggling to keep up her GP work, she'd decided to rest at home. He was glad. The pain of three miscarriages over their time together was still pretty acute. 'When' was easy – as soon as possible.

The train stopped. Springing out onto the platform, he trotted along. He wanted to see all he could of Springwell.

Macdonald reached Springwell late in the evening. His host's cordial greeting helped him relax. He declined the 'proverbial nightcap', and opted for a mug of cocoa.

After the small talk, Macdonald said, "Wonder what the Royal Commission will come up with."

"Dunno. Reform's long overdue. You know Jamie, I've been ashamed of some things I've been party to." Kenney gulped his drink. "We need more emphasis on trying to help patients, less on protecting the public."

A surprise. He'd assumed Kenney would defend the system. "I agree. They should report soon. The grapevine tells me they'll move in that direction." He sipped his cocoa. "What brought you to psychiatry, Liam?"

"I was a biochemist when my wife died giving birth prematurely. Our baby lived a few hours. Life was hell. I threw myself into work, felt an urge to be a doctor and got interested in psychiatry. I came here as a consultant only three years ago."

"Quite a new boy then?"

Kenney smiled. "Yes. My promotion to Deputy in July got a strong protest from one of my peers, who's been a consultant here for decades. Poor man's been off sick most of the time since, and, to rub it in, wasn't shortlisted for the top job."

"Really." He wanted to know of any undercurrents. "Who is this?"

"Theo Godsell – whom they call 'the god'. Our paths haven't crossed much."

"Aye, tricky." He drained his mug. "How goes the 'Acting'?"

"Early days. My spell at the helm is of course a holding operation and I'll retire soon after." Kenney's expression lightened. "Enough of me. What of you?"

He liked this man. Maybe he'd stay on as Deputy? But now wasn't the time to broach this. He talked about himself – his motivation, experiences and hopes.

They discussed the morrow. Kenney would introduce him to key folk in the hierarchy, then act as guide on a tour round the male wards.

Macdonald sat at breakfast, savouring his mug's aroma of coffee beans. "Anything I should look out for on my tour?"

"I'll tell you one or two things – a bit delicate to mention on the wards." Kenney had sensitivity. "Go on."

"We've always had our share of violence, but you should know about a couple of recent incidents. Last month, some male patients tried to escape and two got out. One's still away – and entitled to stay outside."

"What's happened to the patients who didn't get out?"

"Put into padded cells on Refractory, then onto that ward. I've never been consultant there and I don't know how these men are now. Oh, there's one exception – a patient who's a peer of the realm. He was returned to Admissions."

"A nobleman – in here? Delusions of grandeur?"

"No, he's a bona fide peer. A story I'll tell you another time."

"And Refractory is for –?"

"Patients with a record of violence. We've a few from Broadmoor. The staffing level's higher than other wards."

Probably needed to be. "There's no equivalent at Dingleton."

"Two nurses sustained injuries, and have got COHSE involved."

He knew of COHSE – Confederation of Health Service Employees – a large trade union, important to most in the NHS except medics. "Sounds grim."

"And last Saturday one of the escapers, a paranoid schizophrenic, wounded the charge nurse on Refractory. The patient had walked into a police station after a day or two, got sedated and brought back here. Somehow he smuggled in a blade and slashed Charge Parker in the neck. Just missed the carotid. Parker'll be off weeks."

He nodded. "On the way round, Liam, can you discreetly indicate the patients involved in all this? I won't mention the incidents. I want to keep a low profile."

"Yes. I'll whisper in your ear. I'll tell you now about the escapers."

"Please." He listened carefully, noting mentally the names.

"Let's go. Brace yourself. Everywhere's locked."

Walking along the corridors, Macdonald said, "This is gloomy, depressing."

"Yes. Needs lightening. I can try to get work started, if that's okay with you. Corridors, Main Hall, wards and toilets. I'll speak with our Hospital Secretary, who heads up admin/clerical, and our Hospital Management Committee Chairman."

"Fine. That all sounds useful."

"I'll take you to the admin block first and you'll meet Ronald Cope, the Hospital Secretary." Kenney stopped in the empty corridor and whispered. "A prosaic fellow, Cope, who thinks he, not the Medical Superintendent, should be in overall charge. His empire includes the Records Officer and the Chief Engineer. Then you should see Bernard Hallman, Chief Male Nurse retiring end of January, and Caroline Dee, the new Matron. It's Caroline's first month in the job. In the boss's absence, I was in on her appointment; she's a breath of fresh air. Oh, there's one absentee – my dedicated secretary Miss Bewlay, who's on leave until next week."

Cope, a tall willowy bespectacled man who eyed him cautiously, impressed with his knowledge of Springwell's administrative workings, but wholly lacked in vision and was opposed to making changes. When Jamie took up office, one priority would be talking with the Secretary, to listen to concerns and try to win the confidence of a man who must be a key figure at Springwell.

Hallman was Neanderthal. Patients must be "Kept well away from the sane folks outside, so need to be locked up in their wards. Except when they're taken to the Shocker or for their leucotomies. We let two wards onto the airing courts twice daily." This man's successor must have a radically different vision.

In contrast, Matron Caroline (forty-ish, highly personable) impressed. He'd expect any Matron to be efficient, but this one exuded passion for reform and clarity of vision. With her as an aide, change would be a less Herculean task.

Entering Male Admissions, Macdonald saw it was empty of patients. "They're all on the airing court, Sir," Charge Nurse Mullen said.

All on the airing court? "Where do they go at other times?"

"They're out on the court mornings and afternoons, for exercise, except when they're having treatment or in for meals. Evenings they're inside, in the day-room." After hearing about Mullen – ex-army, newly-promoted – and getting an overview of routines, staffing and the patient population, he asked about lengths of stay. As he'd suspected from Mullen's patter, some patients had been on Admissions a long time (and one 'trusty' for decades).

Admissions should be about shorter stays – not keeping patients to suit staff.

"I'll take Dr Macdonald to the airing court," said Kenney.

When the door was unlocked, he followed Kenney into a large drab courtyard with high walls. Great-coated men with peaked caps stood at the corners watching patients slouch round. A scene he associated with the old asylums and prisons.

"Grim. Up north we got rid of these long ago."

Kenney shrugged. "The boss liked them."

Later, he stood in a corner while patients came in for lunch. He noted the ill-fitting institutional clothing and patients suffering the indignity of clinging to their trousers at the waist. "So's they can't escape, Sir," was Mullen's explanation.

They left Admissions. "Let's have lunch," said Kenney, and led him to a small, pleasantly furnished room with a waitress and choice of menu. "For psychiatrists and other senior staff. But ears are too long for talking business."

Macdonald's afternoon tour started with Male Infirmary, where he saw rows of beds, some unoccupied. Charge Nurse Macnamara, a youngish man with an Irish brogue, sat with him in the office and spoke about patients and approaches to their treatments.

He noted Macnamara's comment about the patient with the bandaged head. "Kong Mackay, one of the would-be escapers. They gave the poor man a leucotomy in town, and I do wonder why. He'd been in a violent incident once before, but sure he was known as a gentle fellow."

"Leucotomy's a last resort, indicated only to relieve unbearable tension."

"Yes. Sadly, it's being used here to suppress troublesome patients."

More confirmation of abuse. This charge nurse sounded caring, frank, knowledgeable.

"I thought there might be buckets of urine around, Mr Macnamara," he said jovially. "But I can't spy any."

"Months back when I came here, they were our number one feature. We've worked on hygiene." Macnamara smiled. "Sure we smell real fragrant now."

On Male Annex, where Kenney was consultant, Macdonald listened to Charge Nurse Williams. "I came up from Devon, started on Refractory, but found my true home here this past twenty years. I knows every patient on here and all their stories."

"How long do patients stay?"

"Some have been in Springwell thirty, forty years, Sir, and some longer. Soldiers from the Great War, some. Most aren't loony, though they might've been when they came in. Forever, mostly, they'll stay. Though not all - they're sometimes sent back to the ward they came from."

"Any violence?"

"Not as I'd call violence. One patient kicked off the other day. He has senile dementia, wanted to go play football. We had to restrain and sedate him and step up his medication. Any violent ones have had leucotomies, and, lost souls, they just sits there looking vacant and sad."

"What about activities for the patients?"

"One patient was a stand-up comic, and we sometimes gets him, with more baccy, to put on an act. Mind you, it's mostly us nurses that laugh. We take some to the dance Fridays in the Main Hall, with patients from Female Annex, and us and the female staff supervise. And one of our nurses brings records in to play."

This charge nurse sounded caring, but lacking any notion of discharge into the world outside. Understandable in the man's work context. Another area to tackle.

On Male Refractory, Deputy Charge Jackson looked elderly and harassed. "I'm acting up while Mr Parker's off, Sir."

From the overview, Macdonald noted a high ratio of nurses to patients was "Needed to keep the patients in their place," and "we expect violence."

The incidents Kenney mentioned. "Any violence recently?"

"There's two attacks on nurses just happened. An ex-Broadmoor patient floored one of our nursing assistants. Another patient weighed in and got hurt. Our man was injured bad and he's still in hospital. And last Saturday, the charge nurse got stabbed by a paranoid. Won't be back for weeks."

"What's happened to these patients?"

"We put them straight into padded cells, Sir. Except Chisholm, from the first attack, that was sent to our Infirmary and is now back on this ward. And Paranoid Moloney, that near killed the charge nurse, got released onto the ward again."

"I see."

"And Sir, Charge Parker, before he went off, wrote in the notes advising they both have a leucotomy. I drew Dr Singh's attention to this, but he wouldn't hear of it."

Good for Singh. Using the leucotomy to subdue folk was criminal. "Uh-huh."

"But Dr Godsell, the consultant, is coming back. He'll think different."

Godsell – 'the god', the long-server overlooked for promotion. "Really?"

"Oh yes, Sir. Dr Godsell keeps troublemakers in check."

He'd discuss with Kenney, though maybe it was too late to help the patients. This was delicate, and traditionally 'no go', to question a consultant's clinical judgment. "One other thing. Why are there so many cells?"

"We have to put some patients in there over staff lunchtimes. There wouldn't be enough of us to cope."

This institution was mainly about using power to control and detain. The cells could be refurbished as single rooms.

He and Kenney walked back down the ward. Patients had come in from the airing court. He felt a nudge, then heard a whisper, "Chisholm, blond hair." Yes, the teacher - gaunt, athletic, face alert but strained. He saw Chisholm stare back at them, and looked away. He nudged Kenney and they left the ward.

In the evening, Macdonald met fellow psychiatrists at a buffet in the boardroom. After, Kenney asked, "What did you make of it?"

"A useful meeting. All the consultants are men."

"Yes. It's hard to attract women suitably qualified. The odds are stacked heavily against them being accepted for medicine."

Exactly. It was ironic that, while Springwell's female population exceeded the male, their fates were in the hands of male consultants. Pretty well mirrored UK psychiatry. "Ingrained attitudes of the old guard prevail, sadly."

"Yes, Jamie. Your wife must be outstanding to have got into medicine."

"She's much brighter than I am. I did meet two women this evening."

"One's Lizzie McVeigh. A registrar, she works with me on both Annex Wards. She's capable, good with patients - men and women. She'd make a fine consultant."

"We'll need two more consultants, Liam. Encourage her to apply."

Over supper, Macdonald talked with Kenney about his tour and the issues of concern.

"You've a mountain to climb here." Kenney smiled.

They'd much common ground. "Liam, I hope you'll stay on as Deputy."

Kenney looked thoughtful. "I was going soon, Jamie. But I like your thinking. I'll stop on a year or two. It's a great time to work in mental health."

The mountain had shrunk. He'd begin the ascent with Kenney and Matron.

"I'd like Cope on board, but he struck me as pretty insecure, even hostile."

"That's how I find him. I hope you can work the miracle needed. Our Secretary has clout with Committee, and he's a close buddy of the Chairman."

"I'll try, Liam. Another thing, much more pressing – leucotomy's being used by at least one consultant to control rather than treat. That's not acceptable."

"Yes, I see the devastating effect on some patients in the Annex. Barbaric. Shall I declare a moratorium on sending patients for the op, with immediate effect? I could type a memo, and, quoting you as well, get it round tomorrow – even though it's the Sabbath – to my consultant colleagues, with a copy to all charge nurses."

"Please do. It's that urgent. Won't help your popularity – or mine."

Kenney smiled. "I've nothing to lose. And your shoulders are broad enough."

On Sunday morning, he sat in chapel with Kenney in a pew reserved for senior staff. Patients from the Annex Wards sat in rows – women on one side of the aisle, men on the other. Nurses were interspersed. Even in worship, there was gender segregation.

He had time for only a whirlwind tour of female wards. Matron Caroline agreed to list the changes she'd want and go on a tour with him when he took up post.

He had a final coffee in Kenney's office. "Any reform Caroline suggests on the female side, I'm happy if you can take it forward. The male side won't change till Hallman goes. And I'll want to be involved in appointing key staff."

"Fine, Jamie. I'll keep you in touch."

On the homeward journey, Macdonald shut his eyes, reflecting on his experiences. For some staff, the changes he intended would come like a bomb blast. At least he'd have powerful allies in Liam and Caroline.

Working on Cope would be important to goodwill. Tension between them was inbuilt structurally. As Medical Superintendent, he was formally, and legally, the overall boss. But some resentment from Cope, and blurring of who was in charge of what, was understandable, as the man effectively controlled everything non-medical.

Jamie wanted to shape a caring community, not a cluster of mini-empires.

Surely high drama and battles lay ahead. He thirsted for the fight.

45

Friday 21ˢᵗ December 1956 – in Springwell.

John lay in a mist. Hell of a lot of Shocker. Struggling to think gave him a headache. Everything was jumbled.

Sometimes he couldn't remember his own name, never mind those of others. He'd witnessed a few scraps, and stayed clear.

"You'll see the god on Monday," the boss white-coat told him.

He'd a bad feeling about this.

Monday 24ᵗʰ December 1956 – in Springwell.

The man looked familiar. Not the god. The turban, the beard – the Asian psychiatrist!

"I am standing in for Dr Godsell, who is off sick."

Dr who? He stood in the office with white-coated escorts. "Uh."

"Mr Chisholm, do you remember me?"

"Yes and no. You look familiar and I know your voice –"

"I am Dr Singh. I have seen you before, several times. Tell me, Mr Chisholm – what are the names of your wife and child?"

Wife and child. Yes. The images were hazy. Names? "Can't remember." His head was solid with concrete.

"What year were you born?"

Stupid questions, that his weary brain wouldn't stand for. "You figure it out."

"Mr Chisholm, you have just finished another course of ECT. It may have benefited you in your mood; but your memory may for now be affected."

"Yes."

"How do you feel, Mr Chisholm?"

"Hellish."

The doctor was gazing at him. "How clear is your thinking now?"

"My head's clogged."

The doctor turned to the boss white-coat. "Mr Chisholm should be transferred. To the Annex. ECT will end now. I will not restart other medication, as he appeared to manage without chlorpromazine. I will approach the consultant on the Annex."

46

Tuesday 25th December 1956 – in Aversham.

On her knees, cooing to Becky, Heather encouraged the tottering steps towards her across the living room carpet. So much for the idea that her child might be backward in development. It was great to see Becky walking without support and uttering recognisable words. Graduating from babe to toddler.

Her eyes misted. John wasn't here, and probably never would be, to see Becky growing up. What sort of miserable Christmas would he be having?

It was wretched enough here. No decorations – what was there to celebrate? Likewise, no stocking from Father Christmas, and no toys, except Teddy the bear and Jane the doll. She gathered Becky up and swayed from side to side, humming.

She'd been invited to Christmas lunch by Elsie and Moira. Elsie asked first and she'd said yes. She was glad. Moira was having folk to stay, while Elsie had no family. Also, Mattie'd been diagnosed with emphysema (bad news, though not as bad as the 'big C' Elsie feared) and might not be around for many more Christmases.

The nappy needed changing. With a "Coochy coo," she laid Becky on the floor and set about her task. She mightn't be doing this much longer.

Her parents too had phoned the shop to invite her and Becky, but she'd made her plans. They'd call for her on the thirtieth to take her and Becky to theirs for New Year's Eve. The festive season wouldn't be a great time for them either, with happy memories turned sad. In more affluent times, they'd gone abroad for the whole period.

She imagined Edward the child and her parents, enjoying their Christmases before the tragedy. She wiped her eyes.

Knocking on the door. The postman, to wish her happy Christmas – and expecting a few pence? "Wait," she called, taking Becky into her arms.

She'd nothing to give him, and anyway it was a student stand-in at Christmas. She and John, as students, both got Christmas post rounds. The year she did Christmas Day, she was paid double time and picked up generous tips from merry customers.

She opened the door. "Sam!"

"Popped round to wish you a happy Christmas."

"Come in." She flung the door wide. He was carrying something.

"I've swapped my briefcase for a rocking horse," he quipped as he entered.

"Thanks. Happy Christmas." She kissed him on the cheek. Becky squealed. "There, darling," she said, nuzzling into Becky as she led the way to the living room.

Newman put the rocking horse down. "Happy Christmas, Becky."

"Becky, it's for you," she said, holding the child over it. "Thanks ever so, Sam, from both of us. This must have cost you some."

"No – I visit families and sometimes pick up gifts for needier children. It cost me nothing and I thought of Becky. It's big for her, but she's growing fast."

Her hero! She wanted a hug. If Becky had been asleep...

"I'll find out how John is, sometime after the festive season." He glanced at his watch. "Must go." In the doorway, he turned to blow a kiss, and left.

Fancy Sam thinking of Becky. Big-hearted. Handsome. And unmarried.

Newman started up the car engine, waved to Heather and was off. A good visit. Great idea, persuading Helen to surrender her rocking horse 'for a needy family'.

At home, Ella greeted him with, "Well, who is she?"

"A family called Chisholm. He's in the asylum and they can't afford toys." He looked towards the corner. "Thanks, Helen." To Ella he said, "I'm going for a smoke to clear my head."

In the garden, the sun shone and the air was crisp. There would be no Christmas dinner. Helen, perky again, was going out with friends. Boiled eggs would do for him and Ella.

On call through the festive season! Last year, he'd found himself amid a drunken family fighting. That was not about madness and he shouldn't have been called out.

Well, next month he'd have company at work again.

"Little to look forward to," he'd quipped, after the panel – despite his strong support for the other man – made their choice. The MOH had scowled.

He lit another fag. Mrs C was delightful as well as beautiful and her vulnerability lent her even more attraction. He'd tried not visiting for weeks. But in his mind, she was there – haunting, consuming him. Those hugs. Her hubby wouldn't ever leave Springwell. If he, Sam, had been single... But he wasn't.

Ella was not suicidal. If he tried overdosing or smothering her, forensics would get him. And pleading euthanasia meant confessing to murder.

Maybe he could surrender to his passion and swear Heather to secrecy. "Because," he'd tell her, "any romantic liaison with a patient's wife means instant dismissal." That was it – the way ahead in the new year.

The phone was ringing. He stubbed out the fag and limped slowly inside.

47

Parker's head was exploding, the telly screen wobbling. He rose gingerly from the armchair he'd slumped into when he got home from the Red Lion's Hogmanay Special. Must have had near a bottle of scotch. He'd always been able to hold his liquor – used to drink the squaddies under the table.

As well he wasn't on duty today. First, the cure he'd learned from his old man. He cracked an egg into a cup, added a sprinkle of pepper and two aspirins, and pinched his nose as he downed the poison; then, hair of the dog – just half a glass.

That was better. He faced the mirror. God, he looked old. No wonder the Chisholm bitch turned him down. A tart, she was. Could have shagged her that day, but for the meddling old hag with the friend on Admin. He'd backed off since. Couldn't risk doing for his career.

At least the neck wound was healed, apart from a scar. He'd wakened in the General, and been told what happened. Where did that bastard patient get the blade? Good job it missed the carotid. He'd been off weeks. "Get yourself fit for the assistant chief interview," the Chief had said.

Better shave. He lathered, and picked up the Wilkinson's sword edge. Bugger this trembling. He straightened up again. "Discipline, Ready," he muttered. Head clearer and vision fine, he crouched over his shaving mirror and completed the task.

It'd been a blow when the Chief said they weren't replacing Porter. "I've done the job with only two assistant chiefs, and now they tell me to manage with none. And Little's been useless. Could've done with Porter, one of the old school."

Well, he was being interviewed for the Chief's job on Friday. Little had gone ("Thanks to a great reference from me, to get rid," the Chief said). So, no competition.

He adjusted his tie in the mirror. Fine – he looked smart, younger.

A knock on his door. He flung the door open. The Chief. "Come in, Sir." He smiled at his visitor.

"Happy new year, Ready." Chief Hallman's weary face had more wrinkles than he remembered. Maybe the proverbial cracked glass at Hogmanay?

He motioned to the armchair. "Sir, take a seat." He held up a glass. "Join me?"

"Don't mind if I do, as Colonel Chinstrap would say."

"Yes Sir." He poured a large whisky. "Colonel Chinstrap was a true blue. Best programme on the wireless, *ITMA*."

The Chief drained the glass. "Needed that. It's hell without any Assistants."

That was why the Chief looked so old. "Sir." He'd make damn sure he got Assistants. "A refill?"

The Chief pushed his glass toward the bottle. "Anyway, I'll tough it out this month. Then I'll be a man of leisure with a nice pension."

"Sir, you've earned it. You're an outstanding example for us all."

The Chief was smiling now. "Thanks Ready. You're a loyal man, made of the right stuff for a chief. Just one or two things to mention before Friday."

Good. The Chief was confirming his backing. "Sir?"

"It's not quite the shoe-in I wanted, Ready. We're seeing Macnamara from Infirmary as well. But I'll be in your corner. We need a man that'll run a tight ship, and I trust you." The Chief scowled. "Can't have patients running amok."

He knew this had been a hell of a blow for the Chief – those scum, thumping nurses and escaping. The boss'd said it blighted his career. "No Sir. I'd keep control, like you do. They couldn't blame you. It was down to Niven, the cocky bastard!"

The Chief was looking at him again, no longer scowling. "You're right. I offered to get a nursing assistant across from the Annex while Mullen was off, but Niven said he'd manage." The Chief downed his whisky.

"Another drink, Sir?"

"No." The Chief rose, tottered, then grasped the back of the chair. Never could take his liquor. "Better go. Med Super Acting, the Sectary and Committee Chairman'll be there. Chairman 'n' Sectary like efficiency, so they go with what I say." The Chief stood gaping, speaking slowly and with emphasis. "Think Kenney's on board. Knows I want you. Can't never be sure. He's a funny one."

"Sir." He stood up to see his guest out.

"'Bye, Ready." The Chief gripped the woodwork in the doorway as he exited.

Parker returned to drain his glass. The headache had gone.

Friday 4th January 1957 – in Springwell.

In the anteroom to the boardroom, Parker sat erect on his chair. Best bib and tucker; spit and polish on his gleaming shoes.

The other man, Macnamara, hunched forward on his seat, was scruffy-looking and unshaved, like he'd had a night on the tiles. The chief scruff maybe, but never the chief male nurse, who needed to enforce discipline.

The boardroom door opened. "Mr Parker." Miss Bewlay's imperious tones. "Follow me."

He sprang to his feet. "Ma'am, after you."

He followed her in. There was the Chief, looking down with no sign of recognition. Fine. Nobody must ever know about the Chief's pledge to him.

"Take a seat, Mr Parker." A Welsh accent, from the far end of the table. "I'm Dr Kenney, Acting Medical Superintendent."

He'd seen this guy around – a right drip. "Sir." He sat down.

"Mr Davies our HMC Chairman, Mr Cope our Secretary, Miss Dee the Matron, and Mr Hallman you know." Kenney waved an arm down the table.

He nodded smilingly at each. Matron was the only one he hadn't met. A real head-turner. As Chief, he'd soon get pally with her.

"And Dr Macdonald, our new Medical Superintendent from next month." Horn-rimmed specs, serious-looking. Damn, why was this weirdo here? "A right queer one," Jackson had said.

"Sir." He sat up straight. He was good at interviews, and the man for the job.

An hour later, back in his quarters, Parker poured a whisky. The Chief had primed him well, asked most questions. The others asked a question each. Simple stuff, apart from that Matron bitch and Horn-rims raising things irrelevant to the job – about a Royal Commission and changes. How the hell could he know about what this Royal Commission, a bunch of interfering pricks, would come up with? But he'd kept smiling, responded to each question, and been rewarded with smiles back. He'd surely charmed Matron, who blushed as he answered her. The Welshman had thanked him, said they'd to see one other candidate, but would let him know soon.

'Chief Parker' sounded right. He'd show them. And settle a score or two.

Monday 7th January 1957 – in Springwell.

Parker poured a large whisky. It'd been hell back at work. That new Staff he was saddled with – Maclean from Infirmary – was a right know-all. The fop Singh was on the ward round, standing in for the god. Leucotomies were banned. What nonsense! The greatest bloody tool for silencing violent bad-uns – and the idiots wouldn't use it! When he was Chief next month, he'd put his oar in.

Paranoid Moloney was in his face. He'd make that patient beg for a speedy death. The madman should be in Broadmoor for attempted murder. At least that prick Chisholm was out of his sight, moved to the Annex.

Knocking on the door. Hallman, to congratulate him? He got up and flung the door open. Yes. "Chief, come in, take a seat. Whisky?"

"I'll need one thanks, Ready."

He poured a generous measure and topped up his own glass. Celebration was due. He passed the glass over and sat down. The Chief looked ill.

The Chief took a swallow and laid down his glass. "Ready, I have bad news. They've gone for Macnamara."

"But you said –"

"I know. I told them you were the only man for the job, and I created hell after the vote. Tied at three-all it was, after Kenney and Matron and the Med Super-to-be went for Macnamara. Then they settled on Kenney's casting vote as chairman. I argued that the Med Super-to-be, who's away with the fairies, shouldn't have had a vote but they said that as a panel member he did." He sipped his whisky. "From then till now I've looked at the constitution, and asked COHSE. It's no bloody use. There's no appeal."

Incredible. That drip Macnamara. "The place'll go to ruin, Sir. No discipline."

"Agreed. Sorry old friend, I must go." The Chief rose and tottered off.

Bugger it. That was his job. He picked up the whisky bottle and gulped till it was empty. Felt better. They'd have to appoint him Assistant Chief.

Tuesday 8th January 1957

Parker sat in his office, cradling his head. The hangover cure hadn't kicked in yet.

"Nosey!" A cry. Had he heard right? Paranoid! He wasn't standing any nonsense – and he'd a score to settle. He strode out of the office.

Paranoid was stood there and Maclean was just gaping. A shit of a nurse, to be scared of a patient.

"Nosey Parker."

He grabbed Paranoid by the lapels, then remembered the last time he'd given the bastard a headbutt. He released the lapels, stood Paranoid up and gave him a straight left on the nose followed by a right uppercut. The old one-two. Felled the bastard. Now for a kicking.

"Sir, stop it." Maclean was in front of him, shielding the patient. Intolerable. He lunged at Maclean, and found himself on the floor in an arm-lock.

"Don't try that again, Sir."

Later, Parker was summoned to the Chief's office. The Assistant's job?

"We have to suspend you, Ready. Moloney's nose and jaw are busted and Macnamara on Infirmary, damn him, is making a fuss."

"But, Sir, it was Maclean struck the patient – and hit me. The man's a bad-un."

The Chief looked like he'd had enough. "Ready, I'll keep you informed."

Friday 11ᵗʰ January 1957

The Chief had summoned him. Parker waltzed out the door. Exoneration and back to work, surely. He knocked on the Chief's door.

Entering, he found the Chief standing by the desk. "Sir."

"Ready, take a seat. It's not looking good. In fact, it's bloody awful. Besides getting Maclean and the patient to say in writing it was you did the thumping, Macnamara's got witness statements – all against you. And he's sent copies to Kenney and the HMC Chairman. They're gunning for you."

"But Sir, you believe me?"

"Yes, my friend, and not long ago I could've done something. Even if you'd near murdered the patient, I'd have swept it under the carpet

– like I've done a few times with complaints about nurses. I've spoken to HMC Chairman Davies. He says it's a sacking offence."

Parker wiped his damp brow with his sleeve, swallowed and waited. "Sir."

"Ready, if it goes to a hearing, you're in shite. Davies reckons, whatever you say, they'd have to sack you." He slapped the desk. "My friend, there's a way out."

"Suicide, Sir?" He wasn't joking. Apart from the disgrace, he'd lose his pension and accommodation and wouldn't get another job.

"No, Ready." The Chief was emphatic. "Another job."

"Sir?"

"Here's how. So far, everything's informal. An incident – your word against theirs. You give your resignation in with immediate effect, to me. No reason's needed – I'm the Chief until the end of this month. I've taken the liberty of speaking with an old pal that owes me – chief at a big Lancashire asylum. You're the ideal man for a charge nurse vacancy they need to fill now and my friend guarantees you the job, with accommodation."

The Chief was a fixer, a man after his own heart. This place stank anyway.

"Sir, I'd take it, provided there's no action against me here."

"I guarantee it. Neither HMC Chairman nor Kenney want a hearing. It's bad publicity. If you agree, clear your room tonight and come to my place. I'll help with removal. I'll ring my pal to say you'll take the job from Monday."

"I'll buy it, Sir."

He took the proffered notepaper, kept his letter simple and handed it to the Chief. Bugger this dump.

48

Heather tucked Becky into her cot, waited till she'd dozed off, came back to the living room and put on Elvis's *Golden Album*. She picked up the library book on child development and stretched out on the settee. In nursery work, she'd found her vocation. Now she wanted a refresher on theoretical thinking about the significance in later life of how toilet training and temper tantrums were handled. Vital for Becky – and her.

A faint knocking on the door? "It's Sam" through the letterbox. Swinging off the settee, she shouted "Coming," paused by the hallway mirror to touch up her hair and adjust her skirt, and flung the door open.

Sam, minus briefcase. "Sam, come in."

The aroma she'd come to like – of Brylcreem. She led the way to the living room and motioned to the table. "Sit down."

But he remained standing, his arms outstretched. "Happy new year, Heather."

"Happy new year, Sam." She opened her arms and stepped into an embrace. She was being drawn into him, and oh, the warm insistence of his body. She felt a kiss on the cheek; then his tongue was in her mouth. This excitement and longing for something she was starved of.

He was pressing her backward, toward the settee, and she felt his full arousal. "No, Sam." She wasn't ready for this. His grip slackened and she moved out of the clinch. His tanned face was red.

"Sorry. I thought that was what you wanted. I love you, Heather."

"You're attractive, Sam, but I still have feelings for John. And he's my husband." All true. "Let's just sit at the table and talk." She motioned to a chair.

Yes, she had wanted it. But deep in her being, shame had won the battle with arousal. *Cool down.*

"Okay, Heather." They sat down opposite each other.

"Have you news for me, Sam?"

"Yes. Your husband's been moved to the Annex and he's allowed a visitor. The next date's 19th January, a Saturday. I could, unless something blows up, take you there. I'd stay out of sight."

"Thanks, but I'd like to try the bus."

"Well – I hope the visit goes okay."

"So do I. Last time was so horrible."

"He was a swine to you. Look, Heather, I doubt they'll ever release him, with his mental condition."

Exactly what she feared. Was Sam going somewhere with this? "Really?"

"Yes, from my knowledge of Springwell, I'm certain. It's sad for you, and for Becky." He paused, gazing at her. "You could have grounds for divorce."

"Could I?"

"Yes. If John's 'of unsound mind' for long enough. I'd then want to propose marriage – but any romance with a patient or spouse means the sack."

"So?"

"Heather, I love you enough to risk my career. If we can express our feelings towards each other fully, here, without anyone else knowing – well, I'd want that." He stood up. "I have to go. Think about what I've said."

Stunning, what he was suggesting. An affair! She rose. "Thanks Sam. I will. Remember what I've said too."

She hung back from the doorway while he said good-bye. She didn't trust her feelings with another hug.

Heather leapt off the bus and walked briskly down Springwell's Hospital Lane. The last few days, a powerful urge to take up Sam's offer had been vying with a longing for the John she'd married. Maybe this visit could help calm her inner maelstrom.

Keys clanked as the imposing front door opened to reveal a familiar face. Jock Mackenzie, whom Sam had called 'one of the good guys'.

"Hurry in lass, out o' the cold. I remember you, Missus Chisholm, from when you came to see your man."

"That's right, Mr Mackenzie. I'm told John's on the Annex."

She followed him to the desk, where the visitors' book lay. They went through the formalities - again irritating, as this swallowed precious visiting time.

Mackenzie showed her to a seat. "I'll ring, and your man'll be brought down."

The hall was no longer spooky! They'd painted the walls in brighter colours and hung pictures. And there was a buzz of conversation - seemed like patients having visitors.

A door at the far end slammed. She looked up. A white-coated man was pointing her way. John was striding towards her. She got up, smiling, but stood waiting, uncertain of how he'd be. Only another few steps. He looked thinner, fitter, and more smartly dressed than before.

He stood facing her, his arms spread wide. "Heather, come here."

Wrapping her arms round his neck, she felt his reassuring strength enfold her. Her lips found his. She stood savouring his intimacy. He was rocking her from side to side, like he used to do. That this would last.

She felt him withdraw and she did likewise. She sat on a chair and he drew up one beside her. She dabbed her face with her sleeve. "How are you, John?"

"Chuffed at your visit." He was frowning? "But I won't blame you if you've shacked up with somebody else."

Telepathy? Her cheeks felt warm. He was waiting for her reply. "No.

When I wanted to visit before, they said you were having shock treatment."

"The Shocker – a kind of punishment. Yes, that finished before Christmas. I couldn't remember much after – your name, or Becky's. My memory's gradually come back, though there might be things I'll never remember." He looked sad, lost.

She put her hand in his and was rewarded with a gentle squeeze. "Gosh, you've been going through it, John."

"I've had one or two adventures, but I won't bore you with these." The frown had gone. "It's been okay since I was moved to the Annex. That's a long-stay ward, and I must be twenty years younger than any of the others. A lot look senile or doped, but I hear some interesting tales."

"Do you think there's a prospect of discharge yet?"

The frown was back. "Nobody's mentioned that. And –" John paused, the furrow on his brow deepening, "they say patients are in the Annex for life."

What she'd feared. "Oh, John." He looked so miserable.

"Apparently only a consultant psychiatrist can discharge a patient – and I've not seen one on this ward yet. They say he's very busy. When I do see him, I'll ask." He bent forward and his face brightened. "Enough of me. How have you been, and Becky?"

She told him about Becky's progress and her work at the nursery. He kept nodding, with a dreamy faraway look she scarcely recognised. Mildly worrying, somehow. She began to speak more rapidly. There was so much to tell.

Mid-sentence, a bell rang. She paused. "Fire alarm?"

"I'll find out." John rose and went to ask a white-coat.

"To let us know to wind up. We've about five minutes." He sat down again.

This awful place! "I've so much to tell you."

He stretched forward, and took her hand again. "Heather, I must have been more unhinged than I realised and had terrible unwanted thoughts. I'm through that, and I pine for you and Becky." He stood up. "Please come again."

Her face awash, she hugged him. "John, I will."

But on the journey home, she still agonised. Had John properly recovered from his breakdown? His eyes lacked that vital spark, so characteristic when he was fit. Maybe they'd never release him anyway. If so, she'd always visit when she could. He was her true love. Yet the lure of Sam's insistence remained strong, nagging away at a primal level. And he too had shown he loved her. Could she go along with Sam's proposal – for now?

Monday 21st January 1957 – in Aversham.

It came as a shock. Heather was confiding in Moira about her liking for Sam, and what he'd suggested.

"Mr Newman's married, with a daughter," Moira stated. "At least he was when I was still working. Sad – his wife had a long-term illness. Unless she's died. I'll find out for you."

Next day, Moira was back on the doorstep. "Me again, Heather. More news."

"Come in, Moira."

"I'll just step inside. Can't stop." Moira pushed the door to. "I've checked on Sam. He lives in a council house with his wife and teenage daughter."

What! "You're sure?" This decent caring man had misled her?

"Absolutely. He's been something of a lad, you know – had other women."

Friday 25th January 1957 – in Aversham.

Heather had just put Becky to rest. The knocking on the door was faint, gentle. She opened the door and peered round it. Yes, it was Sam Newman.

"How did your visit go, Heather?"

"Okay thanks, Sam. Look, I won't invite you in." She gulped. She'd rehearsed for this moment. "About your proposition, the answer's a definite 'no'."

"Why, Heather?" He looked puzzled, deflated.

"I love John. And I know you're a married man with a family."

"But –" He gesticulated with his hand.

"Thanks for all your help, Sam. But there'll be no romance. And it's better you don't come round here again."

"But –" Was he going to cry? And was she?

"I must go. 'Bye, Sam." He was still standing there. She closed the door, then ran to the living room and, weeping silently, threw herself into the armchair.

Sam Newman limped into his car and sat in the dim lamplight, fumbling for his fags and lighter. Hell of a shock. And she'd shut the door in his face! He looked back at the door. He felt like going and banging on it, breaking it down. After all he'd done for the bitch. And she'd led him on! How did she know he was married?

Blowing smoke rings, he calmed. Maybe in a month or two he'd go round, try persuading her to change her mind about an affair. The husband wouldn't ever get home anyway. He started up and moved off slowly, back to Ella and Helen.

49

Tuesday 5ᵗʰ February 1957 – in Springwell.

It was Jamie Macdonald's second morning in the job. And this was a vital meeting, with key folk that he needed to go along with him.

"There'll be a bloody revolution," said Davies.

"Yes – bloody, literally," added Cope.

Macdonald decided not to break the silence. This response to the vision he'd outlined – of a caring institution, without locked doors or padded cells or barriers to community involvement – was expected. He'd figured neither the HMC Chairman nor the Secretary would embrace radical change.

Chief Macnamara came in. "Sure, there needs to be a revolution in patient care. Some of our practices are from a bygone era, before we had the chemical cosh and effective anti-psychotic drugs."

"Blind us with jargon if you like. It's not safe," said Davies.

Matron Caroline spoke. "I understand your fears. We'll have to go carefully, and staff will need a lot of reassurance. But let's remember that we're a hospital, to treat and care for our mentally afflicted fellows. Any one of us" – she looked round the room – "could have a breakdown. Would we want to be cooped up, imprisoned, and thrown into isolation if we behaved oddly?"

The debate ran on. With solid backing from his two Heads of Nursing and Kenney, he secured the reluctant cooperation of the two doubters.

Wards would be unlocked from Monday 4ᵗʰ March. Seclusion in padded cells was to be used only for patients likely to harm themselves. And he'd bring proposals to Committee for refurbishment to transform them into small single rooms. Here again, the support of his three allies would be vital in swaying the lay members - and the Chairman and Secretary agreed not to vote against the changes in Committee.

Wednesday 6th February 1957 - in Springwell.

Another critical meeting - for all staff this time - in the Main Hall. Macdonald outlined his proposals to abolish pillars of the old regime - the locked wards, the padded cells and the airing courts. Then, from the platform, he and his three lieutenants - Kenney, Matron Caroline and Chief Macnamara - listened to comment and joined in the (often heated) debate. It was memorable, atmospheric and, for much of the time, uncomfortable.

Unlocking of wards went down like a blunt knife on granite. Reactions ranged from disbelief and ridicule (with one male nurse saying, too audibly, "Guy's a nutter" - and getting a ripple of laughter), to more rational objections: "Impractical for us to keep control" and "unsafe - for the patients, us, and the outside world."

Abandoning padded cells was marginally less controversial. "Mayhem," "needed for violent lunatics to let out their madness," and "vital to cool the bad boys and teach them a lesson," were among the comments.

The phasing out of airing courts wasn't too popular either. "How will they get their exercise?" and "it'll be murder for the lot of us - having them cooped up all day," were two of the comments.

The loudest protest came from the COHSE branch chairman. "I am astounded by this madness. This is the lunatics running the asylum." The man, a pompous nursing assistant with powers of oratory, added, "Chaos and murder will ensue. Our Union will support any members in industrial action." The applause was roof-challenging.

Matron Caroline spoke quietly, passionately. "Working with mentally afflicted folk in here is one of the toughest and most worthwhile jobs anywhere. Remember, for long enough we've had the chemical cosh to subdue the violence – as a last resort, when somebody's out of control. Physical restraints of the past have no place in modern psychiatry." She got mild applause. Was this a measure of support for the changes, or a spontaneous response to Caroline's charming eloquence?

Joe Macnamara said, "And the phenothiazines herald a pharmacological revolution that gives real hope in treating psychoses."

Macdonald went on to outline his vision. Springwell would evolve into a truly caring community. Occupational therapists and art therapists would be appointed, to provide helpful activity for patients. Barriers to the world outside would be lowered and community involvement encouraged. And psychiatric social workers would be appointed to work with patients and families, and help rehabilitate patients identified for discharge. The change process would extend over months, years.

At the end of the meeting, he'd been encouraged to hear some applause. Polite and mild, but better than the boos and catcalls he'd feared.

Monday 4th March 1957 – in Springwell.

Macdonald had remained firm through lobbying and protests. All wards must be unlocked as from today.

Morning, he toured the male wards with Macnamara, speaking with the charge nurses, listening, supporting, debating – and on Refractory, having to insist the ward door be unlocked. Matron and Kenney toured the female wards – and their cautiously optimistic report indicated less resistance there.

Afternoon, they all toured again. A fight on Male Refractory had been diffused via the chemical cosh. A couple of wandering patients from Male Annex were found in the corridors and escorted back. Maybe there was a case for locking the Annex wards to keep senile patients secure?

It was now evening on this momentous day.

The internal phone startled him. "Jamie Macdonald."

"Caroline." Matron. "Trouble, Jamie. Sister on our Annex has reported a patient with senile dementia, Nellie Morgan, missing from the ward. She was last seen about two hours ago. My Assistants and I have searched the building and walked round the outside, with no joy. Sister blames the unlocking of doors, and says this would never happen in the old days."

Blast. Resistance from nurses, backed by COHSE, could derail his plans. "We'd better inform the police."

"I can contact them if you like?"

"Aye. Thanks." Made sense, as Caroline would have the patient's details.

"I'll keep you posted and send you a report about the incident. And I propose no disciplinary action against Sister or her staff – unless any are found to be deliberately negligent. They've been short-staffed today."

This Matron was outstanding – not only ready to take things on, but a brilliant ally in reforming. She had, with Kenney's backing, begun the change process before he arrived. And the tour round with her on his first day was a heartening experience.

The internal phone again. He snatched the receiver. "Jamie Macdonald."

"Caroline, Jamie. Police with dogs are on their way. They're coming to my office for details. I'll bring them straight over."

He sat waiting.

He'd known it wouldn't be easy. Mac Bell had made bold moves in the right therapeutic direction by unlocking Dingleton for the world's first open-door mental hospital, and trying to involve the community in its life. But the changes had inevitably brought difficulties, which Mac was honest about in last year's paper for the *International Journal of Social Psychiatry*.

Matron appeared, with two great-coated policemen and their dogs.

"Matron's briefed us, Sir," the sergeant declared. "We've each got a lamp and a torch." They set off.

265

"I'll stay in my office for news, Jamie."

An unusually strained expression on her finely-cut features reflected the seriousness of this situation. "Thanks, Caroline."

Again, he sat waiting.

Thank God Caroline was Matron. With her talents and passion, she'd have been effective in the skin of a monster. She was also so damned attractive. If he'd been single... Wed to her profession.

"An unclaimed treasure," Uncle Frank would have said. A phrase the young Jamie had unthinkingly taken as a tribute to an unmarried woman's beauty.

He remembered the moment of enlightenment. Sitting in a quiet corner of Mackie's in Princes Street with fellow student Gill, meaning to sympathise with her over the death of her unmarried great aunt, the phrase slipped out.

Gill had stood up. "What patronising bilge," she hissed, her cheeks colouring. "You profess to support women's rights and equality. Back to claiming goods and chattels, are we?" She stomped off to the ladies' lav.

Stunned, he'd sat in silence, eyeing the table, feeling the stare of Edinburgh's tongue-waggers, realising everything he'd heard was true, hoping this woman he fancied would come back to join him.

She did. And, leaving the café together without ordering, they apologised to each other (he for a naivety that didn't reflect how he saw women, she for a rash public outburst that didn't reflect how she saw him) as they walked hand-in-hand along Princes Street.

That had been make-or-break with Gill, and the frankness drew them closer.

Maybe he'd write up his experiences at Springwell after a few years. The psychiatric community was too damned conservative. And the legal framework needed a drastic overhaul. As in Scotland, where the main substantive law was Victorian, in England the 1890 Lunacy Act still applied. Ludicrous!

Aye, the 1930 Mental Treatment Act had re-named asylums, advocated setting up outpatient clinics, and introduced a 'voluntary patient' category. Folk could go into a mental hospital without having to be certified. Big deal. Most institutions had kept harsh stigmatising regimes, and voluntary patients bold enough to try leaving without psychiatrist blessing often found themselves certified and detained.

In Melrose, he'd looked impatiently to a committee being set up to recommend a new legal framework for Scotland. And here in England it was a Royal Commission, set up in 1954. Subsequent law should sweep away anachronisms and improve the lot of the mentally distressed. But he wasn't waiting for that.

Someone was knocking on his door. The police or Caroline? He leapt to his feet. "Come in." It was the sergeant, with dog on leash.

"Sir, we've found the body of an elderly female floating in your pond."

Alas. He dialled Caroline. "Bad news. Come to my office."

At midnight, Jamie dragged his weary frame out of the office. For the first time in many years, he'd felt like drowning himself in whisky. It was a blessing that his desk drawer did not (unlike that in Manchester) conceal a half-bottle. Now, in his emotionally flat state, the yearnings for that instant solace tugged compellingly at him.

Nearly home. He hoped Gill was awake so that he could unwind with her. Up north she too had enthused about unlocking wards, and she'd been active in encouraging the local community's involvement in the hospital. At some point, she would set about doing for Springwell what she'd done for Dingleton. Her GP work was only two days a week.

The lights were on downstairs. She'd be up. Nonetheless, he tiptoed in.

"What the hell have you been up to, Jamie?" Gill was dressing-gowned and unsmiling.

He'd forgotten to ring, keep her posted. "I was winding up, when Matron rang me."

"So? Confession time, laddie. You didn't think to ring me, did you?"

"No. Sorry." He needed a tirade like a bullet through his head. But he must tread carefully, as Gill's sadness at the latest miscarriage had verged on depression. And she too had probably noted Caroline's good looks and charm. "I didn't think."

"You didn't think!"

No welcoming cocoa – just a grilling. He didn't feel like apologising. "Okay, thoughtless! But you could have rung me."

"I did – after being sick with worry – and they told me you were in conference with Matron. I told the man who I was. But he said it was a confidential matter, an emergency. You'd left orders not to be disturbed by anyone. I slammed the phone down. Confession time!"

He'd told switchboard: 'No more calls, except the police'. Couldn't risk the media or anyone else nosing. Gill thought he was having an affair with Caroline!

"Well?" She was scowling at him.

"Matron reported a female patient missing. The police came, and found her dead – drowned in the pond."

Gill was looking intent, and her expression changed.

"I've had to deal with this. And I'm to blame for insisting all doors be unlocked, without giving thought to the frail, elderly wanderers in the Annex."

"Goodness, Jamie!" She hugged him. "The kettle's boiled. I'll get the cocoa."

Minutes later, sipping from a steaming mug and holding Gill close on the settee, he continued his sad tale. "It's grim. Poor Nellie Morgan – she was so emaciated. The fence was down at one end; we assume that's how she got into the pond. There'll be a post-mortem and an inquest."

"Had she family?"

"None recorded, Matron says. Apparently Nellie'd been here over forty years. She came in depressed after a stillbirth."

"Tragic."

"Aye. And I feel damn guilty. Ready for bed?"

She acquiesced and they went upstairs. In bed, they prayed – he saying the words. "Almighty God, I'm sorry for the death of Nellie Morgan. May she rest in peace. And be with all affected by her death – ward staff, fellow patients, Matron. And give each of us strength to face this coming day..." He pondered adding a prayer for the success of his policies, but that didn't seem right.

They kissed and said goodnight. He felt calmer, but his mind stayed alert. Matron had said the ward sister was distraught – blaming herself for the death of "A sweet lady, a trusty for years."

He'd agreed to go onto the ward with Caroline tomorrow. They'd seek out anyone affected and try to help with their distress. He'd insist the blame lay with him. And he'd agree to both Annex wards being locked pro tem.

The pond was a place of beauty, and now of death. He'd talk with Cope and the Chief Engineer, and have it drained.

Ammo for the old guard. Could derail his plans. If there was a big enough outcry... But he'd push ahead, monitoring the 'open door' progress and difficulties. The first psychiatric social worker and occupational therapist appointments would be made next week. And he had plans to start involving the community.

The press! He'd no experience dealing with them. The police sergeant had warned him. "Bloodhounds'll love this and yap at your heels." Terrible publicity.

"No such thing as bad publicity," Mac Bell would say.

Well, the media would give him hell. But he could get from this an airing on the dire state of provision and the need for reform.

He'd take the initiative, ring the local paper and offer a world exclusive.

He began formulating how to approach this, what messages to give. Next thing, he was being shaken.

Gill was stretching across their bed. "Jamie, it's 5.30. The alarm's gone off."

50

Monday 11th March 1957 – in Springwell.

"Our consultant's a-comin' tomorrow – especially to see you," said Charge Williams, the boss white-coat.

Consultant – at last! John could feel the shiver of excitement. "Ah – the god?" he half joked.

"Our consultant's the god, right enough. He says what treatment our patients are to have."

Hell. This charge nurse was an earnest fellow. Dead earnest, And this was leuco heaven? "That monster nearly crucified me. Must I see him? I want home."

The Charge's face had reddened. "Our patients stay here and we looks after them for all their days."

He'd joined the lifers.

Tuesday 12th March 1957 – in Springwell.

John had just finished breakfast when Charge Williams called him into the office.

"This is John Chisholm, Doctor," the Charge said to a man seated behind the desk, and went to stand in the far corner.

This white-haired weather-beaten guy behind the desk was not the god.

"Mr Chisholm, I'm Dr Kenney, Consultant Psychiatrist." The man smiled, then glanced down at a file spread open on the desk.

A different kind of god? "Hello, Dr Kenney."

"I'm sorry not to see you for a chat before now, Mr Chisholm."

Hey, a consultant psychiatrist apologising to him. "Okay." But – beware of Mister Nice Guy. Could be even meaner than Mister Nasty?

"How are you feeling now?"

"Great, by comparison with how I was."

"Right. I see that in January, you reported memory loss."

"After the Shocker. I began remembering things sooner than I expected. The trouble is I've no idea what I've forgotten."

"Hm. We can't monitor any memory loss properly." The doctor closed the file. "I'd like us to consider your mental state when you came into Springwell. There's not much in our records. You hated your wife?"

"No. I was convinced she had a lover."

"On what basis?"

A voyeur? "She'd been distant toward me since Becky's birth. And my suspicion grew. Any man near her – I thought there there was something between them."

"Now, what do you believe?" Not a 'dirty old guy' question!

"I don't think there was a third party."

"And I read in your file that your thinking started bothering you?"

"Thoughts came and went."

"What do you mean?"

This didn't feel like any kind of grilling. Nice Guy looked earnest. Really wanting to know. "My head would get crammed with negative thoughts that'd vanish, like they'd been snatched."

"And now?"

"No such problems. I think clearly without interference. Oh, another funny thing hasn't happened for ages. I thought sometimes people were reading my mind."

"And the notes say you were depressed."

"Yes, I had thoughts of suicide. These haven't been around for ages either."

"Good. What troubles you now?"

"No leucotomy?"

"Heavens, no." Doctor looked shocked.

A genuine nice guy, who cared. "I can go home then?"

"No, it's not –"

"Why ?"

The doctor rose suddenly and threw out a hand. "Just noticed the time. See you next week."

John sat, seeing the hand dangle a moment then withdraw as the doctor breezed past him and exited. What? Did he scare this decent consultant?

Charge Williams escorted him out to the ward.

Tuesday 19ᵗʰ March 1957 – in Springwell.

John sat with Dr Kenney in the Charge's office; a one-to-one in easy chairs. No desk barrier. And the Charge had, at Kenney's request, left them alone.

"Sorry I left abruptly last time. I remembered I should be elsewhere. And today must be brief, as I've squeezed in your session. We'll have longer next time."

"It's okay." Time to make his move. "Why can't I go home?"

"I have to be satisfied you're ready. And your wife..."

"I'm ready. And I'm sure my wife will want me."

"We'll see. Any more questions?"

"Why was I diagnosed schizophrenic?"

"There's little in the notes. Your beliefs about your wife were seen as delusional – fixed and without foundation. But they sound like over-valued ideas – that are common in the general population and don't indicate schizophrenia."

"So I've not had schizophrenia."

"Well, it's possible you have. Thoughts crowding into your head and being stolen, and believing others can read your mind, could be diagnostic. But I'd have needed to see you clinically at the time."

The doctor looked at the notes again. "There's no record of you hearing voices you couldn't account for. True?"

John nodded. A pity the doctor was rising to signal an end to a useful dialogue.

Tuesday 26th March 1957 – in Springwell.

John sat with Dr Kenney – in easy chairs, as last time.

"And how's life on this ward?"

An opening he hadn't expected. "I feel so young, Doctor! But I'm grabbed by older men's tales. Anecdotal history. And it's nice to wear clothes that fit."

"Happy staying here forever?"

He searched the doctor's face. Not even a twinkle. "No!"

"I don't want misery here, young man." The doctor rose, his face crinkling into a smile. "John Chisholm, you are fit for discharge."

What? He grasped Dr Kenney's hand and crushed the man in a hug.

He stepped back. "Sorry." The doctor smiled and straightened his tie. "That's okay. You'll be free to go once arrangements are made. This'll take time, as your wife needs consulting. I'll ask our new psychiatric social worker to contact you about this."

The doctor sat down again. "Take a seat. We've a few more minutes for questions if you want."

"If it was schizophrenia, could it come back?"

The doctor scratched in his hair. "I don't know. There's reason to hope not. It doesn't seem to recur in a fair proportion of younger folk."

"And maybe you guys got the diagnosis wrong?"

The doctor shrugged. "Maybe. In psychiatry we're uncovering the tip of the iceberg. We rarely speak of curing, or having answers. Oh, and your depressed state might have indicated a schizo-affective disorder."

More jargon. "What on earth's that?"

"A state that doesn't present firmly as schizophrenia, and where your mood is abnormally exaggerated – in your case, depressed. As for

273

the depression – broadly speaking, did this come out of the blue, or were there things you felt caused it?"

"Definitely the latter. I was pretty stressed, both at work and at home."

"Again, reason for optimism. Sounds like the stress triggered your breakdown – and indeed your troubling experiences could have been an understandable though exaggerated reaction to severe stress." Dr Kenny smiled. "Enough psycho-babble!"

John shook the proffered hand as they rose. He leapt out into the ward. And the rest of the day he kept whistling his favourite tune, the Song of Liberty.

After a brisk walk in the sunshine and a celebratory coffee at The Stars – a new cafe at the top of Hospital Lane – John got back to a message from the staff nurse.

"A nice-looking woman called after you." Staff chuckled. "Says she's Maggie Lee, the new psychiatric social worker. I'll ring and tell her you're back."

So this woman would be the crucial link for him.

A few minutes later, a fair-haired young woman appeared, spoke to the staff nurse, and came his direction. "John Chisholm?"

"Yes, hello."

She was good-looking when she smiled. "Maggie Lee, PSW – stands for psychiatric social worker. You can call me Maggie. Let's go to my office for a chat."

Friday 12ᵗʰ April 1957 – to Aversham.

D-Day. Yes, Discharge Day. And now, nine a.m., he was en route home in Maggie's car. "The road needs all my attention," she said. "I haven't long passed my test."

She was crawling along, and kept hitting the brake. He stayed quiet!

Wednesday evening at half-past eight, Maggie had come to the ward. "I've just visited Heather and we had a long chat. The way's clear to go home this Friday."

He'd nearly hugged her. Clouds of doubt over whether he'd be welcome home had gathered. Though he and Heather hugged warmly on her fortnightly visits, and talked together so much - mainly her telling him about Becky, the nursery, her friends Elsie and Mattie and Moira - they hadn't touched on him coming home. Even on her last visit, he'd been pessimistic about his chances of discharge. And her response to his mention of shacking up with another guy had left him wondering.

Yesterday had been a tying-up-of-the-ends day. Dr Kenney made an outpatient appointment at Aversham clinic and showed him the discharge letter for his GP.

"One last tip, John," said Dr Kenney. "If you get over-stressed, try and find somebody you can trust to talk with about what's bugging you. But if that doesn't work, ring and I'll fit you in at outpatients."

He'd asked about Ginger. "Discharged. And the Baron insisted on taking, as companion, Mackay - the man you'd know as Kong, who sadly was like an automaton after a leucotomy - back to live on his estate."

Great news! He'd also been given the okay to see old pals on Lilac (ex-Refractory) Ward. With each, sadly, he encountered flat rejection. Pat darted glances around and shambled away with his head down, hands in pockets. George whispered protest that being visited would identify him as the famous author.

He jerked forward, bumping his head on the windscreen.

"You're home," said Maggie. She waved. Heather was in the doorway. "I won't stop. I'll call again soon."

"Thanks Maggie." He shut the car door behind him and bounded towards Heather. He'd a lot of catching up to do.

EPILOGUE

Thursday 4th *October 1962 – in Aversham.*

Two-fifty a.m. John lays down his fountain pen. Part One of Springwell: A Memoir *is nearly completed. This will catalogue his journey through the institution. Identities are disguised through name changes – but the tale is revealed, unexpurgated.*

He could continue, finish Part One. At college he'd swot till four a.m. and tackle exam papers later that morning. But now, a librarian facing the public from eight-forty-five a.m., he seeks rest.

He wants to go upstairs and join Heather in their cosy double bed. But no matter how softly he treads, the stairs and upstairs floorboards will creak. Heather mightn't notice – she snored through a thunderstorm the other night – but he'd have to pass the children's bedroom and could waken them. Baby Liam is a particularly light sleeper, with a lusty cry.

He settles in the armchair and closes his eyes. He drowses, but does not sleep. His brain urges him into reflection. He knows resistance will espouse restlessness, and that anyway sleep will eventually prevail.

Part One has, in the writing, proved more harrowing than expected. He knows that writing about traumatic experiences is a tool sometimes used in therapy. The recently qualified PSW Mac (Angus) Macleod, now his closest friend, is encouraging him in this approach, and is helpfully being available to listen and discuss.

Mac (his old acquaintance Browncoat Mac) expresses no regret over having gone into psychiatric social work and not clinical psychology. "I messed up the finals – and am I glad now! Getting around to see folk and the families in their own homes is a heck of a lot more my style than sitting holding hands in therapy."

It's great to have Mac around, and sometimes they laugh about the dirty laundry and talk about the old days – including the escape. He loves discussing the radical ideas Mac has picked up. "These three guys, John – Ronnie Laing and Thomas Szasz, psychiatrists both, and the Yankee sociologist Erwin Goffman – are like heavyweight nuns in our hallowed psychiatric monastery. Aye, they persuade me that we mental health foot soldiers rely far too much on medical approaches."

He's considered how such ideas could relate to his own experience. Had he been ill, or was his breakdown a problem of living (in unbearable stresses), to do with events and relationships? Maybe in practice it doesn't matter too much.

Or maybe it does. He agrees with Mac that diagnoses, while essential to the medical approach, can become labels that influence how folk view you socially. He's occasionally been aware that his 'label' is inhibiting. "Reductionist – how we mental health guys can still talk," says Mac. "It's our historic culture, and public attitudes."

He sees very clearly the relevance to Springwell-as-was of Goffman's 'total institution' concept. In his memoirs, he sometimes refers readers to this and other literature sources.

He's talked with Mac about the suicidal thoughts he had. Thank goodness the means didn't present. Mac reckons that if life gets bad or meaningless enough for anyone, doing themselves in can seem the best move.

He's also read about The Samaritans, a movement started in London by an Anglican priest who believes talking in confidence with somebody can help folk feeling suicidal or upset. He wants to get a similar service going locally.

His anger is often near the surface. The savagery and oppression in a supposedly caring institution with 'hospital' in its title, the destruction to lives, the waste of talent among his fellow patients. But he no longer feels bitterness on his own account. Without the passage through Springwell, he might still be teaching, with a breakdown about to happen. As it is, he's enjoying work that he's suited to, and that allows him to find time for reading and study.

At home, he savours being with Heather and their children. Life was unexpectedly rocky at first, and he owes Maggie for her work – listening to him and Heather and helping them sort things. Becky is settling in at school. He'll always carry the pain of missing out on a year of her infancy. Heather says she loves the work at nursery. Now NNEB-qualified and Deputy Matron, this is her career – interrupted only by the births of their two youngest. Her pay's not great, and neither is his, but they manage. And the child benefit's a bit of a life-saver.

Right now's not brilliant for Heather. She's spending a lot of time with Elsie across the road. Mattie has died and the funeral's tomorrow afternoon.

John's not looking forward to it. There's a good chance he'll cry. He liked Mattie, and spent time with the old man in the latter stages of gasping with emphysema.

Perhaps it's this triggering him into melancholic reflection – re-playing his childhood bereavements. And his whole being shakes at re-living the scene of Dave's parting "See ya bruv". A happy moment preceding unspeakable loss. This is the memory that gets him weeping. He's not told Mac of his intensifying sadness, but he will. Hopefully after tomorrow he'll pick up. And if he's descending into depression, he'll contact Dr Singh, his consultant at outpatient clinic.

After the kids were in bed last night, he and Heather had a weep-in. Not just about Mattie, and Dave. Heather's lamenting Edward, the brother she never knew, and her parents having to move into a home for the elderly mentally infirm in Aversham. He never got on with her folks, but he wouldn't have wished that on them. Heather really feels for Elsie, who befriended her and Becky while he was in Springwell. Elsie dotes on Becky and is great with their other kids. She's like a grandma – and in fact, at Heather's suggestion, they call her Grandma (and Mattie Grandpa). Heather's own parents are Granny and Granddad.

He's studying the history of mental health law and policy as grounding for his MA thesis at Manchester. He learns that in their nineteenth-century conception, the city and county asylums were built to provide a haven ('asylum' being Latin for 'place of refuge') for mentally afflicted 'lunatics'. From 1930, the change of title to 'mental hospital' signalled the main intended purpose as caring. He notes that sadly, with few exceptions, the institutional emphases were (in line with prevailing public attitudes) on containment – locking eccentricity away from the public and using physical restraints, sometimes brutality, to keep control.

Part Two of his memoirs will focus mainly on the radical changes at Springwell, pioneered by Jamie Macdonald and supported by the Royal Commission findings and the '59 Mental Health Act. As Chairman of the Friends of Springwell Hospital – a group Gill Macdonald set up and is active in – he has periodic meetings with Jamie, Deputy Medical Superintendent Lizzie McVeigh, Matron Caroline Dee and Chief Male Nurse Joe Macnamara, to review how the reforms are working out and discuss initiatives for involving the community. He admires Jamie's dedication to creating a therapeutic environment for the patients, and to schemes ensuring that discharged ex-patients are supported. And Caroline, with her single-minded commitment plus strategic ability and vision of a caring hospital, is also inspirational in the Friends.

On the community schemes, Mac, who with Maggie heads up a department of eight social workers, plays an important part. Through Mac, John hears of Sam Newman, Aversham's Senior Mental Welfare Officer – who, with fellow mental welfare officers from borough and county, goes monthly to the hospital's social work department for training seminars and a review of discharged patients. The mental man! John has no ill feelings now (towards Newman) about being bundled off into Springwell. The man was doing a tough job, and on reflection didn't seem the bullying type. Poor guy – apparently pretty crushed after being widowed recently.

John's work for the National Association for Mental Health – he's on their National Executive – will also feature in Part Two. He plans to continue part-time study for a PhD, surveying ex-patients' experiences of their stays in mental hospitals.

The Macdonalds are now personal friends. He and Heather enjoyed an evening with them last week. A lovely couple, older than they. Jamie told him, over the after-dinner coffee, of their deep sadness at the miscarriages and, with Gill past childbearing age, their application to adopt.

An alarm's going off upstairs. Without sleep, the day ahead – at the library, then the funeral – will be tough. But John knows he will survive.

The End

279

The 1950s English Mental Health Context:
A Brief Note.

The **administrative settings** and people's **job titles** were different then. An outline of these should help you appreciate nuances in formal relationships.

Within the NHS were the **Mental Hospitals** – built in the 19th and early 20th centuries as the city and county asylums (and re-named in the 1930 Mental Treatment Act). In each of these the boss was the **Medical Superintendent**, a consultant psychiatrist by profession. The institutions varied a lot in their regimes. Many still reflected the harsh containment approach of most asylums, despite recent developments in drugs known to alleviate and control the worst behavioural symptoms of the major afflictions. Others (probably a minority) were relatively enlightened, with fewer constraints on patients' behaviour and efforts to heal and rehabilitate. As you'd see in the latter part of this drama, a Medical Superintendent's attitudes and personality would greatly influence the nature of a regime.

Within each local authority was the **Health Department.** Heading this up was the **Medical Officer of Health (MOH)**, a public health doctor by profession. In the MOH's empire were public health inspectors, health visitors, home helps, district nurses, midwives, and at least one duly authorised officer in mental health – the DAO (who carried enforcement powers).

Mental health liaison between hospital and local authority tended to be quite minimal. In 'Mad Worlds', at least our fictional MOH valued cooperation with Springwell, and DAOs could attend psychiatric lectures to student nurses. By the early 1960s, some close partnerships were developing – e.g. between hospital social workers and local authority mental welfare officers (as the '59 Act renamed DAOs).

The **legislative context** would soon change. Still in force was the 1890 Lunacy Act, reflecting a legal approach, with two main underlying premises – that only folk certified insane should be taken to an asylum, and that the public must be protected from such 'lunatics'. To safeguard liberty, lay magistrates would be involved in certifying. The 1930 Mental Treatment Act modified this to allow people deemed 'of unsound mind' to enter as voluntary patients, and advocated the setting up of outpatient clinics. The name 'mental hospital' also came in then. By the 1950s in some areas the JP bowed to medical opinion. The DAO, with mental health knowledge and experience, was increasingly a key figure in emergencies. But the 1890 Act was not repealed until the 1959 Mental Health Act, which reflected a medical approach (without JP involvement) and was aimed at helping 'mentally ill' people. In 1956-7, when the main action in this novel occurs, the 1954-7 Royal Commission on Mental Health was yet to report, and have its main recommendations adopted in the 1959 Act.

Bill Douglas

Acknowledgements

I have lived with and nurtured this novel from its conception through many drafts over several years.

I wish to express thanks to the many who have helped me at some time or another by commenting or simply listening. You are too numerous to be mentioned here. Among you are my children and their partners. My main support throughout has come from my wife and fellow-writer Elisabeth, an ever-patient listener with helpful suggestions.

I will mention others who also have read through and fed back comment (always constructive and helpful) on earlier drafts, or provided especially valuable resource material:- Margaret Brunskill, Peter Buckman, Ian Clark, John Cossins, Anne Eckersley, Barbara Fryers, Tom Fryers, Val Harrington, Tony Higginson, Patrick Janson-Smith, Richard Jones, John Nelson, Marjory Ramage, Chantel Scherer-Reid, Geoff Seale, Peter Sharkey, Rob Watkins.

I've drawn further support for my writing from Writers' Bureau, Lancaster University (mainly my tutor and fellow students on an on-line starting-your-novel course), the writers agents publishers and book doctors I met at Writers' Workshop and NAWG Festivals, and from Formby Writers.

Finally, my thanks go to the publishing team at Troubador/ Matador. It's good working with you.

Bill Douglas